The Hub City Hoodlum

PaPa Sab

2012

ETCHED N STONE

BOOKS & ENTERTAINMENT

THE HUB CITY HOODLUM

PaPa Sak

INTRODUCTION

First and foremost I want to point out that this is a fictional novel based upon real neighborhoods. This particular neighborhood was the set where I grew up and represented. For many years I avoided telling street novels about my own personal neighborhood on the East Side of Compton. I didn't want people to think that I couldn't write about other things besides my own hood. So I thought it wise to write about the street politics all over Los Angeles County and touch on Compton from time to time. My first novel touching on Compton was the hood classic 'Them Laney Boys' about a family of Crips raised by a single mother. The culture of Compton is unique in the fact that it is a relatively small city that has a notorious reputation because of rap groups such as N.W.A. A woman visiting from another state was excited about visiting Compton because of what she heard even though there were no real tourist landmarks. I explained to her that it was my home for many years and it is a ghetto like many other places throughout the United States. What makes this city different is that it is really a working middle class community. I grew up in a house with three bedrooms, a den, a backyard, a kitchen and two bathrooms with running hot water. I never missed a meal nor did I lack decent clothing. I lived with adults that went to work every day and paid bills responsibly. But when I walked out of my house it was an entirely different story. Life was hard when you roamed the Compton streets even for a kid. Many people died young and many mothers cried at funerals of children that were killed way before their time. Not only was I a part of this world, at some point I thrived in it. I learned how to be ruthless and I embraced being a hoodlum from the Hub City. I never lived in the projects and my mother was never on welfare. But the anger and frustration that surrounded me made me adapt and become one with the hostility. The culture for Compton that made Bloods and Crips different particularly in the 1980s and 1990s was that we many times grew up together to grow up and be enemies. We were so close to each other but from different sides so it was a different element. In Los Angeles they had a little more room to spread out in their neighborhoods and streets. In Compton we were a little more compact. The last thing that separated us from all other cities was that most people outside of Compton hated people from Compton. Many Crips didn't get along with Compton Crips and many Bloods had problems with Compton Pirus. It is still like this to this very day. So I had to write a fictional account of where I come from so you could see it through our eyes. So you can understand why we were so proud to be where we were from.

I would like to thank Donnie-Ru and Lisa Clay for posing for the cover of this fiction novel. I would also like to thank Shannon Fisher and Proverb C Wisdom for their gifted photography and eye. I also would like to thank Rasta Asaru Escott El for his great and brilliant graphic design for the book cover. You did your thing homeboy. I would like to thank my cousin Meika Caddell for introducing me to Lisa Clay and being a cool as cousin. I would like to thank Big Tupp his contribution and support of this project. I also would like to thank my big homie Homer-Ru for his love and support. I lastly would like to thank my mother, my brothers, my grandparents and my entire family. This book right here is for Holly Hood-Forever My Lady.

PaPa Sak
The Kingpin of the Inkpen!!!

TABLE OF CONTENTS

I'm from broken families and dried up tears after divorce
Where bitterness is settled in and pain stings its recipient with force
Where daddy is a no-show so mama attempts to be both
While her son searches for manhood while death creeps close
Where peers become role models and life can be war
And teenagers become killers in the cause they fight for
Where I'm from drugs is a conduit to act out violent whims
And you had to have respect in the street to roll around on rims
I'm from the crack epidemic when Reaganomics was the trend
And the CIA was the ones responsible for bringing cocaine in
They fueled the arms race and murders escalated in the street
And red or blue Chuck Taylor's is what we wore on our feet
So the sheriffs are another gang and the police are dirty
And you had to know how to throw ya hands to be considered worthy
Where I'm from slumlords charged high but amenities is low
And ghetto mechanics found a reason for you to visit them once more
Where colors were for real and you better not be afraid to ride
Where I'm from, we wore our rags on the right hand side
I'm just saying, where I'm from it was all about respect
And you might find a heavy weapon under the bed of a Vietnam vet
Reservoir dogs and incarcerated locs that might date your daughter
And never showed mercy when they smelled blood in the water
I'm from the hub city, where life can be shitty
Some of the finest girls are witty and the concrete is gritty
Where rent parties are thrown and the neighborhood drunk is known
And hood rats show up smelling musty while they got perfume on
With smeared lipstick where the depraved cops is the normal piggy
And Malcolm X and Dr. King have been replaced by Tupac and Biggie
And sex is introduced to you while you're just a pre-teen
Where pregnant teenage moms become a part of the routine
Babies raising babies so the whole community is affected
And domestic violence is a pattern that everyone has accepted
The common folk are prisoners and it's stated again and again
But the question is when we are going to clean the mess we've gotten ourselves
in
Where I'm from

REST IN PEACE

D-DOG
EARS
BOO-RU
FOO-RU
POKEY
OG MOUSE
FAT LARRY
BABY TOO LOK
E-BONE
CHAVA
DIRTY RED

Never forget where you come from

1
WHERE I'M FROM

Don't ever underestimate an enemy, and that's on Piru!
Big Sam

"Grumpy! Grumpy! Wake yo punk ass up, Blood."

I felt someone shaking my leg while I lie asleep in bed. My eyes foggily began to open as I tried to make sense of what was going on. The last and final tug shook me completely out of my slumber because I almost fell out of my bed. All I could see was red though my eyes were still blurry. At least it wasn't someone trying to kill me I considered. When my eyes focused the face became clear to me and I let out a long and annoying sigh.

"Why the fuck you waking me up for, Blood?" I yelled at my older brother.

"Where the fuck is my Pendleton? I saw you with it on when I was with my bitch Sharon. I didn't say anything then because I was going back to the house but you need to come up out of my shit."

"Yo punk ass woke me up for that bullshit? You could have just gone in my closet and grabbed the shit. You be tripping Blood and that's on P-Fonk."

"Who the fuck you calling a punk?"

My brother grabbed me by my tank top and lifted me from the bed. I was already irritated about him waking me up, now this. When he lifted me to his level I socked him in his mouth. I knew the punch wasn't going to do anything but piss him off. Sometimes I just don't give a damn. His head snapped to the right then he took several steps back on the nappy carpet. He looked up after a couple of seconds with a smirk on his face. That was my way of knowing that he was mad as hell. He came back within arms' reach and released a two punch combination. I had already braced myself for the pain so I released a three punch combo in the middle of his two punches. I was still the one that slammed into the wall. I almost flew through the window but the wall caught me and you could hear the strain of my weight on the plaster. All my punches landed true but his punches were more effective. The wind was knocked out of me briefly from the wall. Though I recovered quickly, it wasn't enough time to catch my brother before he rushes up on me and grabs me. It wasn't a way to win the fight at this point. My brother was holding seventeen to eighteen inch arms and we were wrestling in a confined space. His stretch in Youth Authority had him holding some muscles that were hard to escape. He was always cock-strong but now it was worse. I wasn't going to just give up. I struggled with every inch of my body trying to find another end to my losing cause. It was almost over before I was saved.

"Do you think I feel like hearing this shit this early in the morning? Dion let go of your brother and Dwayne you need to get up any damn way." My Mother barked into the room.

My brother loosened his brace slowly as I regained my breath. It was a small victory, considering that I didn't just quit. I had to fight until there wasn't any more breath. Maybe my mother knew that about me so she cut it off before it went too far. You have to be that way where I come from. My mother bought a house with my pops back in 1975 on the East Side of Compton. My brother was born three years later before she started working at the Post office. My pops was caught cheating on my mom by having a baby on her by some woman that lived in Orange County. We got a half sister that's six months older than me. My mother didn't find out about it until her third trimester or I might not have ever been born. She kept the house and he moved out with the woman that he had the daughter with. He tried to come around for a little while but my mother told us that he always tried to get back with her. When he realized that wasn't going to happen he stopped coming around as much. So he left two black boys alone to grow up on the East Side of Compton.

The neighborhood we grew up in became Blood territory when gangs in Compton began choosing sides. Some of my big homies originally got into it with the original Pirus from Leuders Park. Eventually though they chose to be Bloods instead of Crips. It was somewhat of a dilemma because we were the only Blood neighborhood off of Alondra Blvd. on the East Side. We were on the front lines. My brother Dion was jumped into the neighborhood when he was eleven years old and they nicknamed him Flintstone. Some niggas said he was as hard as stone and that's how he got his name. I would get put on the set about three years later. My brother named me Grumpy because he said I had a look on my face like I was always mad about something. It was a name that stuck. When my mother was in a playful mood she would even call me Grumpy.

We as Pirus called ourselves P-Fonk and sometimes we wore burgundy to represent what kind of Bloods we are. All Bloods out of Compton were Pirus and there were a few other hoods outside of Compton that claimed Piru as well. Naturally my mother wasn't too fond of us gangbanging but it wasn't much she could do about it. At this point of our years in the street my brother had got locked up and did a little time. I would be the one that would bring a lot of pain to her door. I didn't want it that way but that's just how it went down.

Grudgingly I staggered over to the closet and tossed Flintstone his punk ass Pendleton shirt. He caught it before it landed on the floor and walked out of my room. I thought about lying back down but I was getting up in another twenty minutes anyway. I think I was dreaming about a fine ass bitch before

Flintstone brought his punk ass into the room. I'm gon' even up with that nigga one day in a head-up fade, I swear.

This day in particular was something that was different for me. We were in wartime with a small Crip neighborhood a few blocks west of our hood. We were putting in work against them niggas and shooting up they block but it made the Sheriffs hot. They started rolling through our neighborhood three or four times a day. The Compton Sheriffs would roll up on us and try to find contraband to get some shooters off the street. Usually a name would ring out but we were doing rotation on those crab niggas. The big homies were putting in overtime and it started over an incident that happened two weeks ago.

I'll get back to the day that changed everything in a minute. First I need to touch on what set up the war. Late one Friday night I was hanging out in the hood with my road dog Pookie-Ru. We were over Turtle's house sipping on some Eight-ball, you know Old English Malt Liquor. Jake-Ru and Nu-Nu, who were around my brother's age, were back there as well. Big Sam came walking up to us talking major shit. I had a nice little buzz so it didn't register with me as quick as it normally would.

"Blood, those crab niggas is posted up over in the apartments on Alondra. We gon' have to serve them niggas and run they asses off."

"What the fuck you talking about, Blood?" Jake-Ru replied.

"It's some Crip niggas serving dope over in the Alondra apartments. We gon' have to run them niggas off."

"How long have they been hanging in the hood?"

"I don't know, but Lisa told me she been seeing those niggas over there for the last couple of days."

That was all we needed to hear. We called Turtle from out of the house and huddled up to face those niggas. When we got there it was four Crips hanging outside. Big Sam walked up on the nigga that looked as though he was calling shots. They were laughing about something before we came.

"What ya'll niggas doing over here Blood?"

"We ain't even tripping off that shit, Cuz."

"Ya'll gon' have to raise up from over here, Blood." Big Sam replied while Jake-Ru handed him a forty ounce of eight-ball.

The man made eye contact with Big Sam but never really acknowledged him. He still had a smirk on his face from what was making him laugh early. Big Sam took one step forward and smashed the bottle of beer into his face. In an instant his homeboys ran out on him. The broken glass tattered all over his face had him screaming. We allowed him to walk off into the night holding his face. We laughed about it all the way back to Turtle's house. Big Sam was leading the pack.

"If a nigga takes off on me and my homeboys run out on me I ain't fucking with them niggas anymore." He laughed.

"Yeah his homeboys were supposed to at least fight to protect him when he takes a fall." Jake-Ru added.

"They were a bunch of bitches." I shook my head.

Big Sam wrapped his arm around my neck and smiled. He was one of the big homies that always had game for the young homies to learn.

"Don't ever underestimate an enemy, and that's on Piru."

I kept that in mind as we walked back to Turtle's house. It wasn't really late outside but it was getting darker earlier in the day. My road dog and I, Pookie-Ru was smoking on some stress bullshit ass weed before we heard Smokey roll up. Smokey was an OG second generation gangster from our hood who drove a pretty ass Jeep Isuzu. He had sounds in his car so you could hear that nigga pulling up about a block away from where you were at. He was the kind of nigga everybody in the hood liked and respected. He had a baby by one of the homegirls from the Park named Nikki-Ru. When I say park I mean Leuders Park. All east side

Pirus represent Leuders Park where I'm from. That's where it all started on the east side of Compton. Most Pirus ended their name with Ru to acknowledge that they were Piru Bloods.

Well Smokey-Ru was the type of nigga people was waiting to see. When he pulled up he was gon' have drink and good ass Kush for the homies to smoke. That's why they called him Smokey, because he always had the bomb. He loved being from our neighborhood and wore it with a bravado that I'd never seen before him. He was about 5'11 with cornrows and a light brown complexion. He had some muscle on him from doing a couple of bids in the penitentiary. He was a well seasoned veteran that even Big Sam, who was one of the founders showed much respect.

He walked in the backyard being followed by Sticky-Ru his road dog and Reddy. Reddy was only a year older than me. She was really of my generation but she had put in work against our enemies at such a young age she got to hang with the OGs. She was a pretty bitch with curly hair like she had Indian in her family. She was called Reddy for two reasons. One of the reasons was because she was light skinned but the other reason was because she was always ready to do dirt. She was the only female that I knew that kept a pistol on her like a nigga would. She was always cool with me because she went to school with me for one year. But she normally didn't hang with the homies that were my age. She also once had a crush on my big brother Flintstone or he was sometimes called Stoney-Ru. She would always ask about him when we would go to school. She followed behind Smokey most of the time nowadays and tonight wasn't any different.

"Ay Blood, I need to holler at yo brother. Tell that nigga to get at me." Smokey said to me while passing the weed.

"I ain't gon' see that nigga until late tonight. But I'll let him know big homie."

I puffed on the weed several times before passing it to Pookie-Ru. Smokey walked all the way to the back to Big Sam and other homies playing dominoes. At the domino table was Big Sam, Turtle, Nuck and Slim. Slim was the only nigga at the table that wasn't a first generation OG. When Smokey walked up Big Sam stood up from the table to embrace him.

"We had to serve these crab niggas over in the apartments earlier today."

"Whose we?" Smokey asked.

"Me, Turtle and the little homies rolled up on them niggas five deep. After making one of their homies eat a forty ounce bottle the rest of those niggas ran off. We didn't need any gun play."

"That's what I'm talking about." Smokey laughed.

I tuned out of the conversation because the weed was starting to kick in fast. I didn't notice Reddy creeping up on me from the side.

"What's happening Grumpy Blood?"

"Aw shit, what's up Reddy-Ru? You gon' ever decide to fuck with a young nigga like me. You pretty than a muthafucka." I replied playfully.

"That's the weed talking nigga. I got a couple of hustles if you down to make some money though, my nigga."

"That depends on what you talking about. Yo crazy ass be tripping about yo money. Remember when you pistol whipped Nick Dog?" I sounded skeptical.

"What you scared?"

"When have you known me to be scared? When those crab niggas had us surrounded who stood tall with you Blood?" I said defensively.

"I know you a down ass nigga but are you down to make this money?"

"Yeah, what the fuck are you talking about?"

"I got a package of dope that I need you to hustle for me. You'll make a nice chunk of paper but you'll be working for me."

"Okay but after the first go around I don't want that shit on consignment. You ain't the type of bitch I want to be owing." I smirked.

"I can understand that. So you down to start serving for a bitch?"

"I told you I was and why ain't you hustling that shit ya damn self?"

"You are lucky I got love for yo young ass because you be talking too much shit. I ain't the type to be posted at a spot slanging and shit. I'll get bored with that shit quick than a muthafucka."

"So why don't you do licks with my brother and Slow?"

"Them niggas keep doing robberies and they gon' fuck around and get caught up. That shit is fast money but it ain't smart money. Slow and Stoney got too much muthafuckin heart. Crack is easy and steady money."

"I told that crazy nigga the same thing but he does everything with Slow."

Slow was a big homie that always was trying to rob someone or somewhere. He always had his eye on who he could stick-up. My brother knew how to hustle just like the next man but he followed Slow for the thrill of the game. I used to call my brother stupid to his face and that would cause plenty of fights. I didn't give a damn though, I was trying to look out for him. Slow was a firecracker nigga that would pop at any minute. Niggas like that will have you caught up sooner or later.

"What Smokey-Ru want with my brother?" I asked Reddy.

"I don't know; ask that nigga." She shrugged.

She probably knew but wasn't going to speak on it because Smokey didn't speak on it. She was real serious about second hand information. I figured I would ask Smokey before we left that night. Sometimes I felt like I had to watch out for my brother even though he was considered an OG. He loved the homies so much that he didn't think about what he was doing before he did it. Some of the homies wasn't going to look out for him like he looked out for them. That's just how it is. The hood got a bunch a niggas that grow up with you so they're supposed to have love for you but that ain't always the case. That nigga Slow was on a collision course and he was taking whoever he could with him.

Reddy glared at me as if she was just now getting pissed off about what I asked her. She was a trip sometimes. Her stare went from the bottom of my shoes to the top of my head like she was sizing me up. She moved closer to me as if she was about to dope-fiend-punch me in the mouth.

"Why in the fuck would I be speaking up on what Smokey wants with Stoney, Blood? You on some different shit. You need to put the muthafuckin' weed down and that's on Piru." She snarled.

"Hold the fuck up Reddy, I ain't a muthafuckin' bitch. How the fuck you gon' come at me like that?"

"I'm just saying nigga. You asking too many muthafuckin questions and that can get you caught the fuck up."

"Fuck you Reddy; don't get knocked the fuck out. I'll toss yo skinny ass up." I snapped.

Our voices weren't getting loud but they had risen to higher than a whisper. A couple of OGs turned to observe but were still preoccupied with the domino game. Neither one of us had noticed that the big homies had looked over at us. We were too busy glaring at each other.

"When the fuck have you known me to fight, Blood. I'm too muthafuckin' pretty to fight."

She then suddenly flashed her three-eighty then her lips curled cruelly. I got a quick glimpse of the gun before she put it back in her jacket.

"You gon' have to shoot my muthafuckin' ass, because it ain't no bitch this way. You need to give me…

"What the fuck is up with ya'll?"

Someone said from the domino table. It sounded like Smokey-Ru's voice but I didn't look up to see.

"I ain't fucking with you Reddy. You can handle yo own business."

I walked on the other side of Pookie-Ru and Reddy closely followed behind me. When I turned around she had a different look on her face. It wasn't that scowl that she had before.

"Aw Blood, I was just fucking with you. Don't even be like that Grumpy-Ru. You know I wasn't about to use that muthafucka."

"You shouldn't even play like that. I ain't fucking with you." I glared at her.

"Aw nigga, you tripping off this punk ass three-eighty. It wasn't even like that Grumpy."

I dragged on the weed for a couple of puffs then leaned against the gate. She had fucked up my whole mood in a matter of seconds. She eased over close to me trying to get at me about the proposal we just agreed on.

"You gon' leave a bitch hanging like that Grumpy? I was just saying that you could have asked Smokey that shit you asked me. You claim the set my nigga, so I ain't really gon' try to blast on you." She smoothly explained.

"He should have asked me what?" Smokey walked up.

She glanced up at me then glanced at Smokey. Smokey's eyes flashed back and forth between the two of us.

"What the fuck are ya'll talking about?" He said impatiently.

"You were talking to the big homies so I asked Reddy what you wanted with my brother so she started tripping." I quickly replied.

"Oh; Reddy is funny like that sometimes. That nigga Stoney wanted to buy a pistol from me." He smirked.

I nodded but was still a little pissed off with Reddy. She was one of those types of people that liked to wig out on a nigga but will give you the clothes off her back. I wasn't in the mood for that shit tonight though. Pookie had passed the urb back to me so I could hit it again. It wasn't any denying Reddy was a pretty ass female that could ride like any man could. I respected her but I wasn't about to deal with her bullshit all the time. It was less stress to not even get into business with her crazy ass.

"Look Grumpy, I fucked up. When have you known a bitch like me to admit I'm wrong? I need a reliable nigga to handle my business on the block." She shrugged.

"Ah snap, Grumpy don't let this little bullshit come between you and Reddy making money. You bee what the fuck I'm saying?" Smokey cut in.

Whenever he changed his Cs to Bs I knew he was serious. Smokey was too seasoned to change his vocabulary to talk like a lot of Bloods do. He had stripes, so he could say what the fuck he wanted to say and no one was gon' question him about it. He was blasting on Crips since he was twelve years old. He only talked like that when he was on a no nonsense type of attitude. He even smiled with a glare that would make you cringe. Have you ever met a nigga like that? This made me give her offer a second thought. I wasn't fucking with her until Smokey called a shot on the subject.

"Alright big homie, I'll fuck with her if you think it's a good thing." I shrugged.

"Yeah, young Blood I think it's a real good idea. Reddy ain't gon' stand on the corner and grind like that."

I smiled because it was a compliment. I had hustled for my brother for a minute until he got stretched on a gun charge. My dope game skills had been honed since I was a preteen. Smokey put his hand on my shoulder and gave me one of his smiles.

"It ain't shit to put in work but every nigga ain't built to go get that paper."

After making that statement he walked back over to the domino table. Not even ten seconds later OG Slim yelled domino. Everybody started getting up from the table to yawn, stretch and finish off the last remnants of beer. I was thinking about calling it a night as well. I glanced over at Reddy then eased up close enough to whisper.

"When are you gon' get at me about that?"

"I'll be at you early tomorrow around two in the afternoon, my nigga."

I looked at her crazy for calling two in the afternoon early. She was distracted because she was watching what Smokey would do.

"Aw Blood, I know you niggas ain't finished playing dominos. I wanted to get in on the next game."

"Nigga you know you ain't any good at dominos. We are ready to take our ass home and get some sleep." Big Sam said to Smokey.

"You gon' put me out there like that, Blood?" Smokey smirked.

"You are good at everything else except dominos Smokey. Everybody knows that shit but no one wants to tell yo ass. Now give me some of love I'm out this bitch." Big Sam smirked.

He embraced Smokey and they play fought for several seconds. He stumbled a little bit right before he got to Reddy and me.

"You too muthafuckin' pretty to be hanging with this hoodlum ass nigga." He said to Reddy.

She just smiled then he leaned on my shoulder. He had been sitting down at the domino table swigging beers and now it caught up with him.

"Aye Grumpy, help yo big homie to his car." Big Sam put his arms around my neck.

We strolled outside the gate with him leaning on me. He was a big man with big ass arms. It was a struggle holding him up but we managed to make it outside. We made it to Smokey's car before he paused for a minute. It was a space almost big enough for another car between him and Smokey's car. He kept glancing down the street like he was looking for something. I was struggling just to get him to his car so I was distracted.

Suddenly I heard the screech of tires. Before I could get a good look at the car I was pushed to the ground by Big Sam. Whoever was rolling up didn't have their lights on. I caught a glimpse of the car on my way down to the concrete. I stumbled on the ground for a few seconds before I started hearing gunshots. Big Sam was a strong dude, so it took some time to recuperate from his heavy handed shove to the ground. When I glanced up at him like he was crazy, his body gets riddled with bullets. Lying on the concrete I watched my big homie's body slam to the concrete. The force of the bullets knocked him to the front yard grass. I stared in disbelief as his blood stained the grass then leaked to the concrete. I was in shock. Incoherent for a few seconds I lied on the ground staring at his body. My mind went blank until I heard Smokey and Reddy yelling something at me.

"Blood are you alright? Ah fuck; they just killed Big Sam." Smokey blurted out.

"This is some bullshit." Reddy added.

Both of them lifted me from off the ground. Now it was me that staggered a little bit to regain my footing. I stared at Big Sam's dead body and everything seemed dizzy.

"What the fuck happened? Some crab niggas came by and blasted?" Reddy asked.

"I didn't get to see. Big Sam pushed me to the ground before I could find out who it was."

"We gon' have to ride on them niggas for this shit." Reddy announced.

"Give me yo muthafuckin' strap." Smokey ordered Reddy.

Reddy looked at him like he was crazy for a moment. When he reached out with his hand she reluctantly handed him her gun. He began taking off his jacket then put his gun and her gun in the jacket but he was holding it like it was a bag.

"Any of you niggas got a strap on you, Blood?"

Two more guns were thrown in the jacket before Smokey wrapped it up. Reddy started acting jumpy before she could find out what he was doing.

"Why the fuck you taking our pistols Smokey?"

"Because the muthafuckin' police gon' pull up any minute and we all gon' be doing some time."

He handed the jacket to Pookie and instructed him to put the guns somewhere in the backyard. And right on cue the Sheriffs rolled up on us with their pistols drawn. We all put our hands in the air while they demanded we put our hands on the hood of the squad cars. Everyone kept quiet besides saying our names until the homicide detective rolled up. Finding no contraband they let us go while we watched the coroner put Big Sam in wagon.

2
THE EAST SIDE

If you gotta do yo dirt, the less people know about it the better!
Slim

Damn near everyone on the East Side of Compton that was Bloods came to Big Sam's funeral. It was really just another Piru reunion. I seen Burgundy flags flashing everywhere throughout the church and at the funeral grounds. He had a lot of respect from OGs all over the East side of Compton as well as L.A and Watts. Fuming on the inside most of the homies from my neighborhood sat in the first four rows of the church. It was crowded for the most part. Gang members speckled the crowd of spectators in the seats and against the wall. A few Pirus from the East side that I thought were in jail were at the funeral as well. Both of Big Sam's baby's mommas were crying their hearts out. It was a sad day on the East Side.

One of the things that are a part of the culture of our neighborhood is to have a barbecue when one of our soldiers has fallen. We all met up at the park on Atlantic Blvd to reminisce about the dead homie. It was once called East Compton Park but now they called it Rancho Dominguez Park. When an OG was killed like Big Sam that carried respect, the whole East Side came out to pay him respect. It was always customary that some of the homies, that couldn't handle their liquor, get stinking drunk. One of the big homies would be manning the grill while we reminisced about Big Sam. It was interesting to hear the many stories about him from some of the OGs. We would pass around the best weed available and blaze away. Gangsters don't cry when they lose one of their own. They vent through alcohol, drugs and violence. The barbecue was what you would call a war dance that included a dance we called the 'Blood Dance'. I was a little tipsy before I even had a chance to sink my teeth into the barbecue. About thirty minutes before we started fixing plates the Sheriffs rolled upon us. They came in from different directions rolling their squad cars onto the grass and close to the picnic area. They were making their rounds after a well known gangster was killed. It was obvious that more violence would ensue as the days followed. Their job was to circumvent as many murders as possible but they knew it was like stopping a force of nature. Revenge was inevitable. So they hopped out of their squad cars with a certain bravado. It was too many people outside for them to begin searching everyone. Besides, we weren't that stupid to be up at a public park with our weapons flashing. Murder would have to be quiet. My brother and Slow were closest to one of the Sheriffs with rank. They were puffing on some Kush so Slow tried to put it out.

"I ain't about to crack you over some punk ass weed Slow. I'll probably get you when you try to pull off another one of your robberies with Stoney." Sheriff Brown commented.

"Aw Brown we just chilling." Slow mumbled.

"You ain't got to put out the weed. Enjoy yo little barbecue and keep the liquor in a brown bag and you won't hear shit from me." Brown said while walking up to another OG.

"Hey Brown." OG Slim said.

"Hey Slim, I'm sorry to hear about Big Sam."

Slim nodded while being flanked by Nuck, Smokey, Turtle and Kay-Kay. They were all OGs and shot callers from my hood. It was amazing how Sheriff Brown knew exactly who to walk up on. I always thought he knew too much.

"I know you might want to go to war with the people that done this to Big Sam but it really ain't worth it. My people already know that someone with respect was dropped the other night so we will be hot for the next few nights."

"Okay." Slim replied.

It wasn't really much that Slim could say after that. Brown was making sure he pulled up on one of the shot callers to stop any war that might happen. Slim was a skinny gangster with muscles that didn't show until he took off his shirt. He was old school in almost everything he did. He only wore Levy jeans, a T-shirt or sweatshirt with a small afro and a hairnet. I very seldom saw him without a cigarette in his mouth. He had a nervous problem so sometimes his hands would shake a little. He was always calm and calculating even when it came down to him saying anything. His complexion would be considered light but it was ruddy and had dinginess to it and his eyes always were yellow or red. Now that Big Sam was dead Brown knew that Slim could make a call to go to war or call it off. When Brown looked at him he had a blank expression his face. Brown glanced around at the faces of all the Pirus. It was damn near quiet except for the music blaring through the stereo. One of the homies had a stereo at the park playing the Stylistics. Brown knew it wasn't much he could do but he tried anyway. He was one of those Black police that had love for Black people. He was respected but still was playing for the enemy team as far as we were concerned. He spoke to damn near everyone in the circle before he got to me and Pookie.

"You must be Grumpy, Stoney's little brother. You look just like him." Brown commented.

"How do you know my name?"

"You got arrested near Whaley middle school a couple of years back with him." He pointed at Pookie.

He smiled as though he had the upper hand on me. I was more worried about him taking the beer from me than anything. He ignored the beer and walked back to his squad car. As the Sheriffs pulled off we resumed our barbecue. I could over hear the OGs talking amongst themselves.

"That muthafucka be knowing too much, Blood and that's on P-Fonk. "

"You knew the nigga was gon' roll on us when we lost one of our own. Fuck what he's talking about Blood." Slim replied.

"He saying they gon' be out tonight." Turtle added.

"Those muthafuckas is out every night." Smokey replied.

"I'm saying we gon' need to be careful." Turtle sighed.

"War is war so we chalk that shit up to the game, Blood."

"We gon' handle the shit right, though." Slim glared at Smokey.

Moments later Reddy came walking up with one of the home girls named Renee. Renee was one of those females that had a brick house body. She had real big titties and a nice ass. She wasn't a toss-up though. She was one of those types of females you had to be her man to get to hit that ass. That was the only female I ever saw Reddy hang with. She was cool with other Piru girls but not enough to hang with. Besides, they balanced each other out. Reddy was a pretty ass girl with something mixed in her family and a cute petite shape while Renee had a banging body but was okay in the face. Renee could whip all the females I knew but Reddy was the girl that would shoot first and fight last. If she wasn't with Smokey she was with Renee. Naturally someone would announce their presence because all kind of niggas was trying to fuck either one.

"Here come Reddy and Renee."

When she got up close enough she walked right over to Smokey. Smokey was still fuming from having the police roll up on him.

"What the fuck punk ass Brown want?" Reddy asked.

"He's talking about the police gon' be hot tonight."

"It's time to eat, Blood." Ronnie-Ru announced.

Everyone made their way to the food. It was our hood and the homeboys from our neighboring hood, since we were at a park in their neighborhood. Besides the color red or burgundy they wore green while we wore beige. The mood changed once all the homies got some food in their stomach. It became more like a party as the music prompted the homies to do the Blood dance. It was definitely a war dance as nightfall began to settle in. Everyone helped pack all the food away and start heading back to the hood.

We met up at Turtle's house once again and it was cool for a couple of hours. We didn't see the police lurking at all. Then Smokey pulled up and parked a few houses down from Turtle's spot. He was with Sticky and Reddy. They got out the car and walked towards the back. Pookie and I were smoking on Kush right outside the gate to the backyard. Smokey had a look in his face. He tugged at my shirt then indicated with his head that I follow him to the side of the house.

"Ay Blood, you ready to put in work on these crabs."

I nodded. He smiled then continued.

"Where is those niggas Stoney and Slow?"

"I don't know, they were hanging out for a minute then they bounced." I replied.

"Well fuck it then we can handle that shit ourselves."

He walked to the front where Reddy, Pookie and Sticky were talking. It looked as though they all had guns in their hand. Smokey looked over at Reddy then pointed his head in my direction. Reddy quickly came out with another pistol and handed it to me.

"Peep this out here Blood. Those niggas is hanging out on Bradfield so we gon' just walk up on them and start dumping. Don't start letting off on them niggas until you see me start shooting. Aye Pookie, you gon' roll with me while Reddy, Grumpy and Sticky walk together. Once we ambush those niggas ya'll gon' finish them off. They killed one of our OGs, Blood."

With that said we made our way to the other side. We kept the guns lowered just in case we had to drop them because of the Sheriffs. When we made it to the block there was some activity going on further down the street. I kept hearing the word Cuz throughout the conversation. I noticed Smokey roll up with Pookie. That's when Sticky told us to hide behind some cars and ease into the crowd as quiet as possible. In a matter of minutes we found ourselves several yards from the targets. Not even a second later after I ran behind a Chevy caprice I heard shots from Smokey and Pookie. They were screaming and falling as the bullets began to riddle their bodies. A few of them ran in our direction while one shooter returned fire. The ones that came in our direction didn't stand a chance. We began to light them up. Reddy caught one on the ground so she plugged him in the head while he squirmed on the ground. We quickly ran off after seeing three bodies on the ground.

I remember popping one that was shooting back at the homeboys. He dropped like a sack of potatoes but I kept shooting. We all made it back to Holly Street in a matter of five to six minutes. With everyone still carrying their piece we met up at Turtle's house. Turtle must have known what we were about to do so he had called it a night. All the lights were out and no one was in the backyard. Smokey hopped into his car and Reddy followed by jumping into the passenger side. They sped off in a matter of seconds. He hadn't said anything about the pistols so I kept a hold of mine. Far as we were concerned we could have started a full blown war. Once they killed one of our big homies war was inevitable. Pookie and I embraced before we went our separate ways home. I strolled to my house on Locust Circle and went through the backyard so I wouldn't wake my mother. The window in my room was open so the breeze of the cool air had filled the room. I turned on KDAY radio station on my small boom box. A few years ago I had caught a Santana Block Crip slipping up at a

Dairy Market off of Long Beach Boulevard. I made him cough up his boom box without having a gun. He was too afraid to fight. I would have socked him up anyway but I wasn't big on beating up on cowards. I jacked him for his radio and gave him a pass. I had his boom box in my bedroom for the last two years.

Turning up the radio slightly I heard 'Boys in the Hood' from Eazy-E. The lyrics danced through my head as I lied on my bed. The pistol was hidden under my dresser. If my Moms were to come in my room she would have to lift the entire dresser to find the gun. She didn't usually bother with our bedrooms because she had her own room. My head had hit the pillow for less than a few minutes before I went into a deep sleep.

The next day I was on in the street to meet up with Pookie. Before I could make it to his house I seen some of the homeboys jammed up by the police. The Sheriffs were outside on the block three cars deep. When I noticed four of the homies being harassed I made my way in another direction. Pookie stayed on the other side of where they had the homies hemmed up. If I wanted to avoid them I would have to go around the block. When I walked a few houses down the street Sharon was outside watering the grass. She was a few years older than me but she was fine as hell. She usually wouldn't say much more to me than hi but today she wanted to talk.

"What's going on with the police, Grumpy? They've been rolling around here hot all day today." She asked offhandedly.

"I don't know what's going on. I just stepped out of the house like five minutes ago."

"Yeah they've been looking for somebody because they've been rolling up and down Myrrh Street since early this morning."

"So why do they have the homies jacked up like that?"

I knew she was trying to get information from me but I switched it around so she might tell me something.

"I think some Crips got killed for what happened to Big Sam. That's all it could be because if they were looking for someone, everyone in the neighborhood would know who they were looking for."

"Yeah that's crazy."

She sort of glared at me for not speaking on anything but she knew better. I stood right outside her yard staring at who they had on the police car. It was one of those gloomy days even though it was humid. The four homies with their hands laid out on the hood of the police car were Slow, Sticky, Kay-Kay and my brother Flintstone. I decided to walk up a little closer when I noticed my brother. It was a bunch of white boy Sheriffs and that meant that it could go anywhere. The wrong thing said or done could cause some problems. I was sporting my white All Star Chuck Taylor's with burgundy shoe strings. I had on some cut off gray khakis, a gray T-Shirt with a burgundy baseball cap. I had it turned backwards as I made my way to see what was going to happen. One officer was searching everyone while the other was asking questions with a notepad. The other two officers stood by their vehicles for back up. I decided to get close enough to hear what was being said since I didn't have any contraband. When I got within a few yards the Sheriff asking questions glared up at me. He had blonde hair with a part in his hair. He was buffed out like he was on steroids with a couple of stripes on his beige uniform. He gave me a once over then proceeded with his questions. He could tell I was young but also knew I wouldn't be stupid enough to walk up on him with a weapon. His back up was ready for anything to go down. I glanced at the faces of everybody on the car and the only one that looked as though he was about to bust was Kay-Kay. Kay-Kay was a real dark nigga with a bald head. He was buffed out as well and holding about eighteen inch arms. He stood at about 6'1 in height. He was institutionalized but he was usually calm and soft spoken. He was one of those niggas that didn't talk loud because he didn't have to. If you were in danger with him there would be no warning signs. I was glad he was on my team.

"We know that your hood was responsible for what happened last night. We want to let you know we will be on your ass from now on." Blondie stated.

"We ain't into gangbanging nowadays. That shit done played out. You barking up the wrong tree and that's on Piru." Slow replied.

"Don't give me that shit Mr. Browder. Murders are murders and you're too fucking dumb to get away with that kind of shit. I will haul…" Blondie continued

"Aye Officer, you need to tell this muthafucka to quit breathing down my neck. He searched me and didn't find shit; so what the fuck?" Kay-Kay cut in.

"Look we ain't Compton Police; we're the fucking Sheriffs so call us that. I'm almost done so shut the fuck up."

I glanced over at the Sheriff that did the searches and he was up too close for comfort. He was practically breathing down Kay-Kay's neck as if to fuck with him. I don't know what he got out of being that close to another man but he was close.

"Fuck he needs to give me five feet." Kay-Kay blurted out.

"What are you going to do about it if I don't?" The second Sheriff barked.

Kay-Kay went into action. He lifted his hands off the hood of the squad car and gave the Sheriff a right hook that landed flush on his jaw. He stumbled back on the black pavement and hit the ground with a thud. I covered my mouth and accidentally released instigating sounds. Blondie drew his gun and pointed it at Kay-Kay while the two other Sheriffs ran up on him to subdue him.

"One of you niggers move and your dead." Blondie announced.

The two back up Sheriffs slammed Kay-Kay to the ground then quickly handcuffed him. One of the squad cars was blocking where they had him but it looked as though they slammed his face into the concrete. When they lifted him up to put him in the car his nose and mouth were covered with Blood.

"This is Piru on mine." Kay-Kay announced.

They dragged him to the back of one of the cars. Sticky, Slow and my brother kept their eyes on the barrel of Blondie's gun. After one of the Sheriffs drove off with Kay-Kay in the back Blondie lowered his weapon.

"Get the fuck out of here." Blondie barked.

He went to help his partner off the pavement with the last remaining Sheriff. Together they carried the knocked out Sheriff to the passenger side then sped off. Once their cars hit the corner we all started laughing.

"That muthafucka Kay-Kay ain't wrapped too tight. That nigga took off on a Sheriff?" Slow laughed.

"You know they gon' beat his ass all the way to the station." My brother replied.

"Yeah he's gon' be beat the fuck up when he reaches the County."

"What's up Grumpy?" Sticky and I shook hands.

"What's up Sticky?"

He shrugged then I glanced up at Slow and my brother. Slow flashed a devious smile then nodded.

"What's up young nigga?"

"About to go holler at Pookie but I seen ya'll bumped up by One Time." I smiled.

"You ain't got a strap on you, Blood? The Sheriffs been hot then a muthafucka." My brother glared at me.

I shook my head but Flintstone kept staring like he was trying to probe to see if I was lying. I dismissed that nigga and started walking towards Pookie's house."

"Blood, don't just walk away from me." He grabbed my shirt.

"Aw Blood, leave that young nigga alone Flintstone. We gotta bee what's happening with our pistols anyway."

Flintstone reluctantly released a hold on my shirt then gave me a slight nod. I wanted to sock him in his mouth, brother or not. I was cool about it because of what Slow said. When I made it down the block to Pookie's house he was already standing outside the yard. He had already put a lighter to the rolled up weed he was holding in his hand. He puffed on it several times then passed it to me while he held in the smoke. Within seconds he was coughing the smoke out.

"This is some good ass weed, Blood." He coughed.

I was too busy taking my hits to respond. After inhaling then blowing out a cool ass puff of smoke I nodded.

"Why did the Sheriffs have the big homies hemmed up like that?" Pookie asked.

"Fucking with them because of that shit that went down last night. Sharon's fine ass said that One Time has been rolling up and down the block all this morning." I passed him the weed.

"When that bitch start talking to you?"

"She was just being nosy. If she would have asked Reddy crazy ass some shit like that, she would have probably been shot." I laughed.

"And that's on Piru." Pookie laughed as well.

We strolled down Holly Street watching our back. I would have had grabbed the strap I had from last night but I forgot about it when I left the house. On any given night Compton could get lit up with someone blasting. Now that the East side was hot we knew we still had to watch our back in the day time. When we got close to Holly and Compton Blvd and went to the back of the apartments of OG Ronnie-Ru. It was a four apartment complex with an up and downstairs. In the back was a large two car garage on both sides. Ronnie-Ru had a weight set in the back so the homies could work out. We figured that was where the homies were hiding since the police were so deep. The Sheriffs would know to go to Turtle's house or somewhere around it after awhile. So we had to change it up. For the time they didn't have a clue that a bunch of hoodlums were hanging out in the back of some pink and white apartments. It was a dice game going on when we walked up.

"My point is nine nigga. I bet I hit a nine or five while ya talking shit up in here." Nuck said.

It looked as though he was talking to Jake-Ru but I wasn't sure. Nuck was a pretty boy type with a shoulder length ponytail. He was always fast talking with a whining voice like he was a pimp. But what irritated you the most about Nuck was his laugh. He laughter was a combination of him sounding like he was coughing and he was a maniacal arch villain in a cartoon or movie. His laughter always made me laugh even though it was irritating. He was a personality that stood out.

"Now I told you niggas I was gon' come back here and break this muthafuckin' dice game but ya'll didn't believe a nigga. I'm OG P-Fonk nigga and Jake needs to stop catching all the muthafuckin' dice. What the fuck you scared, Blood." He laughed.

"Fuck you Blood and roll the dice."

"I need some brand new shoes so give me that muthafuckin' Nina Blues." Nuck rolled the dice.

He hit a six then he hit a five and his next roll was a nine."

"Fuck!!!" I heard several people say.

"Yeah nigga I'm an original East Side nigga. I do what the fuck I say I'm gon' do. Now watch me hit the seven on you niggas."

His next roll was a seven. Grunts came from the circle of dice players. I watched from a little distance because most niggas didn't like you close behind them if you weren't getting in the game.

"Hey Grumpy, let me holler at you for a minute." Slim tapped me on the shoulder.

I followed him close to the brick wall that stood about eight feet high. He was sporting a tank top with Levis and Stacy Adams. His Levis were starched and ironed so hard they could have stood in a corner by themselves.

"What's happening big homie?"

"I got love for that nigga Smokey but don't go running after that nigga like that. He can be wild sometimes. I ain't telling you to speak up on the dirt that was done but it doesn't make sense that everyone in the neighborhood got a good idea he had something to do with it. Even civilian muthafuckas nowhere near the game knows what he's doing. He's out there that much."

"We did what we had to do big homie. Those crab niggas killed Big Sam right in front of me." I frowned.

"Yeah, sometimes we got to lay some nigga down but everybody doesn't have to know. You bee what I'm saying young Blood?"

I nodded. I didn't want the whole world to know that I was putting in work. He wrapped his arm around me as we walked towards the dice game.

"Murder cases never close Grumpy and Smokey's crazy ass is out there with his shit and no one can tell him anything. You're a smart young nigga so don't get caught up in being out there like that. If you gotta do yo dirt, the less people know about it the better."

"I hear what you saying big homie."

"Alright then...now let's watch this loud mouth nigga Nuck break up this dice game." He smirked.

3
DEATH AROUND THE CORNER

Nah Pookie I want a fair one with this nigga!
Grumpy-Ru

Roccy was suffering another night of not being able to sleep. His nigga since Kindergarten was getting buried in a few days. They came up Crippin since they were damn near toddlers. He was young but Roccy had developed a reputation as a shooter. So was his homeboy C-Bone. At least he went out shooting when he was killed. The Pirus that blasted on C-Bone and other homeboys came in on both sides like an ambush. It was a constant war that was growing harder to quell.

"Punk ass slob niggas!"

It was a number of Crip sets off Alondra but there was only one Blood set on the East Side off Alondra. They were on the front lines against all the neighboring Crips but they managed to stay alive.

"We should have been knocked them niggas out the box." Roccy muttered.

He lifted himself from his twin sized bed and yawned. The digital clock sitting on the dresser read 3:47am. His fingers swam through his wild and curly afro. His girlfriend helped him take out his braids before she had to go home. He strolled in the kitchen wearing a blue wife-beater, blue basketball shorts and blue corduroy house shoes. He opened the refrigerator breaking the darkness of the house and grabbed the pitcher of water. Looking around first to see if the coast was clear then he took a swig of the water out of the pitcher. The cold water calmed his heated temperature so he fixed himself a glass then went back to his bedroom. Roccy sat on the edge of his bed and stared blankly at everything on his wall. The large poster of NWA hanging on his wall complimented the bedroom's décor. Next to the poster was a large blue handkerchief pinned on all four corners with thumb tacks. On the dresser next to the digital clock was his model car low-rider collection. His assorted colors were only different shades of blue and one black 64' Chevy Impala. Building those cars was the only time he felt at peace. His mood was mostly war especially when walking the Compton streets.

"It's Crip or die, Cuz!" He muttered.

The various pictures of him and his homies flashing gang colors and gang signs littered the wall. He sipped on the water taking in what he had committed himself to. He stared at the wall until he heard commotion going on in another room. His older sister's room was right next door to his so he was able to tell instantly that it wasn't her. When he glanced at the clock again it was a few minutes past four in the morning. His mother usually got up at that time to go to work. Motherly instinct must have sent her straight to his room. He heard the muffle sound of house shoes scooting in his direction on the carpet. She peaked into his room and noticed him sitting in the dark.

"Boy, are you okay?"

"Yeah, I'm good."

"Are you are still thinking about what happened to Corey? I know he was your best friend but baby life goes on."

"He was more like a brother to me, mama. You don't understand."

"I can't say I do. You young people are killing each other a lot faster than when we were coming up. It seems like no one ever fights in your generation anymore."

He wasn't in the mood to hear what she had to say. The thoughts of what was going on in his neighborhood consumed his mind. It was hard to explain to her all the details of the life he was committed to.

"Well you need to know that I love you and I need you to be careful. I can't watch you every second of the day so I need you to be careful. Stay in the house and watch television or go up to the park. But you need to stay out of the streets." His mother firmly stated.

Roccy just nodded as though he was in a trance. A war was about to take place and he had to decide how he was going to handle it. Those slob niggas can't smoke one of our homeboys and think they can get away with it, he pondered.

"Rashad, do you hear what I'm saying boy?"

"Yeah mama!" He snapped.

She stared at him for a moment then sighed. She walked down the hall to only find out that the bedroom door was locked. Now she was a little irritated but she had to be at work in an hour.

"Rashad, tell yo sister that I will buy her some new bras when yo daddy's child support check comes in."

By that time Roccy had lied down in his bed. He nodded then turned over on his side opposite of the door.

"I'll tell her."

He didn't get up from his bed until he heard her walking out the door. Roccy quickly dug under his bed and pulled out something wrapped tightly in a blue flag. He unfolded the Flag to reveal a long nosed chrome forty-five pistol. His lips curled upward wickedly as his thoughts wandered on his enemies.

"It's time to put in work."

Later that day he sat on his porch with his pistol tucked inside of his belt. He had only been on the porch for thirty minutes but he had seen three squad cars from the Sheriffs. That made him question if he should leave the porch while carrying the pistol.

"I might have to wait until it gets dark." He whispered to himself.

Right then his older sister came busting out the screen door. Her name was Rameka but everyone called her Me-Me. She had a pretty chocolate complexion with thick eyelashes. She wore her hair long down her back. To match her pretty face and pretty hair she also had a phenomenal body. Her good grades had her mother bless her with the latest clothes and freshest shoes. She came on the porch looking comfortable in a blue T-shirt, jeans and K-Swiss tennis shoes.

"Where are you about to go?" Roccy asked offhandedly.

"None of yo business." She rolled her eyes.

"See Cuz, I was gon' tell you what mama told me to tell you."

"What mama told you to tell me?" She stopped in her tracks.

"Ain't any of my business."

"Come on Rashad I'm about to go to Lisa's house. You need to have yo girlfriend come and do something with yo hair. You look like somebody scared you or something." She chuckled.

"Mama just told me she would get you some bras when Pop's child support check comes. And I'm waiting on Pam to come to the house. I didn't go over there because the police is too muthafuckin' hot." He sighed.

"Well I'm gone. I'll see you later. When is Corey's funeral because Lisa wanted to know because we was gon' go together."

"This Friday but you know the homies gon' be Crippin' real tough that day. The big homie Bear is gon' have a barbecue."

"Yeah that's what I heard. We plan on being there for all of that."

She said the last sentence while walking out of the yard. The phone rang from inside the house so he ran inside to get it. He was able to pick up the phone by the third ring.

"Hello?"

"Hey Roccy, this is Pam. My mama got me washing dishes before I can come over to braid your hair. Give me another hour baby and I'll be over there."

"That's cool, Cuz. I'll walk to the store and by the time I get back you will be on your way." He replied.

"That's why I love you baby."

He hung up the phone and went to wrap the blue flag around his head Aunt Jemima style. He knew it might be too much but he was feeling that way. He threw on his blue Nike's and locked the front door behind him. He would usually walk to the store with his road dog but that wasn't happening today. He strolled down the street while Mrs. Jackson just shook her head at him while watering her grass. That old lady needs to mind her business. He hit the end of the block and ended up on Alondra Boulevard. He turned to pick up some grease so it will be easy for Pam to braid his hair. He'll grab a bag of chips and chill out until he could see his girl. He walked inside and looked around for future items he would buy. Roccy took his time through the aisles because he had time to kill. Finally reaching the aisle for the grease he quickly grabbed a small jar then walked to the front of the store. He snatched up a bag of Doritos then slid a pack of gum in his pocket. He smiled at the middle aged cashier while he paid for the two items. After she bagged everything he strolled out. Roccy didn't make it all the way out the door before he spotted enemies.

"What's happening, Blood!?!!"

"Just keeping it Crippin' Cuz!" Roccy retorted.

"Oh Blood, we gotta catch a head up fade."

"Fuck this crab nigga Grumpy. Let's beat the shit out of him." The second Piru cut in.

"Nah Pookie I want a fair one with this nigga. Don't jump in on this shit."

Roccy accepted that he was outnumbered but he wasn't expecting one of them to want a head up fight. He had to claim where he was from or be marked a coward. They were about two yards away but Roccy figured they would still jump him so he braced himself for the worse.

"If this crab nigga had the upper hand he wouldn't give you a fair one." The second Piru protested.

"Look Pookie, I want a fair one with this nigga. Just because crabs are that way doesn't mean we have to be." Grumpy glared at Roccy.

"Fuck Slobs cuz, this Compton Crip foe life!!!" Roccy announced.

"This crab nigga got heart." Grumpy's lips curled up wickedly.

By then Grumpy had taken two steps forward and was in close enough range to swing. Without thinking they both went into the fray with both hands flying. No one gave ground for a few minutes then Grumpy landed flush on the chin. Roccy stumbled back a few paces only to retaliate with two more punches. It seemed as though Grumpy blew through his fist like the wind. Grumpy followed with a three punch combination that laid Roccy's ass on the parking lot Asphalt. Roccy was a little shaken by the punches but he quickly shook it off and rolled over to regain his footing.

"Get yo punk ass up Blood. Fuck crabs this Piru on mine." Grumpy barked.

Roccy stumbled awkwardly to his feet and threw up his fist. His breathing was labored but he pushed forward to fight. Grumpy glanced back at Pookie who was observing the exchange but eager to jump in. Grumpy's lips curled up one more time.

"I told you this crab nigga got heart. Fuck yo hood Blood." Grumpy growled.

The Piru was able to have the advantage because Roccy hadn't fully recovered. Roccy bravely put up his guard and prepared for Grumpy's second brutal assault. This time the blows rained down on him harder and easier. He was only able to get two or three punches in before he found his ass on the rugged asphalt of the parking lot again. Blood leaked from his mouth while he lied on the ground stunned and numb. The Piru he knew as Grumpy stared down at him with a look of disdain. There was also a slight grin of satisfaction decorating his face as well.

"Let's stomp this nigga out before somebody calls the police." Pookie rushed towards him.

Grumpy caught his homeboy before he could get close enough to do any damage. Grumpy pushed Pookie back then turned towards Roccy.

"This nigga got heart and he's down for his set. He could have ran or tried to pull out a knife or strap but he stood tall. What they call you?" Grumpy directed the last question to Roccy.

"They call me Roccy with two Cs." Roccy replied.

He tried to show some form of strength even though he was soundly defeated. He wiped the blood from his swollen lip. He was grateful that Grumpy didn't let his homeboy stomp him out but hated that he lost the fight. Satisfied that he had won the fight, Grumpy and Pookie walked away and left him on the ground. Roccy's equilibrium was slightly off as he used one hand to lift his body up. His head throbbed while he tried to shake off the dizziness of the blows that were thrown. He went back to the front of the store to see that his bag of Grease and Doritos were still lying on the ground where he left them. The pain was still throbbing as each step pushed him closer home. There would be another day to even up the score. His thoughts carried him all the way home. He was already home before he knew it.

Roccy rushed into the bathroom and washed his face with cold water. He put Neosporin on his busted lip then collapsed on the couch. He made sure to grab some of his mother's aspirin out of the medicine cabinet. He swallowed two before he fell off into a sleep. While in dream land a tatter on the front door shook him out of his slumber. He staggered to the door to see Pam staring at him. She was a sight for sore eyes. Pam was definitely a bombshell with a pretty cocoa brown complexion and a mole right above her lip. Her deep dimples would flash if she gave the slightest of facial expressions. She was top heavy with a firm butt that was round and plump. She was sporting a blue corduroy mini-skirt and a white and blue half shirt. Her thick lips were glazed with lip gloss while her shiny chocolate legs were complimented with blue open toe sandals. Her pretty feet had a fresh pedicure with a royal blue coat of paint on each toe.

"Damn you are looking good than a muthafucka." Roccy blurted out.

He opened the screen door and let her inside. All his troubles flew out of the window after seeing her at his door. He had totally forgotten for a moment that he was just in a fist fight with an enemy.

"What happened to you Roccy?" Pam frowned then touched his face.

"I got into it with some slob niggas at the store."

"You were by yourself?"

"Yeah, I had to roll alone."

"Oh I'm sorry baby. Let C-Bone Crip in Peace." She shook her head.

"Yeah I miss that nigga and that's on the set." He somberly remarked.

"And those slob niggas ain't anything but cowards and shit. Jumping my baby like that when you lost yo road dog." She frowned.

He didn't think it was wise to tell her that it was a head up fight. He knew that you could win some and lose some but he didn't want to taint her image of him. He laid his head on her plump bosom and tried to get some solace from that. That led him to kissing her on the neck and finally their tongues met. He easily slid his hands down on her heavy breast and his hand slipped under her bra. One of her chocolate boobs popped out of the bra. He sucked on the mocha flavored nipple until he was able to ease both of them out. He began playing with them while they sat up plump and perky. She glanced up at him like she was ready for whatever. She wanted to please him in every way possible. He quickly undressed her while pulling his clothes off as well. He slipped his pole between her breasts and began pushing up and down.

"Now suck on it."

She followed his instructions until he decided to bend her over the couch. He felt her tight wet walls as he hit it from the back. She was a virgin before they started dating. Now she knew how to back it up and work it herself. It was harder for him to hold it in before long. And just like that he exploded inside of her. They both collapsed on the couch breathing hard and panting. She laid her head on his sweaty chest.

"Can I have some water?"

Roccy got up from the couch and fixed a couple of glasses of water. After taking their time with the water and lying naked on the couch. Roccy glanced over at the clock on the wall and decided to get up.

"My mom gon' be home in another two hours. Can you braid my hair?"

"That's why I came over here."

"That ain't the only reason you came over, was it?"

"Not really."

The homies were huddled near the alley later that night. Roccy made sure he was out the house before his mother made it home. A couple of niggas was standing near the big homie Sticks' blue 1963 Chevy Impala. Sticks was a seasoned gangster and a respected Compton Crip. He had a few of the homies curb serving for him so he hung out while watching his money. Roccy smiled while taking a peak at his pistol secured in the belt of his pants.

"I'll holler at ya'll niggas later cuz." Roccy suddenly announced.

"Where are you off to, little nigga?" Mookie asked.

He didn't get a response from Roccy. By then Roccy had pulled the black knitted beanie from out of his back pocket and began sliding it on his head.

"Cuz is about to go put in work." Sticks replied offhandedly while puffing on weed.

Roccy made his way down to Alondra and crept up slow across the boulevard. The people he was after lived right around the corner and more than likely were hanging out there. He was only halfway down the block in enemy territory when he heard voices. He walked up on a crowd of gangsters at a distance of ten to fifteen yards then pulled out his pistol. He stared at who he was about to start shooting and never saw a familiar face. He was hoping he caught the nigga that was with Grumpy. He hated to admit it but he had a little respect for Grumpy. He wanted another head up fade but he would have to touch up his skills before that happened again. Besides, as long as he had his pistol he wouldn't have to fight. His aim was steady but he hadn't really pulled a trigger before now. In a matter of seconds when he thought he had a few enemies in range he pulled the trigger back. He let off all bullets in his gun then he heard the pistol click a couple of times. Noticing a few of his foes laid out on the ground he took off running back to his neighborhood. He didn't bother to stop and check on the homies but went straight home.

Once Roccy made it to his front yard he slowly walked onto the porch. He sat on the chair and thought about what happened. A chill went through his body as he grinned devilishly.

4

GAME RECOGNIZE GAME

*And the more pressure that cracker makes the more snitches gon'
start popping up!*
Reddy

    It's always hard to make money on the streets when it's a war going on. I was on the block for a week curb serving for Reddy. She was giving me dope on consignment and I would hustle that shit until I was sold out or it was three or four in the morning. I was missing a lot of days at school because I was on my grind. I was supposed to be going to Centennial High School on the West Side of Compton. It was only three high schools in Compton and two of them were Crip schools. Dominguez and Compton High were schools I couldn't attend for anything in the world. I would have Crips waiting to get me the moment I stepped on the campus. So I had my mother check me into school at Centennial where the Bloods went. Sometimes certain Blood sets liked to set trip on each other because it was Bloods from all over the place going to that school. Sometimes there was issues but for the most part it was the school to be at if you were a Piru or Blood. I had pulled this female named Denise who everyone called Neicy. She was sexy as hell with a cute shape and pretty ass eyes. She grew up over in Ujima Village which was on the west side of Compton. Their hood was called Village Town Pirus. That was the only thing that bothered me about missing so many days. I didn't get to see Neicy as much as I liked to. She would call me at the house but I was never at home. I decided I would have to go up there one day this week. While I contemplated my high school career going down the drain, Reddy pulled up. It was always unexpected with her. If she was in a good mood she was one of the coolest muthafuckas you could know. If she was pissed off or irritated then you don't know what would come from her. She pulled up in front of Pookie and me in her Cadillac. She jumped out of the car with pep in her step. She was in a good mood.

"What's happening P-Fonk!?!!"

"Soowooop!!!" I replied, that was the known Blood call.

"What you got for me today?"

I pulled out a wad of money that added up to twelve hundred. She looked down surprisingly at the money and cracked what appeared to be a slight smile.

"You are a sound muthafuckin' hustler, Blood."

"Yeah, well I would have more for you but the Sheriffs been rolling around this muthafucka deep lately."

"Yeah because we warring with these crab niggas. Don't trip though; you put more in my pocket than what I was hoping for. The rest of that dope is yours huh?"

"I'm almost out though."

"Don't trip I'll bring you some later today. I'll cop some of that shit later and get back at you tonight." She nodded.

"Tomorrow I'm going up to Centennial because I haven't been to school for the last week or so."

"Aw nigga, when have you been big on school? You going up there to fuck with some bitches or something. You are doing good right now. Don't let these bitches throw you off yo game." Reddy smoothly suggested.

"Don't worry about it Reddy, I'm gon' have yo money. I'm still gon' be on my grind no matter what." I grinned at her.

"I'm just trying to put you up on game, my nigga." She shrugged.

"I know what you're trying to do but I got this. But I'm gon' need that package as soon as possible so…"

"One time!" Pookie announced.

The Sheriff's pulled up in one squad car with two Sheriffs inside. They hopped out like they were about to swing on one of us. They made us all put our hands on the hood of the car. Naturally we were irritated. The dope was stashed so all we had was money in our pocket. They slammed the wads of money on the hood of the squad car.

"Where did you get all that money from Reddy?" One Sheriff asked.

"My mama told me to hold that money because rent is coming up." She quickly replied.

"What about you?" He said to me.

"I'm saving up to buy a car."

"Okay like we're fucking stupid. I'm not here about any dope but I better not catch any of you Pirus with a gun because I'm going to bury your ass. I could give a damn if you kill each other but after awhile people will think we're not doing our damn job. Give me your names since you are clean for right now. I already know your government name Reddy, Sheila Jones." He sounded irritated.

"Dwayne Pittman!"

"Kevin Johnson!"

"So you are Dion's brother? So Flintstone has his little brother in the streets stupid like him." He said to me.

I didn't have anything to say. I was hoping they would let us get our money back and they did after letting us go. Reddy walked back over to the sidewalk with us.

"I had my muthafuckin' strap in the car. That was punk ass Sheriff Cole. Fuck that peckerwood pig." She whispered after they left.

"They came out of nowhere."

"Yeah it's getting real bad when Cole starts putting the heat on niggas." Reddy reflected.

It seemed as though she knew something that we should know. Reddy was a testy bitch so I was a little reluctant about asking her but I needed to know.

"What's up with that pig?" I asked.

"It's getting real deep when Cole starts patrolling the hood. Did you trip how he knew yo brother? He gon' start locking niggas up on petty shit if this war doesn't stop. And the more pressure that cracker makes the more snitches gon' start popping up. I'm out; I got to get at Smokey about this shit."

"You gon' bring that through tonight, right?"

"Yeah, and ya'll need to make time to see the homies in the hospital. Tell Flintstone to roll ya'll up there." She replied.

"I thought all the homies was fine. It wasn't any serious shit."

"Still Blood, you need to holler at your homies." She opened her car door.

She hopped in her Cadillac and sped off a few seconds later. I wasn't tripping about going to see the homies in the hospital unless they were on their death bed or injured badly. They had flesh wounds and shit like that. Whoever the shooter was didn't get up close and finish what he was doing. He shot two of the young homies that were around my age Buck and Kool-Aid. They were hanging out over Turtle's house and got caught on Holly Street. Pookie and I would have been over there too if we wasn't around the corner hustling. I had a fight with a crab nigga earlier that day. The fight ran through my head and I cracked a smile. Pookie must have read my mind.

"We should have stomped that crab nigga down. The one you beat up the other day at the grocery store."

"Nah, because I respected the nigga for claiming his set." I replied.

"He had to represent his set he had a flue rag on his head." Pookie sneered.

Bloods never say the word blue because it represents Crips. Just like Crips never say red but they say dead instead. We called them crabs and they called us slobs. It was a part of the everyday lingo of gangsters. As for Pookie, I didn't know where he was going with this line of thought because it wasn't going to change the outcome.

"He got his ass beat so what difference does it make? Besides, that nigga could have took off running when he seen the two of us but he stood his ground."

"I don't know Grumpy; if it was in reverse then he wouldn't have gave either one of us a head up fight. Whenever those niggas got the upper hand they're always ready to jump a nigga." Pookie bitterly replied.

Pookie had been jumped several times by the Crips at Roosevelt Middle School. Since we were the only Blood set off of Alondra our neighborhood kids were assigned to Roosevelt school district. It ain't cool to have a bunch of young gangsters waiting for you every day after school. In those situations we never got a fair one.

"Yeah but that doesn't mean we have to be like them. I wanted that nigga to know that when the odds are even for him he still didn't have a win. He has to live with the fact that I had my homeboy with me and we didn't jump him and he still got his ass whooped." I shrugged.

Pookie didn't have a rebuttal for that. In fact he smiled at the thought of Roccy being humiliated.

"He still could have been one of the niggas that put in work against the homies. If we would have stomped a mud hole in his ass he would have been in the hospital so he wouldn't have been able to blast on the homies."

"Come on Pookie, Blood. First of all, we don't know if he was the one that blasted on the homies. Second of all, if he would have been in the hospital today then he would have gotten out in a few days and he still would end up blasting on some of the homies. We are in a war right now."

"Alright Blood...fuck it. You think you know everything."

I smirked at his comment then served a twenty piece of dope to a smoker. That was what Pookie and I did from time to time. We would argue, smoke some weed then slap box. That was how we sharpened each other's skill. I couldn't hang around a bitch nigga that didn't have what I had just in case we were caught in the trenches. I wanted to be seasoned in the game like the big homie Smokey. I had to hang around a nigga that thought like that too. I wanted to be nice in the streets like Magic Johnson was nice on the basketball court. When it was time to fight I can throw my fists. When it was time to shoot I can put in work. When it was time to hustle I could make that money. When it was time to holler at a cute bitch I could do that too. Every aspect of being a gangster was what I was striving to be the best.

I didn't hear from Reddy until around ten o' clock that night. She walked over to the spot instead of driving in her Cadillac. The sun was hot and warm during the day but now the chill of the cold air was fucking with a nigga. I had my Pendleton shirt on but the wind was still piercing through that shit. I saw her creeping up by the tall brick wall that had graffiti written on the wall. WELCOME TO EAST SIDE HOLLY HOOD PIRU GANG. It was written in big and bold black letter but hard to make out in the dark. I was down to a couple of pieces of dope which I knew was going to sell out any minute. She glanced around to make sure no one was creeping up on her then walked up on me. She pulled out a small 380' before she slid it under some shrubbery nearby. I shook my head and cracked a smile.

"What's so muthafuckin' funny Blood?"

"Yo crazy ass. You make sure you keep yo heat on you." I replied.

"I'm always Reddy. Get used to it my nigga. You been knew how I get down…now here's this package I got for you." She flared up.

"Calm yo ass down, Reddy. I don't feel like dealing with yo shit right now." I remarked while she handed me the dope.

"You are lucky I got love for yo ass." She shook her head.

"Maybe yo ass is lucky I'm yo homeboy."

She couldn't do anything but laugh. That lightened up the mood between us right away. It was always good to see Reddy smile because she was so damn pretty. She just so happen to be a killer.

"Where's yo road dog Pookie? I know that nigga didn't leave you out here by yourself and we're warring right now." She looked around.

"Nah, he went to the truck for us to snack on something while we make this money."

"He hit that burrito truck on Compton Blvd. and Pannez Street?"

"Yep!"

"Damn I knew I should have left when I first planned to. I wanted me a burrito like a muthafucka."

"I'll give you half of mine when he gets back with the grub."

"I got love for yo ass Grumpy. You a sound ass hustler too."

"You ain't got to tell a nigga that." I smiled.

She shoved me with her fist and smirked. A few moments later Pookie walked up with a bag of food.

"Cole came back around here since earlier today?" Reddy asked.

"Nah, I haven't seen him." I replied.

Pookie shook his head as well. The burrito truck always cut their burritos down the middle as if they knew you would share it with someone. I broke off half to Reddy and we all dug in. I wasn't that hungry so half of that big ass burrito would do me good. The warm food felt good going down the belly while standing in that cold.

"I got some of this bomb if ya'll feel like smoking." Reddy suggested.

"What took you so long?" Pookie replied.

She lit up well wrapped Kush in Zigzag papers. She had it hanging on the bottom of her lip while flicking her lighter.

"At this rate ya'll niggas is gon' be balling. I keep up the supply and ya'll keep putting down the hustle niggas is gon' eat for a minute." Reddy smiled.

"Damn where you get this bomb ass weed from? This shit is right." I commented.

"That's all Smokey be having is the bomb. That nigga ain't smoked stress weed in years." Reddy replied.

"Yeah that nigga is a real muthafuckin' gangster." Pookie said with admiration.

"And he likes both of ya'll young niggas." Reddy smiled.

"Blood, why do you be acting like you that much older than us? You only a year older than me and Pookie." I shook my head.

"I was talking about Smokey looks at ya'll as young niggas. Besides, ya'll the only two niggas in our age group I fuck with. I don't be fucking with Kool Aid, Loko and them." She waved her hand as if to dismiss them.

"Kool Aid and Loko is some riders though." I replied.

"Yeah, well why you ain't gone to holler at Kool Aid yet? He laid up in the hospital and you got all kinds of excuses." She retorted.

"Because I'm out here making this money." I shrugged.

"You lucky I got love for yo ass Grumpy." Reddy smirked.

The rotation was on me so I dragged on the weed. It felt good as the weed smoke went into my lungs. I was the coolest muthafucka on the planet."

Once we finished the weed Reddy was ready to leave. She had a little bit of conversation for us but not much. Her blazing that weed with us was her way of telling us she appreciated our hustle. She wasn't that big on compliments so I knew she meant that shit. I didn't know when she was gon' wig out so I figured it was best that she leaves. Reddy's crazy ass had a very short fuse and I was one of the few niggas she could tolerate.

The next day Loko rolled up to my house in a stolen car. He already had Pookie in the car when they pulled up. It was the same time I was supposed to leave to go to school. I was walking out the door when Pookie came walking into the yard. Flintstone peaked outside behind me.

"That stupid ass nigga gon' catch a GTA charge." He mumbled.

I turned around to see him walking in the kitchen. He hadn't totally woke up yet because he had yawned when he made his comment. I reluctantly walked outside to greet Pookie in the yard.

"He stole that car?"

"You know he did. I guess he did that shit by himself because Kool Aid is still in the hospital."

We walked toward the car while Pookie replied. I was a little reluctant to get in the car after that because I didn't know how long the nigga had the car.

"Blood, how long have you had this car?" I asked through the passenger window.

"Since the day before yesterday."

"So they've already reported this muthafucka stolen." I replied.

"So what Blood, I'm getting rid of it today. What you scared to get in or something? We going up to the Ten to get at some bitches." Loko replied.

He was referring to Centennial High School when he said the Ten. I hadn't seen Neicy in a minute so I jumped in despite my better judgment. When we got up to the school it was females everywhere. I had almost forgotten why I went to school in the first place. I wasn't even worried about Neicy until she walked up on me. Loko, Pookie and I were leaning on the stolen car acting like we paid for it off the lot. We were having fun before school let in laughing and clowning around.

"What's up with you Dwayne?"

I turned around from laughing with the homies to see Neicy staring at me with her hands on her hips.

"Damn Neicy, what's up with you?"

Neicy was a cute broad from the West Side. She lived over in Ujima Village so she was claiming Village Town Pirus. I couldn't help but to notice how good she looked. She was wearing a red silk blouse with a jean mini-skirt. She had on some Puma sneakers that were black with a red stripe. Her shape was showing through her cute little outfit. The way that ass was sticking out of that mini-skirt made me want to take her back to the house. My eyes thoroughly scanned her from head to toe.

"I'm about to go to class. Where have you been?"

"Trying to get paid. You know how it is." I shrugged.

"Well I ain't...

"So what's up Neicy are you going to class or what?"

We both turned around to see a stocky nigga with real bad acne. He was kind of mean mugging me but I just folded my arms and stared back at the nigga.

"Here I come Turbo damn." Neicy sighed loudly.

"What's up with that nigga?"

"Oh that nigga likes me. What are you jealous or what?"

"Game recognize game. I ain't gotta be jealous to recognize that you've been giving him some attention or he wouldn't feel he could speak up on you like that." I shrugged.

"Come on Dwayne, you ain't been to school in awhile. You ain't called me or anything and you expect me to just wait around. I always liked you though."

"Well fuck that nigga then. Show me how much you really liked me by coming to my house this weekend."

"Okay are you gon' come pick me up?"

"Yeah I'll come get you."

I didn't know how I was coming to get her since I didn't have a car. She nodded and smiled after I said that so I went along with the program. I guess I would have to cross that bridge when I got to it.

"We'll hook up on Saturday then." She rubbed my chest and walked to class.

Both Loko and Pookie were staring at me with all smiles. I played it cool but I was eager than a muthafucka to fuck with Neicy. I seen that little body walk off and I could feel the lust in my tongue.

We were hanging out up at the school but never went to any classes. It was always a spot where the gangsters could hang without going to class. When school let out we were out in the front again flirting with the girls. Neicy came out the front to talk to me for a moment and confirm that we would hook up on the weekend. She gave me one of those seductive sexual hugs that let me know she would be with the business if we hooked up. Pookie and Loko was spitting at females just the same until the campus pretty much dried up. Then we hopped into the car and made our way back to the neighborhood.

We decided to roll down Rosecrans because that's the route we always take. It was always the way back to the East Side for us.

"That bitch wearing the black spandex pants had ass, Blood." Loko commented.

"Yeah her name is Trina. I'm trying to fuck that bitch as soon as possible. Her people is from Fruit Town. What that one bitch you was hollering at with big ass titties?"

"Oh you talking about Shonda. That bitch be playing hard to get. I was trying to holler at Cynthia that runs track for the Ten. That bitch got body."

"Yeah she had a banging ass body. That nigga Grumpy trying to act all faithful with the one bitch what was her name…"

"One Time!" Loko whispered loudly.

"That one broad with the mini skirt…did you say one time?" Pookie asked.

"Where they at Loko?" I asked from the back seat.

"They right behind us."

"Fuck, we gon' get locked up for Grand Theft Auto on a bucket." I retorted.

"Those muthafuckas gon' have to catch me." Loko replied.

"Nigga if they behind us they running the plates right now." Pookie glared at Loko.

"Yeah they running the plates." I added.

"I don't give a fuck what they doing. I'm gon' hit the corner at this muthafuckin' light and dip on they ass. Once I get a distance we gon' jump out and every man for himself."

Pookie turned around to look at me. If we didn't have the same thing on our mind it was close to it. Why did we even fuck with this crazy ass nigga? That was when the Sheriff cut on his lights for Loko to pull over. He skirted out by hitting the corner hard making a right turn. I glanced back and seen the Sheriffs right on his tale. He hit his brakes once letting the squad car ram into the car we were in. That slowed the Sheriff down since he was by himself. But I could tell that he was making a call for back up. Loko punched on the gas and gave himself a little distance.

He made a quick left after side swiping another car and almost crashing into oncoming traffic. The Sheriff tried to follow but was tangled up for at least a minute. That was all Loko needed. He hit the brakes then pulled up on the curb and put the car in park. We all jumped out the car in a matter of seconds and ran in three separate directions. By the time the cop made it to the side street we had all went in different directions. He didn't know who to chase after. I hopped over a few fences then climbed in a couple of back yards until I found myself close to Compton Boulevard. I was nervous for more than just the police. I was in enemy territory. I figured it would be safer if I just made it to Compton Boulevard. Hopefully the Sheriffs wouldn't scour the Boulevards but the back streets instead. If I was walking down a main boulevard while the police were looking for someone they might think I just got out of school. Plus I didn't have any contraband if they stopped me. The other reason I thought hitting the Boulevard would be better was because enemies normally hung out on back streets. Even though it was broad daylight who would hang out on a main street and take the chance of getting caught in a drive-by? I hit a couple of more fences and found myself in the parking lot of a commercial business.

With as much ease as I possibly could I walked out of the parking lot. The exit was only a few steps from Compton Boulevard so I casually strolled onto major street. I had about five or six blocks before I was in neutral territory. That sounded like a breeze considering it was in the middle of the afternoon. Once I cleared my second block I noticed two men walking toward me in the distance. They were about a half block from me and walking fast. They were pretty much preoccupied with their conversation but I noticed them right away. They weren't wearing anything significantly blue but they wore black. That's always a tell-tale sign when you are walking up on Crips. A Blood will always wear some red to let you know what team he's on. If they were wearing neutral colors like black, gray or white more than likely that meant they were Crips. I wasn't wearing a lot of red but I did have on red shoelaces. My belt was also red but you couldn't tell because it was covered by my white T-shirt. I didn't have enough time to cross the street and they were moving up on me. Once they were in a short enough distance they couldn't help but notice my shoestrings. Both of their brows wrinkled up quick as we drew closer to each other. There was no way I was getting out of this so I might as well dive right in.

"What set you from, Cuz?"

"Holly Hood on mine, Blood."

I swung on the one to my left and my blow landed true. He stumbled back and almost fell. I turned to his other homeboy so me and him had an even exchange. He wasn't a pushover type of nigga. It was a struggle just to have an even exchange. He landed the last blow to my jaw but I went with the punch. His homeboy was able to recover and he smelled blood. I nailed him in the jaw one more time before splitting the two. This time he didn't stumble but absorbed the pain of the punch and countered. We exchanged several blows before we found ourselves locked in a wrestle match. My heart was pumping harder than normal. The sun was out but the wind was sharp and chilling. The exchange went on for a few seconds before his homeboy came and picked up a bottle from a nearby trash can. It was a small green bottle of Night Train. He crashed it right into my forehead and blood gushed out the side of my forehead but I didn't fall. They both hesitated to see the effects of the bottle. I stumbled down the street then took off running. I turned around several times to see if they would follow but they didn't give chase. I jogged all the way to the intersection of Compton Boulevard and Long Beach Boulevard. I crossed the street and let out a deep sigh once I made it across the street. My face was bleeding but I was able to walk the rest of the way home.

5

BATTLE TESTED

Don't ever come in arms reach of a nigga talking shit!
Grumpy

I wasn't fucking with Loko like that again. Fortunately for us we were all able to get away. I'm the only one that ended up with a cut across my forehead right under my hairline. It wasn't anything but a punk ass scar but I was really mad at myself. It was only the day before that Reddy told me she didn't fuck with them niggas like that. Loko would do shit just for the sake of doing shit. He wasn't getting any money by stealing cars. You know how most niggas will strip the car down and sell the parts or take it to someone that can strip it down; Loko wasn't that type of nigga. He was the type that would steal the car just to joy ride in it. Occasionally he might steal a car to do a drive-by but that was about it. He was a knucklehead nigga for the sake of being a knucklehead and I didn't get down like that. He wasn't a bitch nigga or anything like that but he was reckless. That was what OG Slim was giving me game about. Don't be all out in the open about it for the sake of getting a name. Put in work then move on to what you have to do to survive.

I was sitting on my porch when Pookie walked into my yard. I was trying to plot how I was gon' get Neicy over to my house today while my mom was at work. He shook his head when he reached the porch steps and cracked a half smile.

"I ain't fucking with that nigga Loko." He shook his head.

"Yeah I'm on the same page as you. I got this big ass band aid on my head because some crabs caught me slipping on Compton Boulevard." I replied.

"That nigga be on some stupid shit Blood. And like dumb asses we rode along with that nigga. I got love for the nigga but he does shit for the sake of doing shit."

I laughed to myself because I felt the same way. He climbed on the porch and sat on one of the empty chairs. Usually we would hit my backyard to lift weights but today we just sat on the porch.

"Are you going over on Pannez to hustle or what?" Pookie broke the silence.

"Yeah later on but I'm trying to find someone that will give me a ride to pick up Neicy. I talked to her last night and she still wants to come through."

"With her fine ass." Pookie replied.

As if on cue Reddy hit the corner in her Cadillac leaning to the side. She pulled up right in front of my house. She hopped out her car wearing jeans, a small white T-shirt and white K-Swiss sneakers. She had her red flag hanging a little bit out of the right side pocket. She stopped short of the porch and put her right foot on the first step.

"What the fuck happened to you?"

"Some crab nigga hit me in the head with a bottle. I was caught slipping over there in the wrong hood and they jumped me." I replied with a shrug.

"I heard you hopped in the car with Loko's dumb ass. Yo brother was talking to Smokey earlier today."

"My brother talks too muthafuckin' much."

"That nigga is a real gangster though. It wasn't like I didn't tell yo ass the other day that I don't fuck with them niggas." She frowned.

"Yeah well I know not to fuck with him now."

"So that's why you weren't on the block last night?"

"Pretty much."

"Now that nigga is fucking with my money. And yo 'follow the leader' ass gon' get fucked up with that kind of shit."

"Who the fuck you think you talking to Reddy. You come up on my porch talking shit."

She thought about what I said then pulled out a cigarette. She didn't smoke a lot but when she did she always showed signs of nervousness.

"I'm just saying my nigga, that you got be smarter than that." She blew out the cigarette smoke.

"I'm already knowing."

"I didn't mean to come at you like that on yo porch and shit. I just thought you knew better that's all."

That was her way of apologizing. The words 'I'm sorry' wasn't about to come out of her mouth but she would show it in the way she acted.

"Since you coming at me like that why don't you help me out with something?" I slyly asked.

"Oh so a bitch is feeling bad about some shit and you gon' try to take advantage of the shit?" She glared at me.

"Nah, I just wanted you to give me a ride to pick someone up."

"Oh so you want me to help you pick up a bitch? What the fuck I look like nigga?" She smirked.

"Look how you get down Reddy. I was caught up with Loko's crazy ass because I didn't have a car to get to the west side. You want to chew a nigga out for rolling with the homie but you ain't offering a ride and most bitches ain't trying to get on the bus anymore."

"What about you getting back on the block?" She fired back.

"That broad ain't about to be here forever. I just want to hang out with her for a few hours then shoot her back home. I'll be back on the block way before it gets dark."

"Ah so you got to take the bitch back home too." Reddy shook her head while puffing on her cigarette.

"If she's getting picked up naturally she gon' need a ride back to the house." I said incredulously.

"Well it's gon' look stupid me picking up that girl while you in the car. You should just roll the Cadillac and drop me off over Ronnie-Ru's house. All the homies is over there." She dragged on the cigarette.

"You gon' let me roll the Cadillac?" I asked in disbelief.

"Yeah nigga but if you get my shit towed, you gon' pay for it to get out the pound."

"That's straight."

"You got some money saved up or you gon' have to work off yo debts?"

"Ain't shit happened in yo car yet. But I always got a stash."

We hopped in the Cadillac and she allowed me to drive. I think she wanted to see how I rolled the wheel before she let me go off somewhere. I had driven my moms' car several times when she didn't feel like driving but she was always in the car. The Cadillac was smooth as I dipped the corner onto Holly Street all the way to Ronnie-Ru's house. When I rolled in front of his house Reddy and Pookie hopped out. I could see some of the homeboys hanging out but most of them were behind the building. I threw up the P sign for P-Funk then rolled up the street to Compton Boulevard. After making a left turn I drove down to Long Beach Boulevard and made a quick right to Rosecrans. Once I hit Rosecrans I made another left and kept driving down the Boulevard until I made it to the West Side. I made one more right once I made it to Central Avenue. I rolled into Ujima Village and to my surprise Neicy was standing out front. I pulled up on her in the Cadillac and she was a little startled. She didn't know if I was about to shoot her or what. It took a few seconds for her to realize it was me once I pulled up in front of her.

"Dwayne? Boy don't scare me like that."

"Aw baby I wasn't trying to scare you." I climbed out the car.

"Yes you was." She playfully hit me on the chest.

I wrapped my arms around her and we began kissing right there. I was grabbing her ass while we kissed. She was in another jean mini-skirt but with a white T-shirt with her name Neicy written on it in red cursive. More than likely she had it designed at the swap meet. After an extended kiss she held on to my hand for a minute.

"Are you ready to go?" I asked.

"Yeah, are we going back to yo house?"

"Yep!"

"Is yo mama at home?"

"Not now."

She cracked a devilish smile and hopped in on the passenger side. As we rolled down the street she looked around as I headed back to the neighborhood. It seemed as though it didn't take as long to get back. I passed by Ronnie-Ru's house but I didn't stop. I went straight to the house without any problems. We walked into the house and I quickly asked her if she wanted something to drink.

"No but you can show me to your room. I want to see how your bedroom looks."

My dick had gotten hard the moment she said that. She said it in a naughty and sexy way. She walked around on the palms of her feet with her ass poked out with one finger in her mouth. I wanted to start taking off her clothes right then and there. She looked around and noticed the posters on the wall.

"Ain't them NWA niggas Crips?"

"Probably so; but they the only niggas talking about real shit right now about Compton." I shrugged.

That made sense to her because she nodded like she had considered that herself. She slowly walked over to me with her finger still in her mouth and wrapped her arms around my neck. We started kissing again. This time the kisses were hard and passionate. Both my hands were grabbing on to her ass at this point. I lifted her mini-skirt so that I could feel on that soft ass. After we lied on my bed she started coming out of her clothes. I helped her take off her shirt then I took off mine. She wasn't too great in the breasts area but she had a nice plump ass.

When she was totally naked I just stared at her for awhile. She posed for me as my fingers made their way down and around her belly button. I lied on the bed and she climbed on top of me. She guided my manhood into the place where it should go. I knew right then that she had done this before. She started off slow but we began to pick up the pace slowly. She got into her little rhythm and began sweating. She had on some grown woman perfume so her perspiration was intoxicating. I stroked her plump soft ass as everything got more intense then suddenly she shook several times.

"Ooh shit Dwayne, that's it right there."

I pushed inside her and she swirled her hips around during a few more of my thrusts. All of sudden she stopped with her mouth wide open as though she was savoring the feeling. I decided to stop when she stopped but I wasn't finished yet. She looked down at me and smiled devilishly at me again.

"You want to do it doggy style?"

I didn't even answer her. I bent her over the bed and smoothly slid inside of her. She worked me doggy style while putting my hand around her neck. She grunted in a womanly manner. It was feeling too good to be true. That was when I felt the nerves in every inch of my body. I belted out a moan then attempted to push inside her a few more times before I collapsed on top of her. She kept pushing her ass into my pelvis as if to help me experience the full feeling of my climax. It was something that I could never believe felt so good in life. I fell to the bed and laid my head on the pillow and she planted her head on my chest. My breathing was labored but relaxed at the same time. My muscles felt loose and my body was floating.

"Why do your homeboys call you Grumpy?"

"My brother says that when I wake up in the morning it looks like I'm always pissed off about something. He even has my mom calling me that now. After awhile it just stuck…Grumpy-Ru."

"You know that nigga you seen me with the other day?"

"Yeah what about him?"

"He says he was locked up with your brother in L.P."

L.P was short for Los Padrinos Juvenile Hall. It was usually where the Sheriffs would take us if we caught a charge and was under eighteen. Sometimes they would release us from the Sheriff's station but that was only for petty shit.

"Oh so he knew my brother?" I asked with indifference.

"Yeah and he talking about you only get passes from niggas because of your brother. He says you ain't battle tested like your brother Flintstone. Niggas would have been ran up on you if it wasn't for yo brother."

That should have been my cue to run as far away from this bitch as I possibly could. If the nigga said it or not why is she bringing this to me. I don't know of a gangster that's gon' have something nice to say about a nigga taking his bitch. All she was doing was instigating some shit. I glared at her for a minute but tried to be cool about the shit. At this point I knew that whatever I said was only going to blow up bigger than what I said. I personally didn't give a fuck except for the fact I wanted to fuck her a few more times.

"If that nigga feels that way then he needs to run up on me for a head up fade." I shrugged.

"Yeah baby he doesn't want to get down with you." She smiled.

She was probably telling him the same thing. I wanted to jump up out the bed and throw her on her ass but I didn't know who I was crossing. Some of these broads got family members that got a reputation or an OG status in their hood. Since she knows where I live she could easily send some niggas to my house and light it up. I had to be smart with this messy bitch. Originally I thought about offering her some food and drink but after that small conversation I reconsidered. We didn't talk about it for the rest of the time she was there but I knew it wasn't over.

I figured out a way to shoot her back to the house without looking like I was rushing her out the house. The phone rang and when I answered it I pretended like it was my mom on her way home. We quickly got dressed and hopped into the Cadillac. I dipped off of Locust Circle onto Holly Street all the way up to Compton Blvd.

"Where are all your homeboys? I don't see any of your homies hanging out in ya'll hood? Is everybody in the house?"

"We have a few kick it spots but you just have to know where they're at. We on the front lines off of Alondra fighting all those crab niggas."

I was telling her that as we passed by Ronnie-Ru's house but I wasn't about to tell her where the homies kick it. She had already made me wary when she brought up that nigga from school. When I dropped her off in Ujima Village she gave me a real nice kiss. She waved as she walked away from the car. She was acting like she was in love. I made a three wheel turn and rolled out of Ujima Village and headed back to the hood. It wasn't surprising to see the Sheriffs jack some gangsters on Rosecrans up. They had three gangsters with their hands on the hood of their own car. It looked like a 1985 Regal Supreme sitting on gold rims with gold spokes. The Regal was a shade of brown that was more than likely a factory made color. They were Bloods but I couldn't tell what set they were from. They were older gangsters probably in their late teens or early twenties. They wasn't wearing a lot of red and that was how I was able to tell they were older but they wore enough to be recognized as Damus. It is only been two lanes on Rosecrans but you also had the gutter lane where cars could normally park. They had them jammed up in the gutter lane. The Cadillac was in the left lane away from the Sheriff's prying eyes. I still watched them as I made my way back to the neighborhood. It wasn't long before I pulled up in front of Ronnie-Ru's house. I parked the car a couple of houses down from his apartment complex.

"What's up Grumpy, Blood?" Loko announced.

I embraced him and noticed Kool Aid hanging out on some crutches. He was sitting on a broken weight bench while a few homies were admiring Smokey's car. He had a beige 1963 Chevy Impala. His tires were white walls and his rims were gold. Glancing inside I could tell that the interior was all original. The car was parked on the grass behind the apartment complex so no one could see it unless they went towards the back. That car was so pretty that I wanted to kiss on her. Reddy hopped out of the passenger side with a wrinkled forehead. She walked around to the driver's side of the car. She tossed a cigarette to the ground and stomped it completely out with her shoes.

"Where's my Cadillac at Blood?"

"It's right outside" I tossed her the keys.

She caught the keys then her lips curled up slightly. She glanced around then eased up close enough for only me to hear.

"You already dropped that bitch off at the house?"

"Yeah and good looking on that." I nodded.

I turned around to see my brother Flintstone, Slow, Jake-Ru, Kay-Kay, Nuck, Slim and Ronnie-Ru drinking on hard liquor. Normally it would be beer but they were passing around Night Train and Thunderbird. The homies from my generation hanging out were Pookie, Loko, Kool Aid and Timmy-Ru. One of the big homies passed me a bottle of Night Train so I took a couple of swigs.

"What you know about that Blood?" Flintstone snatched the bottle.

I pushed him and he almost stumbled and fell. When he regained his footing he tried to rush at me but Smokey caught him before he could get in arms' reach.

"I'll fuck yo young ass up Blood."

"You act like I'm about to run from yo ass."

"Nah Blood, ya'll niggas is brothers. And ya'll from the same hood."

Smokey was right but I was probably a little salty about what Neicy said. That was why I probably always picked a fight with my brother because I wanted to prove to myself I was just as down as him. When he calmed down Smokey let him go and he took a swig of Night Train. Reddy shoved me a couple of times then whispered in my ear.

"Why you always starting up shit with yo brother?"

"That nigga snatched the punk ass bottle from me." I said incredulously.

"You know what I mean nigga." She glared at me.

"Whatever Blood."

"You gon' hit the block in a little bit?"

"Yep, I gotta make some paper."

About an hour later I hit the block with Pookie. We didn't call it a night until close to three in the morning. I linked up with Pookie close to noon and we caught the bus up to Centennial High School. He wanted to holler at this female he was talking to. We decided to hang out in the back until lunch time then we would make our way on campus. He found the girl he was looking for so we posted up while he got at her. I turned around to see a pack of four gangsters coming in my direction. I thought for sure they were about to jump on some Crips somewhere but I couldn't predict where they were headed.

"Blood, ain't you Grumpy-Ru from Holly?"

"Yeah, who wants to know?"

I noticed Pookie break his embrace with his girlfriend thru my peripheral. He eased closer to me as we both sized up all four who came at us.

"They call me Mack-B and I heard you wanted a head up fade." He eased up in arms distance.

My right fist slammed into his jaw. He stumbled backwards a few steps but didn't fall. I didn't give him any time to breath. I followed that up with a three-punch combination to his mouth. He hit the pavement so hard that he slightly slid on the ground. He stumbled to his feet quickly.

"Let these niggas handle it head up, Blood." Pookie announced.

This time his guards were up and he rushed at me. His equilibrium was off so he wasn't throwing his best at me. I had to admit to myself that this nigga was tough. Since he was already dazed I decided to just pummel him to the ground. Two more punches followed after he swung at me and missed. Instead of just falling to the ground he grabbed a hold of my T-shirt and dragged me down with him. Before I could fall all the way to the ground I snatched loose of him and hit him in the mouth while he was on all fours. That brought him to the ground leaving him open for me to stomp on him.

"Nah Blood, I ain't gon' let you stomp the homeboy like he's a crab." One of his homeboys stepped up.

"Nigga yo homeboy lost a head up fade Blood. He gotta take his ass whooping how it comes or me and you gotta get down." Pookie barked at him.

I leaned down to see that Mack-B was in no condition to fight. I squatted down while he tried to recover.

"Don't ever come in arms reach of a nigga talking shit. If you were a crab nigga I would have stomped yo ass out and that's on Piru." I stood up.

Pookie and I walked out of the school as quickly as we could. He didn't get a chance to say bye to his female friend. When we made it a couple of blocks down the street Pookie tugged on my shirt.

"What was that about Blood?"

"That bitch Neicy being messy. When I fucked her the other day that bitch gon' tell me some nigga was going around saying that I wasn't battle tested. Only reason niggas ain't running up on me is because of my brother Flintstone."

"So that bitch is running back between the both of ya'll?"

"Yeah, but I ain't fucking with that messy ass bitch. Broads like her will get a nigga caught up in some shit. If she was there I probably would have smacked the shit out of her just for running off at the mouth."

"Well that nigga gon' think twice next time he wants to say you ain't battle tested." Pookie smirked.

6
HOODRATS AND HOES

That still don't mean I'm gon' get at any random bitch!
Loko

In the hood you go through stages when you are in the streets. The first stage is being introduced to the game. Whatever attracts you to the game is what makes you want to be in the game. Some niggas like squeezing triggers so the thrill of shooting a gun seduces them. Then you have niggas that want to make money. A sound hustler can make serious money in one night if it's a good night. Some people that get in the game love having homeboys around that they can kick it with. Whatever it is that makes you become a part of the streets you hold on fast to that and it is what keeps you going. The next stage is the pain stage of the streets. That's what tests who you really are in the streets. It could be prison, getting shot or stabbed or stomped on by an enemy that starts determining your character in this concrete jungle. Compton is a city that will show you the most brutal and violent things the street has to offer. A man will be tested on what he says he is at some point in the Hub City and I'm no different.

Women can be any man's downfall. There are so many women in the game that it can distract you from what you trying to do or be. All I ever wanted to be was the ultimate gangster. Some niggas go into this game half ass and don't fully commit to what they say they are about. I couldn't look in the mirror living like that. So now I started getting calls from Neicy every other day. I was skeptical about even talking to that messy bitch. One afternoon I decided to pick up the phone only to hear Neicy's voice on the other end.

"What's up with you Dwayne? You ain't answering my calls now? I let you fuck and then you stop calling."

"Because I don't fuck with messy ass females. You've been going back and forth between Mack-B and me." I calmly replied.

"So you were the one that beat up Mack-B? I ain't got anything to do with what's between you and him."

"Yeah right, you told that nigga that I wanted a head up fade. It wasn't a problem for me but I bet he won't be quick to run up on a nigga like that again." I smirked.

"I didn't tell him shit. All I told him was that you and me are talking. So he would know that I got a boyfriend."

"When did we say that we were together?"

"Come on Dwayne, we ain't together?"

"I'm just saying."

"I could be pregnant and you pulling this shit. That's just like a nigga."

"Pregnant!?!!" I began coughing

"Yeah pregnant."

"The baby ain't mine! We only fucked once."

"It only takes once. I just missed my period and I ain't fucking anyone but you."

"Oh so you and Mack-B never fucked around?" I asked like I already knew the answer.

"Nah that nigga just liked me."

I just sighed through the phone. It might be possible that this bitch just might be telling the truth. I wasn't ready for a baby. Neither her or I spoke through the phone for several seconds.

"Well if you find out for sure let me know."

"What about us? Are you my man or what?"

"Yeah that's straight. We can be together."

She sounded happy when she got off the phone but I didn't really give a fuck. I wasn't in any stage of my life to have one girlfriend and a baby. It wasn't in the plan. I stepped outside to see Kool Aid limping down the street. I didn't want to be bothered with anyone but he noticed me on my porch and walked over. He had slowed down a little bit after getting shot. He and Loko were still road dogs but he was trying to calm down. When he walked up I stepped off the porch and we embraced.

"What's happening Blood?" He nodded.

"I don't know, just trying to dodge games by these crazy ass hoes. How you feeling walking on that leg?" I sincerely asked.

"That shit hurts sometimes but I'm getting better. My grandmother says it's gon' really hurt when I get old. I don't even know if I'm gon' make it to twenty-five and she's talking about getting old." He shook his head and smirked.

I looked at him curiously because I never considered what he was saying until then. I didn't know how I would be at twenty-five because it seemed so far away. He pulled out a wrinkled joint of weed and slid it in his mouth. It hung on the tip of his bottom lip while he talked.

"You want to hit this shit Blood?"

"Yeah let me hit that. What kind of weed is that?"

"This is that Buddha Tai weed. This ain't the shit that Smokey be having but it's still bomb ass weed." He puffed then passed it to me.

"Yeah they call that Skunk weed."

"Nah they call that shit the Chronic now." Kool Aid glanced at me.

I took a few puffs of the weed and passed it back to him. He was glancing around as though he was watching out for someone. At first I assumed it was because he had been shot recently.

"What's wrong with you, Blood?"

"Ain't shit wrong with me." He glanced around again.

He walked over to my porch and pointed to one of the chairs. I quickly nodded then climbed in the other chair. My eyes scanned his movements because he didn't seem the same. He had a paranoia thing going on. I wasn't with that kind of shit because you don't know when your time will come. It doesn't make sense to dwell on it.

"What's up with Loko's crazy ass?"

"I haven't got at that nigga today."

He puffed on the weed then passed it to me again. The skies were gloomy even though it was a warm day. California weather was funny like that sometimes. Living on Locust Circle was sometimes deceptive as far as being a nice neighborhood. It was in the cut and you had to drive on Holly Street in order to get to Locust Circle. If the homies decided to hang on the circle it was hard for enemies to find us. They always caught us slipping on Holly Street. My thoughts wandered as my brother walked up to the yard.

"What's happening Blood?" His deep voice bellowed.

We both returned the greetings while Flintstone put one foot on the top step of the porch. Kool Aid had the weed in his hand when Flintstone arrived.

"Let me hit that."

Kool Aid passed him the weed and he took a few puffs then passed it back to me. The rotation was going cool. Kool Aid stuck his chest out a little more when Flintstone walked up. He obviously had a lot of respect for my brother and my brother pretty much liked him as a young gangster.

"Where is Loko and Pookie?" Flintstone asked.

"I don't know where that nigga Pookie at and he ain't seen Loko." I replied.

"Oh. We served those crab niggas for what happened to ya'll." Flintstone said to Kool Aid.

"That's good looking big homie. It's time I went out there and handled my business with these niggas."

"Yeah but wait until you ain't limping. The homies gon' have yo back but don't rush into that shit, Blood. We know you a down ass nigga."

"Yeah."

"Aye Grumpy let me where your Brim hat tonight. We gon' be hitting up Skateland and that hat matches my other shit."

"I don't give a fuck. How are ya'll getting up there?"

"Reddy, Sly and me are rolling with Smokey up there. It's gon' be bitches up there tonight." He cracked a half smile.

"We might try to go up there tonight if we can." I smiled.

"Alright then."

He ran inside the house after that to get his clothes ready for the night. I knew how my brother got down. He had been making money with Sly from jacking people for their rims and parts. They would sell the parts to a mechanic then sell the rims on the street. So he had some money in his pocket to floss with the females. If a Blood wanted to meet some women and didn't have to worry about the enemy, Skateland was the place to be. It was on the west side of Compton off of Central Blvd. next to Dootos. Dootos was also a club but it was a landmark for Pirus because it was where OG Bartender was killed. He was one of the founders of Leuders Park Pirus. Skateland was now the spot that Dootos once was. All those thoughts flooded my mind before I glanced over at Kool Aid.

"We gotta go up to Skateland tonight and get at some bitches."

"Yeah that shit will be tight but we can't catch the bus up there." Kool Aid shrugged.

"I'll figure out something before the night is over." I replied.

Later that evening while I was at the spot Reddy walked up. She came by to drop off another package even though it was a slow night. She was already geared up when she approached. She had on a red Gucci shirt, some tight 501 Levi Jeans and a pair of all red Adidas. It irritated me a little bit because I wanted to go where she was going.

"Damn Reddy, I forgot you got a little ass back there." I playfully peaked at her ass.

"Whatever Blood. You might want to put that shit away." She handed me the dope.

I put the dope in one of my stashes then handed her a wad of money. She smiled then leaned on the wall.

"So you going up to Skateland tonight?"

"Yeah, how did you know…Flintstone?"

"Yeah that nigga came walking up earlier wanting to borrow some shit while I was chilling with Kool Aid. I want to go up there tonight with ya'll." I replied.

"I thought you were about making that money. I'm telling you Grumpy, chase after the money and these bitches will follow. By the way, I heard you got down with Mack-B from the West Side over a bitch."

"Hell Nah, that nigga got at me talking about he heard I wanted a head up fade with him. When he came in arms distance I put hands on him."

"Yeah some of my homies from around the way told me you beat his ass. Niggas can't really trip about it because it was head up. I heard Pookie stepped in when one of his homeboys tried to break it up."

"Damn how do you know all this shit? You might as well had been there." I replied in disbelief.

"I got homies that from all over the place since I've been locked up in juvenile hall and everything. You a down ass nigga Grumpy and I got love for yo ass." She half smiled.

"Well if you got love for a nigga then let me drive yo Cadillac up to Skateland tonight. You can still roll with Smokey and I follow behind ya'll."

"Oh so I let you roll it to get at a bitch now you want to drive the shit all the time. Just because I gave yo ass a compliment don't mean you gon' run all over me, Blood." She flared up.

"It ain't like that Reddy; I was gon' roll behind ya'll. I'm just trying to go up to Skateland and have a good time like ya'll. You know what I'm saying."

Reddy glared at me then put her head down for a moment. She had that way of analyzing some things like she was about to hunt you or something. I made sure to give her eye contact because me backing down would have made her look at me like I was scared or something. She always kept it gangster and looked for signs of weakness. She developed that habit from hanging around Smokey because that's how he was.

"Blood I'm gon' give you the keys and you better put some gas in that muthafucka this time."

She handed me the keys then walked off. I walked off also but in the other direction. Suddenly I remembered that I had the stash hidden somewhere so I came back to get it. I couldn't take the chance of someone finding it. After I grabbed the package and practically ran down Holly Street until I made it to the circle. That was when I ran into Kool Aid, Timmy-Ru, Loko and Boney-Ru. They were sharing a couple of forty ounce bottles of Old English Malt Liquor.

"Blood, what the fuck are you running from?" Loko asked.

"Nah I'm going to the house so that I can roll Reddy's Cadillac up to Skateland tonight."

"Ah shit, Reddy said you can roll her Cadillac?" Kool Aid laughed.

"Yeah, have any of you niggas seen Pookie?"

"I ain't seen that nigga all day today." Loko replied.

Everyone pretty much gave the same response by gesturing with their head. It was heavy on my mind of what could have happened to him. I couldn't wait on him because I had to hurry up to catch up with Reddy.

"Ay Blood, can we roll with you?" Loko asked.

"I don't give a fuck." I shrugged then ran in the house.

I took a quick shower and slapped on some cologne to blend in with my gear. I had on a white T-shirt, with beige khakis, white Reeboks with thin red laces and a San Francisco 49ers Starter Jacket. When I walked outside all the YGs were waiting outside of my yard on the sidewalk. They followed me around the corner down to Ronnie-Ru's house. I knew that was where everyone would meet up to roll out. When we made it over to the big homie's house Smokey and everyone else was piling up inside of his truck. I ran up to the passenger side to holler at Reddy. My brother and Sly were sitting in the back seat.

"What's happening Reddy?"

"Damn Grumpy, you almost got left."

"What's up with the little homies?" Smokey interjected.

"They were gon' roll with me." I replied.

Reddy glared at me when I said that. She was playing it cool but she was kind of pissed off that I had invited the young homies. That wasn't part of the deal. I shrugged a little bit hoping she would still hand me the keys.

"Fuck it let all the homies roll and I'll even pay for those little niggas to get in." Smokey announced.

That's when Reddy's facial expression changed and she handed me the keys. All of the homies piled in the Cadillac and we were rolling five deep. Once we made it to Skateland it was already packed. You could see red lined up outside the door. Bloods from different neighborhoods were standing in the long line to party and talk shit. We found a place to park then stood in line nine deep until we were able to get inside. It was pretty ass women everywhere. They had on their red just like everyone else. It took us about thirty minutes to get inside.

Once inside the dance floor was already filled with people gathered in small packs dancing in the dark. The dance floor was downstairs where skating would usually take place on certain nights. Upstairs was where the DJ booth stood and on both sides were the latest video games. Directly across from the DJ booth was the concession stand to order different types of food. There were ramps on both sides of the booth that led down to the dance floor and on the other side of the concession booth was where everyone sat to eat their food. No one was allowed to bring food onto the dance floor. Once you hit the dance floor there were sets hanging out with each other in small packs. So if you had beef with someone more than likely he was with all of his homies. Then there were people from other sets that you had love for. Some you went to high school with or was locked up with at one time or another. For instance, Loko was locked up with a few people on a juvenile stint so it was Bloods from LA and Watts that had love for him. Since Damus were outnumbered 2 to 1 in all of Los Angeles County, they got along once they got locked up together. After all the reunions and reconnections we partied until the late night. I went upstairs to the concession stand to run into this pretty ass girl. She had a pretty caramel complexion with hazel eyes and a fat ass. She stood about 5'2 in height with the cutest dimples. She sort of giggled as we tried to pass each other. She had on a one-piece jean dress that tightly wrapped around her body.

"Damn baby, you must be trying to get to know me."

She smiled without saying anything. I pushed up closer to her and decided to start whispering in her ear. She was nodding to everything I was saying then a disruption incurred.

"Bitch, you fuck with my man again and I'll kill yo ass."

A heavy set female with big ass titties and a short bob hairstyle started swinging on another female. She basically toppled the girl to the ground and began beating her down while the girl was laid out on the floor. The heavy set girl didn't show her any mercy either. By the time security came to break up the fight there was blood all over the floor. That was my chance to wrap my arms around Portia. That was the name she gave me after sliding me her phone number. She welcomed my advances as my hand wrapped around her small waist. When I pulled her closer to me she whispered in my ear.

"You got some of yo homeboys with you? I'm up here with three of my homegirls so I wanted to know if ya'll want to kick it."

"Where we gon' kick it at?"

"At my homegirl's house. Her mom is out of town for the weekend. We can go back there with drink and everything."

"Yeah I'm with it. Get at yo homegirls so we can make this happen and meet me by the DJ booth."

I found all the young homies hanging together checking out some cute high school broads.

"Man that little bitch got ass." Kool Aid shook his head.

I glanced in the direction to see a little chocolate girl smiling at him. I walked up to the homies excited.

"Ay Blood I thought you was gon' bring back some chili cheese Fritos?" Boney-Ru asked.

"Aw Blood I forgot all about that shit. I got at this cute little bitch upstairs and she got some homegirls. They want to go back to their house."

"They some crab bitches?" Loko asked.

"At Skateland?" I glared at him.

"That don't mean shit."

He had a point but I wasn't trying to hear what he had to say. I pushed him to the side and began my spiel with Kool Aid and Timmy-Ru.

"She got to have some cute ass friends. At least let's go check them out and if they tore up then we won't fuck with them."

That made sense to Kool Aid and Timmy-Ru and Boney-Ru followed even though he couldn't hear what I said over the music. As we began walking off Loko grabbed me by the arm. I almost lost my temper until I turned to see his facial expression. He had a worried look on his face.

"Grumpy you don't know those bitches."

"Look nigga, either you like pussy or you like dick. What do you like, Blood?"

"Pussy! That still don't mean I'm gon' get at any random bitch. And the big homies are around here somewhere. We can't leave without them." He pried.

"We came with the big homies but that don't mean we have to leave with them. Are you coming or what?" I was irritated.

He followed behind me as we walked up the ramp and found ourselves gathered around the DJ booth. Portia and three of her homegirls were already waiting on us. Two of them were cute but one was kind of on the heavy side. She had big titties like the girl that was fighting earlier. Someone would have to take one for the team while someone else didn't get a bitch at all. I had pulled the baddest one in the pack. When I glanced at the clock on the wall it was already one-thirty in the morning. Skateland closed at 2am. It was a perfect time to leave before it gets too crowded to get out in a hurry. All nine of us made our way to the parking lot. Portia was happy to see me driving even though she was on the passenger side of the vehicle she was in. I didn't care about that. I pulled up close to her and she told me to follow them. They were rolling in a gray 1988 Cutlass Supreme.

We must have made it into the East Side of LA but I was a little nervous when the car started jerking. I glanced in the rearview and Loko was sitting in the back seat pouting. When I glanced at the road the girls had gotten a little distance so when I punched on the gas the car fizzled out. We were stuck in the middle of the street. There was a grocery store down the street in a shopping center. After turning the ignition several times it was obvious we had ran out of gas.

"We should have gotten gas on the way up there." Kool Aid commented from the passenger side.

"Let's just get out and push this muthafucka into that shopping center parking lot." I replied irritably.

We pushed the car down the street until we made it into the parking lot. The Cadillac was heavy but we managed to park it.

"Are those bitches gon' come back?" Kool Aid asked.

"Man fuck those bitches. How are we gon' get back to the hood?" Loko growled.

"Let me see if she got a gas can up in here. We can put our money together and get some gas to get back to the hood." I suggested.

When I popped the trunk there was nothing we could use to put gas in the car. I let out a sigh after realizing we were stranded. The females that were with Portia never turned around to see what was up with us.

"It looks like we gon' have to walk back to the hood." I admitted.

"Blood we stuck on the East Side of LA. You know how many crab hoods we got to walk through to get back home?" Loko snapped.

"Fuck you Blood, we all stuck in this shit. You had us caught up the other day behind that stolen car."

"Fuck you Grumpy. That's what the fuck I'm about to do now is steal me a car so we can get back to the hood."

We almost got up in each other's face before Kool Aid came between us. He was frustrated himself but he was more sensible than the both of us.

"Let's just worry about getting back to the hood." He frowned.

We walked about six or seven blocks before we heard a bunch of niggas hanging out. I didn't even know what hood we were in before we were spotted. It was confirmed that it was Crips when one of them said something.

"Aw cuz, who are these niggas."

They were older than us and bigger. The number was about even but they could have had one or two more gangsters than us. That was the first time I was really scared but I couldn't show it.

"What set ya'll from Cuz?"

"Holly Hood Piru, Blood!" Kool Aid announced.

"Aw we got slobs in the hood, cuz."

That was all I heard before we were quickly surrounded. I swung on one of the Crips and my fist landed true. Next thing I knew we were in the middle of a brawl. I felt something sharp pierce my skin but I kept fighting. I glanced around and saw three of my homies run off into the night. I looked to my side and the only one standing next to me was Kool Aid. He stood his ground with me.

"Yo own homeboys ran out on ya'll slob ass niggas. This Crip on mine cuz."

"This Piru on mine Blood." I replied.

Kool Aid and I put our backs to each other and stood our ground. They were coming at us now with all they had. That's when I seen the blade that had cut me. One of the Crips was lunging in at one of us every chance he got. He didn't have much heart because he didn't just start stabbing away at us. I was surprised that no one had a gun. It wasn't much doubt in my mind that we were going to die today. I wanted to cry but I couldn't let my enemies see me weak like that. Tired, sleepy and fatigued we were breathing hard but still standing. We didn't know if they were going to get more guns or was the one with the knife going to stab us to death. I was too tired to run and too tired to fight. There was no choice in the matter so we would fight until both of us were dead.

"Holly Hood Piru Gang Blood!" I announced before jumping into the fray.

7
A LONG DAY

My brother is in the muthafuckin' hospital and these punk ass little niggas ran out on him!
Flintstone

We were trapped and outnumbered at least six to two. If I'm to die tonight let me at least die fighting and as a man. I felt the blood leaking from my side. It wasn't all the way through but I felt the pain. My breathing became labored but I stood tall with Kool Aid back to back with me. He was holding off three or four Crips coming in his direction and he still walked with a limp from being shot in his leg. The one with the knife made his pass towards me again. I knew I was a goner this time around.

"One Time!"

One of the Crips announced before they all took off running. Suddenly the siren chirped on quickly and the Los Angeles Police rolled on us. They parked the squad car in the middle of the street and hopped out. By that time Kool Aid and I had slumped down to the curb both exhausted and wounded. They lifted us up from off the ground and slammed us on the hood of their car. I winced in pain while burning from hot hood. One of the police began searching me while the other searched Kool Aid.

"What were your homies running from? Wait a minute, this one is bleeding."

"They ain't my homies." I managed to reply.

He instantly turned me around and stared at my gang attire. After making a once over of my entire wardrobe he took a step back.

"You are in the wrong neighborhood." He said shockingly.

We were in no position to resist whatever they were trying to do in searching us. His partner finished searching Kool Aid then they walked closer to each other to talk. We were on opposite sides of the squad car so Kool Aid and I leaned on the car and kept quiet. The wind had picked up and even though I had on my 49ers Starter Jacket. I noticed it had a rip in it from the wound.

"Okay we are taking you to the hospital. Do you want to press charges against the people that stabbed you?" He asked me.

"Nah." I shook my head.

He opened the back door and tossed Kool Aid and I in the back seat. His facial expression showed that he expected me to say no to his question. They dipped a few corners and headed up to Martin Luther King Jr. Medical Center on the west side. It was known in Compton as Killer King. You would go in there alive and leave dead. My wound bothered me but I was more exhausted than anything.

"So what are a couple of Bloods doing over in Crip territory?"

"Going home." Kool Aid replied.

"What are you a couple of Athens Park Bloods or what?"

"Nah, we Pirus." Kool Aid replied.

He sounded a little offended in his response. I glanced at Kool Aid and shook my head indicating to him that he had answered enough questions.

"What are Pirus doing over in this neighborhood? You are supposed to be somewhere in Compton."

This time Kool Aid didn't reply. I was wounded but I wouldn't have replied even if I was in a perfect bill of health. The pain was irritating so I managed to give a moan to distract the pig from asking more questions.

"Okay don't die on us, I will get you to the hospital in a few minutes." He sighed.

They escorted us into the emergency room then they turned around. It took almost four hours before we were admitted in to see a doctor. It didn't take him long to patch me up but he offered me a bed. I called the house on the phone since my mother had insurance on me. The phone rang several times before someone picked it up.

"Hello?"

"Dion, it's Grumpy."

"Man, what the fuck happened to ya'll niggas last night? I heard ya'll went chasing after some bitches." Flintstone growled through the phone.

"Yeah but Reddy's Cadillac ran out of gas in crab territory. We got caught slipping by a bunch of niggas in L.A."

"All of ya'll?"

"Loko, Timmy-Ru and Boney-Ru ran out on us. Only Kool Aid and I stood against them niggas and one of them stabbed me."

"Ah fuck that Blood. Those niggas is in violation for running out on my muthafuckin' brother. Where the fuck are you right now?" He barked.

"I'm at Killer King but I'm alright after they patched me up. The L.A. pigs rolled up on us before they could finish us off. They threw us in the back seat and gave us a ride to the hospital." I replied.

"Nah fuck that Blood, we on our way up to Killer King then we gon' have to handle those little niggas for running out." He slammed down the phone.

After hanging up the phone Flintstone threw on his red Pendleton and rushed out the door. He hopped in his 78' Regal he just purchased and rolled off Locust Circle to Holly Street. He didn't bother to stop at the stop sign. He pulled into the driveway of Ronnie-Ru's apartment complex to see the homies hanging out.

"What's happening Flintstone, Blood!?!!" Slow announced.

"My brother is in the muthafuckin' hospital and these punk ass little niggas ran out on him."

He walked over to Loko and smacked him with his open hand. The plastic cup that Loko was drinking from flew out of his hands and slid on the cement spilling its contents. Momentarily stunned, Loko jumped up from the crate he was sitting on.

"I didn't run out on anybody, Blood and that's on P-Fonk."

"Blood sit yo ass down and shut the fuck up." Smokey emerged from a car.

He was sitting down on the passenger side of his Chevy. He walked over to Flintstone after barking at Loko.

"What the fuck happened?"

"My brother called me from Killer King because some crabs had stabbed him. He said Reddy's Cadillac ran out of gas so they had to walk through crab hood. He said Loko, Boney and Timmy-Ru ran and only Kool Aid stood tall." Flintstone glared at Loko then at Smokey.

"Blood, let's roll up and bee if Grumpy is fine then we will handle this hood shit. Reddy, let's roll so we can put some gas in yo Lac. You drive Flintstone and we'll go up to Killer King together."

Just like that Smokey had given instructions on what should be done and the homies fell in line. That always amazed Flintstone since they've both put in work for the hood. Smokey was just one of those take charge type of gangsters. Reddy and Slow climbed in the back seat and they rolled up to the hospital. When they arrived the lobby was almost empty. It was a Mexican woman holding a small child and in the corner was Kool Aid. He had nodded off into a slumber with his mouth wide open. All four walked up to him and towered over him.

"This is too easy." Slow chuckled.

"What's happening Blood?" Smokey announced.

Kool Aid blinked his eyes then shook his head to clear his vision. Once they were in focus he slowly stood up to greet them.

"P-Fonk Blood! What that bee like?" He said groggily.

"We hearing that you were the only one that stood tall with the little homie Grumpy-Ru." Smokey replied.

"I was just being down for my homeboy." Kool Aid replied offhandedly.

He hadn't regained all of his mental functions yet. He still was trying to recover from not getting any sleep the night before.

"Why didn't you call yo moms or something to come and pick you up from the hospital?" Smokey continued.

"Because Grumpy is still up in here."

His tone was of uncertainty. He didn't really understand the question. He rubbed his eyes then looked around for the water fountain.

"This is a down ass little nigga, Blood." Flintstone declared.

"Let Blood get some water." Reddy suggested.

He staggered over to the water fountain and allowed the water pressure to splash all over his face before taking a drink. He was a little more sure footed when he returned to where the homies were standing.

"Blood, what are ya'll doing here?"

Everyone busted out in laughter. Kool Aid cracked a smile but he didn't know what everyone was laughing at.

"What's so funny?"

"You Blood! We came up here to pick up you and Grumpy. When we get back to the hood you need to take yo ass home and get some sleep. Let's go get Grumpy." Smokey replied.

They made their way up to the third floor. Reddy went up to the nurse's counter to find out what room Grumpy was in. Five gangsters echoed the halls of the hospital with their footsteps until they reached the room. When they walked into the room Grumpy was wide awake glaring out the window. Everyone piled into the room talking loud.

"Aw Blood, I didn't know ya'll was gon' get here so fast. I'm ready to bounce up out this bitch."

"Come on then let's roll. But we gon' handle those little niggas for running out on you and Kool Aid." Smokey replied.

"What's up with yo Cadillac, Reddy?" Grumpy asked.

"We're about to go get that muthafucka right now so we can put some gas in the tank then roll back to the hood."

We piled six deep into Smokey's Chevy Impala and headed over to crab territory to pick up Reddy's car. I was a little reluctant but I was the one responsible for having it stranded. Five minutes into the ride I glanced over at Kool Aid and he was sound asleep. Flintstone, Kool Aid and I were sitting in the backseat. Smokey was driving with Reddy and Slow sat in the front seat. When we pulled into the shopping center to my surprise the Cadillac was still parked in the spot we left it. Slow let Reddy climb out of the car on the passenger side and she checked to see if there was any damage.

"Everything is straight, Blood." She announced before climbing inside.

Smokey made his way back to the closest gas station. He had a gas can in the trunk of his car. When we made it back to the shopping center Reddy handed the gas can to me.

"You the nigga that ran out of gas." She smirked.

I grudgingly put the gas in the tank. Smokey left the car running while he watched us put the gas in the tank. I decided it would be more comfortable to hop in with Reddy when we left. I was hoping she didn't talk any shit.

"Aw Cuz, what set ya'll from?"

I glanced around to see two Crips walking towards us. I had on the same clothes from the night before so it was obvious that I was a Blood. Reddy wasn't as obvious as me but she had on red shoelaces and a matching red belt. The two Crips were older than Reddy and me by at least four or five years. They were sporting their colors as well. One of them had a little size on him like he had done a bid in prison. He was the one that hit us up. The second Crip wasn't that much smaller. He had some size on him in the muscle department as well. They both stood about six feet in height. I turned around for a confrontation forgetting that the homies were four deep in another car.

"East Side Holly Hood Leuders Park Piru Gang, Blood!" Reddy announced

"What the fuck did..."

Before the first Crip could finish his question I heard five or six gunshots let off. The stockier enemy was hit and fell to the ground hard. The second one quickly ran for cover ducking under another car. As I advanced toward the passenger side my eyes turned toward Smokey and he was the one waving the pistol.

"Let's roll Blood!" He yelled.

Reddy started up the engine and sped off in the parking lot after I hopped in on the passenger side. Everything happened so fast that I didn't have time to think. We were following Smokey in a direction I wasn't too familiar with but he found his way to a freeway entrance. We were in a two car caravan all the way down to the 91 freeway until we exited Atlantic Avenue. I was on pins and needles wondering if someone noticed us. In broad daylight Smokey had shot that nigga. If he wasn't dead he probably was seriously wounded. Reddy acted like she had taken a shot of adrenalin.

"That's what the fuck I'm talking about Blood. We was in that crab niggas hood and we still served his ass. That's how we get down Double H for life." She yelled.

I stared at her like she was crazy. I was tired and sleepy and the last thing I wanted was to get bumped up by the police and I hadn't had any real sleep. My wounds were okay but they were still tender. A good six hour nap would do me some good.

"What's wrong with you nigga? You act like you had love for that crab nigga."

"I ain't had any sleep and I'm still wearing the bandage from when I was stabbed. Last night was enough excitement for me."

Reddy busted out in a loud laughter. There was nothing funny to me. She leaned back in her driver seat once we turned on Holly Street.

"I know where you coming from Grumpy. But that nigga hit us up first. It wasn't like we started that shit. We was gon' put gas in the tank then roll back to the hood."

"Yeah that shit just caught me off guard. When he started blasting on that crab nigga I was like what the fuck now? I need to take my ass to sleep."

"Alright, I'll roll you to yo house on the circle." She smiled.

It was pleasant to see Reddy smile. Sometimes I would be reminded how pretty Reddy was. She was a gangster so to get her to smile was difficult. She was different to me because she was one of the few gangster girls that I would love to fuck. It was girls that claimed the hood or other sets that were down to put in work, carried themselves butch. The feminine women were just fucking one of the homeboys but they wasn't really down to put in work like Reddy. When she pulled up in front of my house I climbed out then leaned down in the window.

"Bee up Reddy."

"Holly Love Blood. And don't worry we gon' serve them little niggas for running out on you." She assured me.

I stumbled into the house and headed straight to my bedroom. I left a trail of clothes from my bedroom door to my twin sized bed.

It would be six hours before I woke up from my sleep. A sharp pain on my side let me know that the night before wasn't a dream. After staggering into the kitchen for a glass of water my brother knocked on my door. My mother must have thought I made it home last night because she hadn't said anything to me. I opened the door and Flintstone walked in.

"We whooped those little niggas' asses for running out on you and Kool Aid. They were in violation for real." Flintstone leaned on my dresser.

"They didn't try to deny that shit?"

"You know they did. Loko tried to say that he was stabbed also but he didn't make it to the hospital. He and Timmy-Ru and Boney-Ru rolled in a car Loko had stolen. They all claimed that they rolled back around looking for ya'll but couldn't find ya'll. Smokey was like 'Blood you shouldn't have ran in the first place.' Nuck was in the background cracking up the whole time."

"Aw shit I bet you that made it worse. That nigga got an irritating laugh. What did Reddy do to them niggas?"

"She just watched me, Smokey, Slow, Kay-Kay and Ronnie-Ru knot them little niggas up. I told you that little nigga Kool Aid was down. I know when niggas got heart and when they are scary. Now Grumpy, now that you've seen other side of this game you now know where you stand. Any nigga can claim to be a gangster but the streets will show what you really are at some point in time. A bitch nigga won't stay true to what he says he is."

"I know Blood." I replied arrogantly.

He shoved me in a playful way. All I could do was laugh because I wasn't in the mood for fighting. Even though I was asleep for six hours my body was still drowsy. Besides I appreciated Flintstone showing his love for me even though I wouldn't admit it to him.

"Well I'm going back to the other room before I have to fuck you up." He stood totally erect.

"Or get fucked up." I quickly replied.

He turned around as he headed for my bedroom door and smirked. When he opened the bedroom door I stopped him.

"Why didn't mama say anything about me not coming home last night?"

"I told her you were asleep and tired as hell so she wouldn't bother you for the night." He nodded.

"Good Looking on that." I nodded.

He threw up the Blood sign with his right hand then closed the door behind him. Staring at the door for a few seconds made me crack a small smile. After that long ass day I knew where I stood with my brother. The glass of water was quickly swallowed right before my eyes closed and sleep had me again.

8
TRACKS OF BLOOD

You ain't ever supposed to speak on someone putting in work!
Baby Blue

The California wind was unusually strong on this spring late evening. School was almost out for the year. A young rider by the name of Baby Blue unloaded then reloaded his nine-millimeter. He was testing it out for the work he was about to put in. His Uncle Spider from LA was telling him how some Pirus from Holly had killed his big homie in broad daylight. His cousin had called him from the penitentiary talking about his dead homie. Spider had Baby Blue by four or five years and he was the first in their family to really start Crippin. He was from East South Central Los Angeles and was his mother's younger brother. The words still echoed through his head from his conversation with his uncle.

"Some slob niggas killed my nigga Monte, cuz. Me and that nigga go back to the sandbox cuz. The homie C-Dog said that it was a broad that yelled out her set in the middle of my muthafuckin' hood cuz. Serve those slob niggas and let them know this is Crip or die."

Baby Blue stood up and walked out of his backyard. Closing the wooden gate behind him he was greeted by his road dog Smurf.

"What's happening, Cuz?"

"We about to serve these slob ass niggas and that's on Compton Crip. Was you able to get that 380'?" Baby Blue replied.

Smurf pulled out a small automatic weapon then nodded. They were standing on the side of the house while they made sure their guns were loaded. They almost made it out of the front yard before Baby Blue heard his name.

"Lorenzo, where you about to go?" His brother Sean asked loudly.

"None of yo muthafuckin' business, Cuz." Baby Blue growled.

It was loud enough to be heard by his brother but he was trying to avoid being heard by his mother. Baby Blue flashed his pistol by lifting up his shirt and that's what made Sean go back in the house. They strolled down the street looking both ways until they reach Alondra Blvd.

"On Kelly Park Compton Crip we're about to serve these niggas." Baby Blue swore.

"Do you still talk to that nigga Dwayne that now claim Holly? Didn't you play Pop Warner with that nigga?" Smurf asked offhandedly.

"Yeah but that was when we were kids and shit. We're on some grown man shit nowadays. If that nigga gets caught slipping then he gon' have to die." Baby Blue shrugged.

"But yo moms is cool with his mom right?"

"I don't give a fuck about that right now, Cuz." Baby Blue snarled.

Once they crossed Alondra Blvd they walked down the major street until they reached Thorson. When they reached Thorson they dipped into the alley that was behind the Alondra apartment complexes. The next street at the end of the alley was Holly. When they reached Holly Street they both drew their weapons. Keeping their pistols lowered so it wasn't so obvious that they were packing. Halfway down Holly Street they realized that no one was out. It was extremely quiet on the block but they kept pushing forward. When they reached Myrrh Street it was still empty. Baby Blue glared at Smurf and all he could do was shrug. Now Baby Blue was beginning to get nervous. They were one block north of enemy territory and there were no enemies to shoot. He couldn't just hang out on the corner so he had to make a decision fast. Smurf was following him.

"Let's keep it pushing, Cuz."

Smurf nodded so they made their way to the next block. Nothing was still going on when they made it to the middle of the block. Baby Blue reluctantly walked north down Holly Street until he almost got to another corner.

"Aye Blood, I'm gon' holler at that nigga tomorrow. I parked my car down the street because I hopped in with Smokey." A voice yelled.

"Hold up Blood I'm going that way so I'm gon' stroll with you big homie." Another voice announced.

"You ain't gon' run out on me are you Blood." The first voice smirked.

Baby Blue gave a hand signal to Smurf for them to get ready. If it worked out the way they planned it would be an ambush. Baby Blue hid behind a truck while Smurf was standing by a tree.

"So the homie Pookie got locked up because he was caught with a pistol?"

"That's what I heard, Blood."

"First offense so he should only get about two and a half to three years, right?"

"It depends; sometimes the D.A. will bring up school attendance at those juvenile courts. If he was a truant he might get more time. They used all that shit against Flintstone when he got locked up."

"Well we'll find out soon enough if…

Boom! Boom!

Boom! Boom!

Pop! Pop!
Pop! Pop!
Boom! Boom!
Pop! Pop!

Baby Blue and Smurf ran off in the night heading down Myrrh and cutting to Thorson. They didn't stop running until they reached Alondra Blvd. The fear and adrenalin rush kept the wind underneath them for most of the way. Once they hit the major street their running became a fast paced walk. Crossing over to the other side of the street they found themselves walking next to Kelly Elementary School.

"You want to hang out at the park, Cuz?" Smurf asked while panting.

"Hell Nah Cuz, are you crazy. I think I killed that big slob nigga."

"I know I hit the other slob with the 380'. Yeah we should probably go in the house."

"Hold the fuck up, Blood. I just heard gunshots and Slow and Loko just went back down Holly Street." Smokey announced.

"Yeah I heard that shit too." Ronnie-Ru added.

"We all heard that shit." Slim said.

The dice game instantly was broken up and everyone in the back made their way to the front. They walked down the street to only see neighbors coming outside. As everyone came out their houses a pack of Pirus made their way down Holly Street. A girl named Kimberly came out to her gated yard and started screaming.

"Someone is over here bleeding."

All the homies ran down the street following Smokey's lead. When they ran up to the body they were stunned at what they saw.

"Aw fuck Blood, the muthafuckin' homeboy Slow is dead. It's gon' be hell to pay for this shit Blood and that's on Piru." Smokey cried out.

"Not the big homie, Blood." Kool Aid stared at the dead body.

"I just called 911." A neighbor announced.

"Aye Kool Aid, take these gats before one-time show up." Smokey ordered.

"Alright."

He walked away from the scene with about four guns. He ran off back to Ronnie-Ru's backyard. Everyone else stayed until Ronnie-Ru noticed someone else squirming nearby.

"Blood that's the little homie Loko."

Loko was shaking but he was obviously alive. Tears fell down his face as he tried to bear the pain of his wounds. It was hard to tell where he had been shot but it was obvious that it was the upper body.

Suddenly paramedics pulled up followed by several squad cars. The Sheriffs quickly hopped out of their cars with their guns drawn.

"Everyone assume the position and put your hands on the hood of the car."

Sheriff Brown hopped out of the third squad car but he hadn't drawn his weapon. He walked over to Slim, Smokey and Ronnie-Ru.

"So who are ya'll warring with the Ward Lane's, the South Side's or the Kelly Park's?" Sheriff Brown asked.

"We ain't talking to the police. Somebody just shot our homeboy so ya'll need to leave us the fuck alone." Smokey barked.

"I know who I should be fucking with. I'm trying to prevent anyone else dying. And you Holly Hood boys have a tendency to want to even up the score."

"Their clean." A Sheriff announced.

"Alright you can go."

Everyone climbed off the car just when they were putting Slow in one of the paramedic vans. They drove him off but it was obvious he was dead. The second paramedic van slid Loko inside the van and drove off. Sheriff Brown walked over to the pack of Pirus and glared at them.

"It was tragic what happened to Ronald Walker but that doesn't mean that we have to have more violence."

No one responded but maintained sullen faces. It was painfully obvious that he wasn't going to get through to them today. He reluctantly climbed in his car while the homicide detectives began trying to question the neighbors. The pack of gangsters turned around and walked back to Ronnie-Ru's house.

"Blood, we gon' handle some niggas behind this shit here." Smokey vowed.

Baby Blue slid his revolver under his bed then lied on his twin sized mattress. He shared a room with his younger brother but it appeared as though Sean was asleep. They were starting to call his little brother Tiny Blue.

"So ya'll put in work on them Holly slobs for Uncle Rick?" Sean asked in the dark.

"Shut the fuck up Sean. You talk too much, Cuz."

"Damn Lorenzo, I didn't say that shit all loud. I was just asking." Sean protested.

"You asking too many muthafuckin' questions. You ain't ever supposed to speak on someone putting in work."

The room went silent and both brothers were left with their own thoughts. Baby Blue felt a surge of power as he lied in his bed. A small smile crept up on his face as he thought about killing an enemy. It was something he could get used to. He didn't see the face of the man he killed but he knew the man was just as dead.

He fell off in a peaceful sleep knowing that he killed an OG enemy.

The following morning Baby Blue woke up to his mother cooking breakfast. He yawned and made his way to the bathroom. When he came out of the bathroom the aroma of pancakes and sausage swelled his nostrils. Peering through the hallway he rushed for the kitchen hoping to catch the last remnants of the breakfast.

"Boy did you wash your hands before you got out of the bathroom?" His mother asked.

"Yep!"

The pancake batter was sitting on the counter and in the pan were two sausages. He quickly devoured one of the sausages while putting margarine in the pan for his batter. After cooking and eating his food it didn't take long for him to get dressed. As he was walking out the door his mother made a remark.

"You know that boy Dwayne that you used to play football with? I was talking to his mother earlier today and she said a boy got killed and he wasn't even twenty years old. Another boy younger than him was shot but he lived. They were friends of that boy Dwayne...do you still keep in touch with him?"

"Nah mama, I ain't seen him in years."

"Well you be careful because she called me to tell me there are a lot of upset people over there right now."

"Aw mama I'm always careful."

He slid out the door before she could talk anymore about it. He didn't have time to feel guilty about killing slobs. That had to be chalked up to the game, he pondered. When he met up with Smurf they walked up to the park to hang out.

"My moms was talking about that shit that went down last night. She still talks to that slob nigga's mama on the phone. She said they're mad than a muthafucka over there."

"Yeah the Sheriffs been hot around here. They rolling up on niggas already. They had some of the big homies hemmed up on my way to meet up with you." Smurf replied.

"Is that why it ain't any one up at the park?"

"Probably so, Cuz."

They hung out at the park waiting for some of the homies to show up. They finally came up to the park hours after Baby Blue and Smurf had been posted. The drama didn't start happening until later that night when they were leaving the park. When they walked home they started hearing gunshots in their neighborhood. They glared at each other and took off in the direction of where the gunfire was heard. When they reached the street a crowd of spectators was outside. One of the big homies K-Bone quickly walked by while they were walking up.

"What the fuck happened K-Bone?"

"One of them Holly niggas got killed so those niggas is riding, Cuz."

K-Bone swiftly left the block while Smurf and Baby Blue came walking into the crowd of spectators. Two of the homies were laid out on the concrete. T-Macc looked pretty bad but C-Rag appeared to only have minor wounds.

"We done started some shit." Smurf whispered.

"Yeah but we can kill niggas just like them."

Baby Blue walked up on one of the homegirls from the hood. She was a cute female with a light complexion. She was the big homie Crazy's baby mama.

"Hey Lisa, what happened to T-Macc and C-Rag?"

"Some slobs rolled up on them on beach cruisers and started shooting. Right when it started getting dark. I think they waited until the Sheriffs stopped being hot. They had dead rags covering their faces."

Baby Blue understood that when she said they had dead rags she meant they had red rags covering their face. From Baby

Blue's estimate she was a down bitch from the hood. He walked over to Smurf who was leaning on a metal fence.

"Yeah Cuz, it was some slob niggas."

"That's what you went over there to ask Lisa? I could have told you that without Lisa." Smurf shrugged.

"She seen the niggas roll up though, Cuz."

"Aw shit, she was there?"

"Yeah nigga."

"Well let's get out of here before One-Time shows up." Smurf suggested.

For the next few nights everyone in the hood were watching their back. The streets pretty much remained empty at night. The Sheriffs were on patrol scanning the streets for any activity. It was too hot to move around at night without either the enemy creeping or the Sheriffs. Baby Blue and Smurf agreed that they would make their movements during the day. The third night into the war word was out that two other homies had been dropped. It was a time of doing what was necessary to survive.

One early afternoon Baby Blue and Smurf were headed up to the store. It was better for them to not be armed considering how the Sheriffs were rolling the street. They were going to the local grocery store to pick up a few things for Baby Blue's mother. The stench of the garbage can filled the parking lot air. The peeling paint of the decrepitated building was a microcosm of the eyesore landscape. It was a clear indication to Baby Blue that his senses were super sensitive today. He tried not to worry about it but it bothered him nevertheless.

"We should have brought our straps; the way them Holly niggas been tripping." He said to Smurf.

"Yeah but the Sheriffs are tripping too. We got a better chance of them niggas not tripping in broad daylight." Smurf assured him.

"I don't know but I'd rather be judged by twelve than carried by six. You understand what I'm saying, Cuz." Baby Blue frowned.

"Try not to think about that shit."

The grocery store was somewhat crowded so it took a little time for them to gather the things Baby Blue was told to get. Then the wait in line always took a long time especially when they only had two checkers open.

"This is some bullshit, Cuz." Baby Blue sighed.

"I'm gon' grab a bag of these M & Ms" Smurf slid a pack in his pocket.

When they finally reached the counter the Latino cashier smiled. Smurf made it a point to flirt with her. She had pretty gray eyes. She barely spoke English but he could tell that she understood what he was saying. She would blush but she was a little older than him. Baby Blue paid for the few groceries then they headed for the door.

"I'll fuck the shit out of that Mexican bitch." Smurf declared.

"Yeah right, she wasn't throwing you any play."

"That's just some shit I'm gon' have to work on."

"Whatever nigga."

"Aye Cuz, why yo moms is buying cornmeal? She's about to fry some fish or what?"

"Yeah, why you asking? You gon' eat..."

"Aw Blood, look at these Crab niggas slipping."

Both Baby Blue and Smurf turned around to see two Pirus staring at them. One of them already had their pistol drawn but the other one hadn't pulled out yet. When Baby Blue glanced at the other he instantly knew who he was. His eyes got big because the Piru with his gun drawn was ready to shoot. The familiar Piru put his hand on his homeboys' gun stopping him from shooting.

"I know that nigga right there so give him a pass Blood."

The Piru with his pistol drawn glared at his homeboy like he was crazy. He stared at him clueless on how to respond.

"Let's smoke these niggas Blood. Pull out yo heat Grumpy."

"Nah nigga, his mom and my moms are real cool. I ain't gon' watch this nigga get killed in front of me, Blood. Give him a pass."

The Piru lowered his weapon while Smurf and Baby Blue stood frozen in the middle of the parking lot. They were too nervous to run so they were stuck.

"Get the fuck out of here Lorenzo." Grumpy barked.

Before he could repeat himself Baby Blue and Smurf scurried off as quickly as possible. They weren't half way down the block before they heard police sirens. It sounded like they were in the same parking lot they just left. They didn't look back to find out.

9
LYNWOOD SHERIFFS

So, what does that mean to me?
Linda

4 years later

I was finally going home after doing four years for a gun charge. To taste freedom was an entirely different thing. There was homies that I hadn't seen in years. My daughter was three years old and I've only seen pictures of her. Neicy is supposed to still be my girl but that broad was more than likely fucking someone else while I was locked up. It wasn't a big deal to me because our relationship was based on bullshit anyway. My mom pulled up moments after they released me from Youth Authority. Scanning the scenery I was glad to be home and free. My mom started in on me right away though.

"Look here Dwayne, you gon' have to put this gangbanging shit out of your life. Dion will be coming home soon and I'm telling him the same thing."

"Come on now Mama, gangbanging done played out. It's all about getting that money." I shrugged.

"Oh so you plan on getting a job? You are eighteen years old so I can legally kick yo ass out the house." She glared at me.

"Aw come on Mama, you don't want to kick me out." I smiled.

"I'm just saying. You have to be about business now that you're an adult." She said lightheartedly.

"Yeah I got a few things in mind."

I turned on her radio and turned it to the station that played oldies. Soothing old school music always calmed my mother down. She leaned back in her car seat and pulled out a Virginia Slim cigarette. Once the cigarette was lit she was in relax mode all the way to the house. Some things never change and that was one of them.

When we made it back to the house my bedroom looked much smaller than I remembered. My NWA poster hanging on the wall seemed corny to me. My twin sized bed seemed old and raggedy. It was time to renovate and make changes to my living space. In fact, I wasn't expecting to stay with my mom's house forever. In the next six months I was going to hustle my money and get my own place. After cleaning up and tearing down the posters I wanted to get some clothes. I only had one khaki suit that fit me because I had gotten a little size since I was locked up. I was almost working with seventeen inch arms. I tried on one of my brother's Pendleton shirts and it fitted. As far as pants I was shit out of luck. I had to roll with the same pants until it dawned on me that I had a savings stashed away in my bedroom. One of the poles on my bed was hollow so I would stash my money there. When I found the money I damn near jumped up and down. After stashing the money in my pocket I walked into my mother's room.

"Hey Mama, can I use your car?"

"Where are you going?"

"To the Compton Swap meet."

"What are you getting up there?"

"Just a few clothes."

"Well don't bring a whole bunch of red shit into this house. I'm serious about that gangbanging Dwayne." She scolded.

"I know Mama."

She tossed me the keys then closed her bedroom door in my face. I hopped into her brand new Honda Civic and cruised off Locust circle until I seen Timmy-Ru. He looked different to me.

Of course he was older but he had a little stock on him in size. He must have done a stretch as well but not as long.

"What's happening, Blood?" I announced.

I pulled up on Holly Street and practically parked the car on the curb. Timmy-Ru turned around for me to see him puffing on weed. It smelled good but I didn't know when I was going to get a piss test from my parole officer.

"Aw shit, Grumpy-Ru finally got released. What's happening with you Blood?"

We embraced. His voice was deeper than I remembered but four years had passed. My voice was deeper to him as well.

"I'm on my way up to the swap meet to get some new clothes. I just got home today."

"Oh then we have to get with the homeboys and have a party or something."

He had let his hair grow out and was rocking braids that went down his back. His thoughts were clouded because of the weed he was smoking.

"You want to hit the weed?"

"Nah, I might get tested when I see my parole officer."

"Oh yeah."

"Where are all the homeboys? Everybody still hanging out over Ronnie-Ru's house or what?"

"Nah Ronnie-Ru caught an assault charge so he was violated. Everybody still hangs out at Turtle's house but only at night. Pookie is home from doing his time. You know that nigga gon' be glad to bee you."

"Yeah, I need to holler at that nigga. Roll with me up to the Compton Swap Meet so I can pick up some clothes."

"Alright Blood, I ain't got shit to do."

I was sitting on over twenty-five hundred so I had to buy some shit that made people notice. I didn't buy that much red except for a belt and a few pair of red shoelaces. I knew that I was a Piru and if anyone hit me up I would represent. My goal was to look clean and not so much on the banging side. But I also had to buy myself a burgundy handkerchief which was Piru colors. I mostly bought khakis, T-Shirts, socks, drawers and six pair of shoes. I also picked up a few pairs of corduroy pants. After getting some 501 Levi Jeans and a pair of Guess jeans my wardrobe was complete. Now I was ready to hit the block. I picked up a few things for Timmy-Ru just for rolling up there with me.

"So what's been happening in the hood? Who have we been warring with lately?"

"We had that war when you was still on the street but that eventually slowed down because the Sheriffs started riding on us. The Lynwood Sheriffs was hot for a long time in the hood." Timmy-Ru replied.

"What's up with Pookie, what has he been up to? What about Reddy, Smokey and Slim."

"Pookie been laying low and doing a little bit of hustling. Reddy is still running around with Smokey and Sly. You know Smokey gon' do his thing no matter what. I think Pookie is slanging for Reddy like you used to. Smokey had to get down with a nigga from the MOB. One of them was set tripping at a party in Leuders Park hood and Smokey knocked his ass out. They tried to make up excuses for they homeboy saying he was drunk when he got knocked out."

And as if on cue, three or four niggas from the MOB ran into us at the mall. Kornbread was leading the pack of MOB Pirus. I always remembered him because he used to try to get with Reddy real tough. She didn't like him that way even though she respected him. He was a few years older than us. We shook hands when he walked up.

"What's up Blood?"

"Nothing; just trying to make sure these crab niggas ain't roaming through the swap meet. We've been hearing these crab niggas been coming up here."

The Compton Swap meet was technically in their hood. MOB Piru was on the border of Lynwood and Compton but considered Compton territory. Kornbread glanced at us to see what we wanted to do but I wasn't in the mood. I had gotten out the same day and wasn't eager to go back so soon.

"So you Holly Hood niggas down to roll up on these crab niggas?"

It was an open challenge to see if we were still representing. I yawned because I knew I was ready to go back to my own hood. I didn't have to earn any stripes with him even though it was a certain amount of respect.

"We were about to go back to our hood." I shrugged.

I didn't really give a damn what he thought. MOB Piru got it's notoriety from the Death Row Records owner Suge Knight because that was his neighborhood. It was respect for Kornbread and his hood but I wasn't about to patrol his hood for him.

"So ya'll niggas is gone."

"Yeah, we're about to bounce. Ya'll bee up." I replied.

Kornbread made a facial expression as though he expected that from us. I kind of ignored it even though I knew it might come back to haunt me later. What convinced me that I made the right decision was the fact that I had all those bags. If I was in a rumble my bags could end up anywhere.

"Do you think those niggas thought we were scared?" Timmy-Ru asked.

"I don't really give a fuck. I know we ain't scared so it doesn't concern me what the fuck he thinks, Blood." I curtly replied

"You ain't changed Grumpy. You the same nigga I remember years ago."

I nodded without saying anything. He wasn't the same to me. He was more seasoned and relaxed about being a gangster than I remembered. Timmy-Ru also seemed as though he was sharper than before. My thoughts considered those things while pushing towards the door. Before I could get out the door I ran right into somebody.

"Damn nigga, watch where you going?"

"Who the fuck…"

When I glanced at her she was pretty than a muthafucka. She had a nice light brown complexion with a nice petite frame. She was little in height and only stood about five feet tall but she was sexy as hell. What really caught me about her was those luscious lips. She kept walking after we collided.

"Hey hold up."

She turned around and glared at me as though she didn't want to be bothered. She was with two of her homegirls. That didn't deter me from seeing what was up with her.

"Hey I'm Dwayne."

"So, what does that mean to me?"

"I don't know yet. Let's find out together what that means to you."

She cracked a small smile and I knew I had her. She wasn't expecting me to come back with a reply like that.

"So tell me your name, Ms. Bumping into people."

"You bumped into me." She fired back.

"I know but I can't take all the blame because I wouldn't feel right."

"Well this ain't starting out good."

"That depends on how you look at it. For me I bumped into someone I wanted to know right away. And that's real good."

"Yeah but you probably say that about all the females you bump into. And you must bump into a lot of people because you don't be watching where you going." She smirked.

Her friends laughed right along with her. At that point I knew who was the comedian of the group. It was always a girl out of a pack of females that made everyone else laugh. If I didn't pull her number she was going to joke for the rest of the day about why she didn't throw me any play.

"Yeah but sometimes that's how things work out. Me and you was probably meant to bump into each other." I playfully shrugged.

"Whatever, I wouldn't even be thinking yo ass if I didn't think you were a little cute." She rolled her eyes.

"Since we feeling each other, give me your number and we can talk more about it."

She thought about it for a few seconds. She glanced down at my bags and that had to intrigue her a little bit. After giving her friend a slight hand gesture, one of the girls broke out a pen and paper. She wrote her number down and folded the small paper. We went our separate ways but I only got a few steps.

"What's your name?"

"Read the paper."

I stopped to open the folded paper and right above a phone number was the name Linda. I glanced up at Timmy-Ru and he was smiling.

"What was her name?"

"Linda."

"She was a cute little bitch with a smart ass mouth." He shrugged.

"Yeah I know but I like that."

When we made it back to the hood everyone had gathered on the block. Word must have gotten out that I had made it home. Only person I thought seen me was Timmy-Ru but me rolling down the street could have gotten me spotted by anyone. When we rolled up in front of Turtle's house the homeboys were hanging out deep. I climbed out of the driver's side to see the homeboys eager to greet me.

"What's happening Blood?" I proclaimed.

All of the young gangsters came up and embraced me but the OGs waited for me to reach them. When I was close to the backyard Smokey, Slim and Nuck were waiting for me. Standing behind Smokey was Reddy with a slight smile on her face. She was glad to see me but she wouldn't openly say it but would show it through gestures.

"So they let you out that muthafucka. How are you feeling Blood?" Smokey asked.

"It feels good to be home and back to the hood." I replied.

"That's what the fuck I'm talking about Blood. This nigga is glad to be back in the hood. We got to throw something for this nigga this weekend." Smokey said while we embraced.

"What's up Reddy?" I nodded.

"What's up nigga? Holly Love."

"Holly Love."

"Now that you out young nigga you gon' need to make some money. All this shit is good until a nigga realize he's broke and shit." Nuck laughed.

Some things never change. Embracing Nuck and Slim it was funny as hell to hear that nigga laugh. It actually felt good to hear him laugh, which meant I missed it.

"Yeah, I plan on getting paper Blood and that's on P-Fonk."

"Grumpy has always been a sound hustler." Reddy cut in.

"Well we'll see young nigga." Nuck replied.

I just shook my head and followed the rest of the homies to the backyard. There was already alcohol in the back when we reached the table. I glanced around to see if there were any changes to Turtle's backyard. He still had the brick wall around his backyard with the metal gate door entrance. The grass was always a tan color from all of us treading back and forth on it. The peeled paint of the garage door was still off white. I knew at that very moment that I had made it home. Smokey passed me a 40 ounce bottle of Mickey's while I scanned the yard. It was a brand new bottle that hadn't been opened. He bought the bottle for me to open and swig first. It tasted really good to drink beer after all these years.

"That bottle is yours Blood."

"Good Looking Big Homie."

I smelled the Kush floating in the air but I knew I couldn't partake. It was good to be home and not on lockdown. Reddy glanced at me a few times and that was always a clear indication she wanted to talk. I walked over to her and gave a slight nod. She led me back over to the garage so we could talk.

"So you ready to start making this money?"

"Hell yeah."

"Well you gon' take over the spot where that nigga Pookie been working." She sharply replied.

"What we gon' be working together?"

"That's up to you but I'm supplying you from now on."

"What's up with Pookie?"

"That nigga ain't a real muthafuckin' hustler like that. Don't get me wrong, he can put in work for the hood and he's a down ass nigga but Blood ain't willing to put in those hours." She sighed.

"That's my road dog Reddy; what the fuck am I supposed to tell that nigga."

"Whatever the fuck you want to tell him Blood." She snapped.

"A nigga ain't been home a full day and you coming at me off the muthafuckin' wall, Blood."

"I'm just saying that ain't a problem I'm worried about and you shouldn't be worried about it either. Some niggas can hustle and some can't."

"Yeah, I'll get at the nigga."

"Yeah you handle that shit because I'm about to give you a package come tomorrow. Be careful though, Sheriff Cole has been roaming around this muthafucka lately. He's been coming down on us Holly Hood niggas tough. A crab ass nigga got his cap peeled back and they been trying to put that shit on us."

"Is the spot still over there on Pannez?"

"Yeah but over there by Compton Blvd. near the Burrito truck. It's been popping over there lately."

"Alright then let's do this shit."

"I'm glad you home, my nigga."

She walked away after saying that. When I glanced around everyone was in the backyard except for Loko and Pookie that was out of jail. Timmy-Ru was nursing some weed when I leaned in to ask him.

"Where is Loko?"

"That crazy ass nigga been different ever since he got shot that night Slow was killed. Your brother Flintstone wasn't the same either but Loko is more of a loaner behind that shit. He comes around but it ain't like before."

"Me and Blood used to have words for each other. It was always love but we used to be like oil and water and now I miss the nigga."

"Yeah I remember how ya'll used to argue and shit."

After finishing the bottle of Mickey's I had a nice buzz. I hadn't drunk any alcohol in four years so it had me a little tipsy. I planned on coming back to Turtle's house but I wanted to put my clothes away and bring back my mom's car. I greeted the homeboys and told them I would be back in another ten minutes. I lived on Locust Circle so walking around the corner was nothing to me even though my mind was a little cloudy.

"Ay Grumpy Blood, you want to carry my strap?" Timmy-Ru asked.

"I'm just going to the house and coming right back."

He shrugged and went back to what he was doing. When I made it back to the house my mom had her door closed so I knocked on the door.

"What?"

"Your keys are on the table."

I slipped on my brother's Pendleton because it had gotten cold and dark was approaching. I barely made it to Holly Street when the Lynwood Sheriffs rolled up on me. I was a little irritated when they demanded that I put my hands on the car.

"What the fuck I do?" I slightly slurred.

"I don't know yet." He replied while searching me.

I let out a sigh to show that I was irritated but he didn't give a damn. After his thorough search he glanced at my face.

"You look familiar. You niggers walk around here like you're too fucking smart, WHAT'S YOUR FUCKING NAME?" He barked.

"Dwayne Pittman."

"Oh so they finally released you. Mr. Grumpy from Holly Hood."

"East Side." I mumbled.

"What did you say?"

I looked up like he was imagining things. He pushed me off the car after realizing I was clean.

"You haven't been out long enough to do something stupid yet. Just know when you do I'll be here to bust your ass."

When I looked at his face for the first time I realized it was Sheriff Cole. I remembered him from the last time he bumped us up on Pannez. I wanted to say fuck him but I wanted to enjoy my freedom a little longer. When I made it into Turtle's backyard everyone had already seen him bumping me up.

"Sheriff Cole's peckerwood ass be tripping, Blood. What did he say to you?" Smokey asked.

"He was just talking shit and called me a nigga. Fuck that cracker, Blood. Let's keep the party going."

10
PUSSY AND PAIN

Yeah but I ended that muthafucka with a bang!
Grumpy-Ru

Money was flowing good now that I was back on the block hustling. Pookie was a little salty about me taking his spot even when I tried to put him on. How many niggas like eating off of another man's plate? Reddy explained it to me that he wasn't dedicated to those long nights hustling on the corner. Pookie wanted to get into some dirt. Believe it or not selling dope on the corner kept me out of trouble. He would hang with me from time to time but he wanted to get into some action. He had been my road dog but since he had gotten out of jail he had been turned up. Most times he expected me to roll with him to do dirt but I was about making money. I didn't want to go into action unless there was a war going on. There wasn't a war going on as of yet but you could always tell when one was brewing. On our side of Alondra all we needed was one of our homies to get out that was a shooter. That meant that it was open war on all enemies of our hood.

Like I said before there are different types of gangsters. There were killers, shooters, hustlers, fighters, players, bangers, gangsters, winos, thugs and criminals. Killers were the type that would go out and kill by themselves. A war didn't have to take place and they were creeping on the enemy every chance they got. Shooters were homies that were openly willing to shoot someone. They might kill somebody but they are more than likely trigger happy. Fighters were the type of homies that would rather fight than shoot but will shoot if necessary. Players were the type of homies that really was about hollering at the bitches. Bangers always wanted to gangbang and nothing else. 24/7 they only represented gangbanging so they didn't have time for nothing else. Then you have the gangsters; who were well rounded about the street shit. Anything that involved the street they were organized and calculating. That's what I always wanted to be. Winos were homies from the hood that drunk and smoked their pain away. They were the homies that always had the weed or alcohol. The common thug was anybody that was just taking up space but getting nowhere in the streets. And last was the criminal; he was the type of street cat that was willing to try any crime once. Pookie was going in that direction and I wasn't about to do some dumb shit just for the sake of doing it. We were all hoodlums but it depended on what type of category you fit in. This was tension that was caused between us besides Reddy wanting me to run the spot.

"We were about to break into Sarah's house, are you down?"

"For what?" I asked.

"They might have some money stashed somewhere and I never liked that bitch, Blood."

"So you don't know what they got for sure and you want to break into their house. That sounds stupid than a muthafucka."

"Fuck you Grumpy, Blood. You always on yo muthafuckin' high horse. If the homies want to ride then you should be down to ride."

"Nigga you ain't riding on nobody. You want to break into Sarah's house because you don't like the bitch? I'm not gon' get stretched on a B & E charge because you don't like the bitch. Then once we get in the house we only gon' find some change and some cheap jewelry. That ain't smart to me." I fired back.

"Fuck it homie, I'll do that shit with someone else."

"Yeah, good luck in finding someone stupid enough to do that shit with you. First thing they gon' ask is what is in there to steal. And you don't even know." I smirked.

"Whatever Blood, what are you about to do?" He said impatiently.

"I'm about to go to the house once this package is done. I'll re-cop from Reddy tomorrow. Neicy's crazy ass is coming through with my daughter. I think she had my daughter calling another nigga daddy. Jada always looks confused when she calls me daddy like she was saying it to some other nigga."

"Well she looks just like yo ass but a little lighter." Pookie smirked.

"Yeah I know."

As we were talking two customers came up back to back and bought my last two twenty pieces of dope. Since that was the end of my package I got ready to pack it up. Pookie decided to roll with me over to the house. When I got there Neicy, Jada and my mom were already sitting on the porch. It seemed as though they were laughing and having a good ole time until we approached.

"Hey Mama!"

"Hey Dwayne, look how big my granddaughter has gotten."

"Yeah she's growing fast."

"Hi Mrs. Pittman!" Pookie cut in.

"How are you Kevin?"

"I'm doing pretty good."

By that time I was playing with my daughter Jada. She was a little more receptive than before. Neicy smiled at me, showing pride that I was playing with my daughter. Pookie shortly thereafter tapped me on the shoulder.

"Hey Grumpy, I mean Dwayne, I'll get at you later."

"Okay homey." We embraced.

When he was a short distance from my house my mother glared at him then glared at me. I knew she was about to speak her mind.

"That boy needs to stop wearing all that red. When are ya'll gon' realize that gangbanging is only killing your own kind."

"Mama gangbanging done played out. Pookie is wearing a little red just to represent where he's from but not to gangbang."

"Well then he should be wearing red, white and blue because he's from America." She replied.

"I doubt if he'll wear any blue Mama. Let that man live his life the way he sees fit. Pookie gon' be alright."

"Un huh!"

She walked into the house after that. I didn't really want to talk about it. Since Neicy was in a good mood I decided to see what I could get out of it.

"Damn baby I missed you. We need some alone time soon."

"Oh so we can fuck?"

"I'm just saying, I've been locked up for a long time and we only did it once since I've been out." I shrugged.

"Is our relationship all about sex?"

"Nah but that's a part of it."

"Well I don't know when we can be alone anyway."

I was starting to wonder if she came by today because she knew my mom would be at home. I was locked down for four years and she supposedly hadn't messed with anyone the whole time. But when I get out she's trying to ration the ass. That irritated the hell out of me even though I was glad to see my daughter. I heard the horn blow a couple of times from a car so I turned around and it was Reddy. She was rolling in a late model Monte Carlo nowadays. I stepped away from the porch and hopped in on the passenger side. When I glanced back at Neicy her mouth was wide open. I didn't give a damn especially since she wasn't giving up the ass anytime soon.

"What the fuck is wrong with her?" Reddy asked.

I turned around to face Reddy because I was glaring at Neicy and her frowned up facial expression. The last thing I wanted to do was fire up Reddy because she was still a little off. Next thing to happen was my baby mama getting shot by her.

"She's mad at me because I'm jumping in the car with you. Don't even trip off that bitch right now."

"You need to let that bitch know that mean mugging can get you killed...what's up with that package?"

"I'm sold out but I didn't sort out what I'm supposed to pay you. I got the money but I ain't divided it yet."

"If you got that shit in yo pocket then count it out now." Reddy quickly replied.

"Hold on then."

I hopped out the car and ran in the house. Neicy was still on the porch when I ran in the house. Of course she was glaring at me when I ran past her. I pinched my daughter on her cheek before going inside.

"Oh so you got bitches rolling up on you like that?"

"This is business." I sneered.

I ran into my bedroom and went to my stash to pull out a wad of money. The exact count of the wad of money in the stash I knew but I would have to count everything that was in my pocket. I dashed outside past Neicy and Jada back inside the Monte Carlo.

"Did yo baby mama just call me a bitch?" Reddy pulled out a three-eighty

"Damn Reddy, that's my baby mama and my daughter is with her. Chill the fuck out in front of my mama's house."

"Alright but you need to check that broad, Blood."

"I need to count out this money." I retorted.

After I gave her what was owed she seemed to lighten up a little bit. Reddy acted like she wanted to talk.

"You know we might go to Skateland tomorrow night."

"Oh yeah, Skateland still be cracking?"

"Hell yeah, but it ain't like it used to be. Back in the day when we used to see Doug E. Fresh, EPMD, Whodini, Queen Latifah and all them it was the shit but it done slowed down now. But it still be having the best music. You should roll."

"Let me think on that shit. I'm trying to save up to get me a ride. So I gotta keep hustling until I can get some shit I can floss..."

"Grumpy, are you going to spend time with your daughter or what?" Neicy yelled from the porch.

"Aw shit, you better handle yo business before I end up shooting that bitch." Reddy smirked.

"Whatever! I'll get the package from you tomorrow."

I climbed out the car and as Reddy was driving off my mother stepped back on the porch. My mother had her hands on her hips glaring at me in an evil way. I already knew she was about to give me an earful.

"So you have women visiting you while your girlfriend and daughter is here?"

"That's Sheila from around the corner. She had loaned me some money and I was paying her back."

"Pretty Sheila that used like Dion?"

"Yeah mama."

"Oh okay, you should have told her I said hi."

Neicy's attitude changed when she realized my mother was cool with the girl. Reddy and Neicy were two different types of females. Reddy would have shot her in the ass just to teach her a lesson. Neicy was one of those types of females that didn't have anything else past talking shit. She wasn't really a fighter type of girl and she probably didn't know what to do with a gun. I chilled with Neicy while trying to set up some time to get some pussy. She was playing so hard to get that eventually it got on my nerves.

"You must be fucking someone else then."

"Or maybe you're fucking someone else." She fired back.

"I'm gon' start fucking someone else if I ain't getting any from you."

"Well do what you gotta do...you know what, fuck you Dwayne."

"I'm out." I shrugged.

I went into the house to kiss my daughter who was talking with my mother. She had a pretty good conversation to be only three years old. She hugged me and said goodbye then I almost walked out the door.

"Where are you going Dwayne?" My mother asked.

"In the streets."

"No you ain't! You gon' drive my car and take Neicy and Jada back home."

"That's okay Ms. Pittman..."

"Dwayne ain't doing anything child. All he's going to do is run the streets with his knucklehead friends. He can at least take you home." My mother said nicely.

Grudgingly we piled into my mother's car. I was glad to be able to roll my mother's car. She would let me drive every now and then but not on a regular. It was kind of quiet in the car to Neicy's house so I turned up the radio. She lived with her grandmother in Fruit Town now. Fruit Town was a Piru set that was on the border of the East Side and West Side of Compton. The niggas from Fruit Town that I knew claimed East Side. The reason it was called Fruit Town was because their neighborhood had a bunch of streets named after fruits. There was Peach Street, Plum Street and one of the streets was Piru Street that ran all the way through from the West Side. Neicy's family actually stayed on Piru Street. When we rolled over there it was a couple of niggas hanging out on the corner. When we got up close I happened to notice a black long nosed 45' in one's hand. He glared in the car but must have realized that it wasn't any danger. Our windows were rolled up and we had our lights on. So he kept his pistol drawn without lifting it to shoot. I breathed a sigh of relief because I hadn't brought my pistol with me and my daughter was in the car.

I pulled up in front of her house and parked the car. My daughter was asleep in the back seat so Neicy and I talked for a minute.

"Are you really gon' start messing with other bitches?"

"Everything is real. I'm a real muthafuckin' man and I need some loving on a regular basis. Besides you fucking someone else anyway."

"I ain't fucking with no one but you. I just ain't been in the mood for all of that."

"How do you expect me to be with just you and you ain't in the mood?"

"Just give me some time."

"Okay but I got to get back to the hood."

I wasn't really listening to what she had to say. She gave me the ass the first night we hooked up now all of a sudden she ain't in the mood. I eased my way out of the conversation then drove off. Of course I didn't bring the car home when I got back to the hood and it was dark by then. When I pulled up to Turtle's house only a few of the homies were in the back yard. Pookie, Loko, Timmy-Ru and Train were hanging out front smoking on weed when I pulled up. Loko seemed a little calmer than usual. The Loko I've gotten to know since I've been out of jail was much more paranoid than before. He wasn't as talkative as I remembered either. I embraced everybody then the weed was passed to me. I puffed on it a few times then passed it to Train. Now Train was a stocky and extremely black homie. He was so black that we called him blue black. But he had a gang of bitches on the East Side loving his ass. He wasn't a pretty boy or nothing, in fact, he had squabbles. He was just the darkest person I ever met in my life with a long ponytail. He had the sex symbol thing going for dark skin cats before Wesley Snipes. Timmy-Ru had developed a temperament like mine in recent times. All his hair was shaved off but he was maybe a shade lighter than me and I was of a sandy brown complexion. I had bitches throwing me play all the time if I wasn't on the corner but I was usually on the corner. Timmy-Ru was kind of shy about getting at the females at this time. Pookie was considered a pretty boy and that was why he was always turned up. It was like he was constantly trying to prove that he wasn't a pretty nigga. Loko and Pookie had the same light brown complexion but Loko looked grimy. His face had a dirty look to it and he was skinny from when he was shot. Staring at the homies from my hood in my generation was a trip to me. We were going into adulthood with different looks and temperaments.

"Blood, let me holler at you for a minute." Pookie whispered.

"What's up?"

I followed him over close to the yard next door to get some privacy. I was reluctant because I thought he was about to suggest some stupid shit again. He was itching to go back to jail and I wasn't.

"I know these bitches that stay close to crab territory that want us to come through. You got yo mom's car so we should roll."

"In what hood?"

"Over near South Side but it ain't in the heart of their hood. They ain't crab bitches either they just live over there. The girl I'm fucking with, her mom went to Las Vegas for a week." Pookie explained

South Side Compton Crips would get notoriety because one of their homeboys was accused of killing Tupac Shakur. In my opinion they were like the Hoovers of Compton. Hoover Criminals were a L.A. gang that were once Crips. They started beefing with everyone so tough they just decided to call themselves criminals that banged against Crips and Bloods. South Side was starting to be a hood that didn't get along with hardly anyone in Compton. I was willing to take the chance of rolling over there though. Pookie was excited about it and it made me just as excited. Now he was talking about doing some real shit.

"Fuck it Blood, I'm with it." I nodded.

We hopped in the car and drove down Holly after telling the homeboys we had to make a move. We sped down Holly Street and made a right on Alondra Blvd until we reached Long Beach Blvd and made a left turn. I started to get a little more alert as we dipped down a residential street. We pulled up to a house on a street that was quiet and dark. Pookie and I crept up to the porch and he rang the doorbell. I could hear the footsteps of someone walking up to the door.

"Who is it?"

"Kevin!"

The door swung open after someone looked through the peephole. They didn't bother turning on the porch light. They couldn't have gotten a good look at our faces. A short chocolate bombshell with thick ass legs in a mini-skirt hugged Pookie. When I seen her face I couldn't believe how fine she was. She led us through the living room until we reached a small flight of steps into the den. Everything was plush and pretty. I wondered where Pookie came across this female until I seen the one he was hooking me up with. She was about the same complexion as me but she had light brown eyes. She was wearing skin tight jeans with an ass nice and plump but athletic. It looked as though she ran track in high school. Her hair was sandy brown and laid straight down to her shoulders. I already was thinking of ways to hit that ass.

"Hey Tamara, this is Kevin and this is his friend…" She glanced at me.

"Dwayne." I replied.

Glancing at Pookie it was written on his face that I had pulled the better of the two. If I could pull her. I walked down to the den and my tongue was thick with saliva. I sat down next to her on the couch and she seemed pleased. That was my cue to start jibbing at her in her ear. Pookie was on his way upstairs with his girl before she stopped and walked up to me.

"Since Kevin is being rude my name is Nichole."

"Oh yeah, my bad." Pookie smirked.

They went upstairs and disappeared in one of the rooms leaving Tamara and I alone. I eased a little closer then she started asking questions.

"You are from Compton or you just came over Nichole's house?"

"Nah I grew up in Compton on the East Side."

"What side of Compton is this?"

"South Side but we don't get along with them niggas."

"So what are they Crips or Bloods?"

"They are Crips and we are Bloods."

"Oh, I ain't ever messed with anyone from Compton before."

"Where are you from?"

"I'm from Carson."

"How did you meet Nichole?"

"We went to the same Catholic school for years until high school. We've been friends all of our life." She giggled.

"So you want to be my friend?"

She smiled and nodded. That was my cue to ease in and start kissing on her. We began kissing passionately in a matter of seconds. My hands found themselves all over her body and she was moaning. Before long I was taking off her blouse that was tucked in her tight jeans. She came up out of the blouse and bra and I started kissing on her titties. She moaned louder as I sucked on her nipples. This was getting good now all I had to do was slide off those tight ass jeans. I was able to unbutton the pants but that was about it. She tapped me lightly to tell me to stop so I stopped. She sat up on the couch and slid the jeans down to her ankles. My dick was on hard already but it was about to break a hole in the zipper of my khakis now. I quickly unbuttoned my Pendleton shirt and slid off my khakis until I was just in my boxers and socks. We started kissing again but this time we were chest to breast and I loved it. Her panties were on the floor bunched up with her jeans so I climbed on top of her and slid my drawers down. She put one of her legs on the back part of the couch while her other foot was on the ground. I pushed inside of her tight wet walls and it felt like paradise. It had been so long that I didn't know what to do. We were kissing, humping and touching passionately. She got into the groove of what she was doing with ease. I couldn't believe I was fucking this fine ass female. She started putting her hips into it by twisting and turning with a swivel of her ass. This felt too good to be true. Her soft skin felt heavenly next to mine. If I was to get sprung on a broad she was pulling it off. My body trembled as the pace began to pick up. It can't come this fast. If I can stop it then I need to act quickly before it's too late.

"Let's do it doggy style."

She bent over the couch and let me push inside of her from the back. This wasn't much different than being on top of her. Her soft but firm ass cheeks bouncing against my pelvis was overwhelming. I need to hold it a little longer. She kept picking up the speed and that wasn't good for me. I was trying to hold it in as long as possible then she let out a small moan. That only turned me on more. In a matter of seconds I had squirted inside of her.

"Ooh shit." She moaned.

"Damn." I shivered.

I was trying my best to savor the feeling as long as possible. After I pulled out she got up and ran to the bathroom butt naked to wash up. I stood in the middle of the den butt naked with a hanging dick. My head was tilted backwards with my mouth wide open. My body was sensitive on almost every nerve. I didn't come out of my trance until she returned to the den.

"Are you okay?" She asked.

"Yeah I'm good." I smiled.

She began getting dressed and made small talk while watching television. Pookie and Nichole were upstairs in one of the bedrooms for another twenty minutes before they came back down to the den. I glanced at an old Grandfather clock and it was only five minutes to eleven. Tamara and I exchanged phone numbers then Pookie and I dipped out. That had really hit the spot so I was all smiles when we got inside the car.

"Where did you meet Nichole's fine ass at?"

"I met that little bitch at the Compton Swap meet about two months ago. We've been talking on the phone but I was always leery about going over in crab hood. But yo bitch was the baddest, Blood."

"Yeah that bitch was fine than a muthafucka. She told me she's from Carson. Her family probably got money, huh?"

"I don't know but Carson bitches always have it going on. Even they mamas be fine, Blood and that's on P-Fonk." Pookie chuckled.

It felt good to chill with Pookie on some homeboy shit. We wasn't disagreeing about something in the street we were just some homeboys that just got some ass. We cruised down Alondra without a care in the world. When we reached Holly Street it looked as though everyone had gone inside. I still decided to roll up on Turtle's house but all the homies had dispersed. That was a cue for me to take it into the house. I was on cloud nine so I knew I was going to sleep like a baby. Pookie jumped out of the passenger side. We stepped out to only be standing in front of Turtle's house on the sidewalk.

"Where's all the homies at?"

"I don't know but I'm about to go in the house and call it a night, Blood."

"It's only eleven o'clock Grumpy."

"Yeah but I ended that muthafucka with a bang." I laughed.

"Yeah you're right. I should call it a night too."

"You want me to roll you down to the house."

"Nah, I can…"

"Fuck slobs Cuz!"

Pop. Pop. Pop. Pop. Pop. Pop.

I attempted to run but I didn't get far as a bullet hit me in the shoulder and another hit me in the hip. Whoever was shooting must have run out of bullets. It didn't dawn on me how close the enemy was until I seen his face. It was that crab nigga Roccy that I had a fight with years ago. He was older and taller with a bunch of hair on his face. He had a blue flag on top of his head Aunt Jemima style. He tried to pull the trigger a couple of more times and that was how I was able to see his face. His dark brown face was scrunched up in hatred as he attempted to finish me off. After hearing the click of his gun a couple of times he glared at me and took off running down Holly Street towards Alondra. That was when the pain of my wounds had sunk in. Tears ran down my face as I tried to consume the hurting.

"Blood, are you alright."

"Nah that muthafucka Roccy crept up and got my ass Blood." I groaned.

"Ah Blood, we gon' have to serve that crab nigga. I'll get somebody to call the paramedics."

"I already called them." I heard a neighbor say.

The pain was unbearable and it felt like I was about to die. To calm myself down I just closed my eyes and pretended to be asleep.

11
STRETCHED

You know you gon' have to get rid of that gun that Reddy gave you!
Kool Aid

Two months had passed since Roccy was able to ride in enemy territory. He had been lying low to plot his next attack. He wanted to kill Pookie but he ended up getting Grumpy instead. Somebody must have been praying for him because Roccy had run out of bullets before he could finish him off. He wondered while sitting on his porch many days if Grumpy had seen his face. It didn't really matter one way or another. They were in a war and if you get caught slipping than that was on you. He had done several walk-bys in the last few years but they had been warring with another Crip set. It was the first time in a couple of years that he actually done a walk by in Holly Hood territory.

"I finally got to serve some more slobs." His lips curled up.

Roccy was beginning to be a well respected shooter in his neighborhood. He had developed a tendency to be a loner because he didn't fully trust all of his homeboys. He would hang out with a bunch of the homies but no one else replaced his road dog.

"If you are alone you can't snitch on yourself."

It was broad daylight and he didn't want any more encounters with any Pirus so he decided to go to Jackrabbit liquor store. There was only Starks liquor store on Bradfield and Alondra and Jackrabbits on the corner of Long Beach Boulevard and Alondra. They would sometimes run into Holly Hoods if they went up to Starks. Jackrabbits liquor store was right in Crip territory. He didn't like carrying his pistol in the daytime because of the Sheriffs so he strolled without a gun. Running across the Boulevard he dodged cars to make it to his destination. When he walked into the liquor store he ran into J-Rocc from South Side.

"What that Cee like Cuz!?!!" Roccy announced.

"You better keep it Crippin' Cuz." J-Rocc replied.

He turned around to see Roccy smiling at him. They quickly embraced then J-Rocc turned to his other two homies.

"Cuz, this nigga right here is a down ass rider. That's on the set and that's on Compton Crip. What's been up with you, Cuz?" J-Rocc chuckled with his hand over his mouth.

"Trying to stay alive and not catch a case."

"Yeah this is my muthafuckin nigga, cuz. Me and him were in L.P. juvenile hall and we were riding on niggas for real. It was mostly L.A. Crips in our unit but Roccy had my back. Where did they send you, I forgot?"

"They sent me to Camp Mendenhall out there near Magic Mountain. I damn near did eighteen months out there."

"Yeah, I just got out of Youth Authority. They tried to charge me as an adult on a murder but I beat the rap. I just came up here to get drunk with my homeboys but you should drink with us."

"Yeah I'm with that Cuz but I can't stay too long. My bitch is gon' come by and spend some time with me. You know how that is." Roccy grinned.

"Yeah Cuz, I just got out three weeks ago and the first thing I wanted to do was get me some pussy. I'll roll you to the house whenever you ready."

Once all the liquor was bought Roccy hopped in the back seat of J-Rocc's blue Monte Carlo. Roccy found himself in the backyard with a bunch of South Side Crips. His hood was considered allies with them but he was still a little uneasy. They had a tendency to set trip and that was the last thing he needed without his pistol.

"What kind of heat you carrying nowadays?" J-Rocc asked after a few drinks.

"I got a six shooter thirty-eight but I need something with more bullets, Cuz." Roccy replied with undertones of frustration.

"Ah Cuz, I got some heat for you if you want to put in work. I can give you one of my guns because I know you gon' put it to good use. You want to serve those slob ass niggas from Holly, huh?"

Roccy nodded with a devilish grin. J-Rocc bounced up from the weight bench they were sitting on and went inside the house. It took him several minutes so one of his homies passed him a 40oz bottle of Old English that was half empty. He swigged it and it tasted a little different. J-Rocc came outside in a few minutes then sat next to him. In his hands was a brown paper bag.

"Here you go, Cuz. This is a nine-millimeter with sixteen in the clip and one in the chamber. You catch a nigga slipping with this shit Cuz; you got sixteen times to miss."

"Good looking on this J-Rocc."

"Ah that ain't shit. If you had some heat and I needed it you would let me use it, right?"

Roccy nodded.

"What's in the beer besides eight-ball?"

"Some of the crazy homies put hard liquor in their beer. I don't drink that shit unless I know it ain't been tampered with. Some of the homies smoke primos and they will try to slide some of that shit to you if you ain't careful." J-Rocc whispered the last sentence.

Everybody knew that primos was weed mixed with crack. Roccy never got a kick out of smoking a lot of weed or drinking. He never messed with crack in his life. He was into shooting his enemies. He hung out with J-Rocc for another thirty minutes then he was taken home. He shook hands with J-Rocc then made his way quickly out the passenger door. To his surprise Pam was waiting for him on his porch. She didn't say anything until she seen the car drive off.

"Was that J-Rocc from South Side?"

"Yeah, I hung out with him earlier." Roccy replied while letting her inside.

"They let that nigga out of jail. I heard he caught a murder charge."

"Yeah but he beat the case."

"What's in the brown bag?"

"Don't worry about all that."

Roccy quickly went into his bedroom and stashed away his new weapon. He already had it on his mind that he was going to sell the thirty-eight and use that to get some dope. He needed money so that he and Pam could get a place. When he walked out the bedroom she was there in the hallway to greet him. She eyed him suspiciously as he closed the bedroom door.

"Why are you trying to hide something?"

"It's just some things that you shouldn't know Pam. That's all I'm saying." He replied curtly.

"Are you serious, as much as we've been through?

"Yeah as much as we've been through there are still things I can't tell you." They embraced.

"What will you tell me?"

"That there is no bitch that comes before you."

She gently kissed him and smiled. They walked into the living room with her still in his arms. He collapsed on the couch carrying her with him and they both laughed. He moved her bangs away from her face.

"You are a fine muthafucka." He jested.

"And I'm all yours Nukka."

They kissed and began getting undressed. It had been a routine the last year and a half since he'd been out of jail. She was more in love with him today than she was when they first got together. He was holding seventeen inch arms and muscles bulged through his shoulders and chest. She rubbed her hands all over his upper torso. He kissed her as she climbed on top of him. They passionately began to undress until they were both on the couch butt naked.

"What time your mother or your sister is coming home?"

"My sister won't be home for another two hours. She's going to Beauty College and they keep her until five and it takes another thirty minutes to get home. My mom makes it in at seven." He whispered.

She grabbed a hold of his manhood and slid it inside of her. Pam grabbed a hold of his chest hairs and let out a soft moan. Roccy pushed inside of her while grabbing her ass cheeks. They quickly soiled the couch as their sweat entangled their ecstasy. Before he could get into his groove he felt himself climaxing. But Pam wouldn't stop sliding down his pole until she let out a loud growl. A moment later Roccy grunted from the same climax she had just experience. She collapsed on top of him panting on his sweaty chest.

"Baby?" She whispered.

"Yeah?"

"Why are you keeping secrets from me? I thought that we would never have anything to hide from one another."

"Some things in the streets shouldn't be spoken about. This is Compton so pillow talking can get you killed. I got enemies and I don't want anyone to have anything on you so I don't tell you anything. That doesn't mean that my love for you ain't real." Roccy calmly explained.

"What enemies you got now? Are you talking about those Holly Hood niggas or somebody else? You are warring with Crips now like Santana Blocc or Neighborhood…what enemies?"

"All of them Pam. But I got personal enemies that want to see me dead."

"Who wants to see you dead?" She quickly asked.

"Niggas I've gotten into it with."

"Like who? Give me some names Roccy. They are my enemies too."

"I'm just saying."

"You are saying who?"

"You just won't let this die, huh?"

"No not until you give me some names."

"Okay Grumpy, Pookie, C-Bone and Tank are a few names. If something ever happens to me you best believe one of those niggas did it." He sighed.

"Grumpy and Pookie who are they? I know C-Bone; and Tank is sitting on seven or eight years."

"You don't know when your enemies might catch you slipping. That's why I stay ready and always keep a piece when I'm walking these Compton streets."

"That's what was in that brown paper bag, huh?"

"See Cuz, that's why I don't want to tell you about certain shit. What I do in the streets and in the hood is some things you don't need to know."

"Okay, Okay but who is Grumpy and Pookie?"

"Just some slob niggas from Holly Hood." He sneered.

It took me awhile to recover from my bullet wounds. Now I was back walking in a normal way. That muthafucka Roccy was beginning to be a problem. The Sheriff's homicide detective came in to question me about who shot me. I wasn't about to snitch even if he was an enemy. If he wouldn't have run out of bullets I would have been dead. I knew from that day forward lying up in the hospital that we were going to bump heads again. The next time we met up we were going to be on equal ground. I dipped into the stash of money that I was going to use to get me a car. Reddy sold me a gun fresh out of the box with no murders. I don't know how she had the connections she had but I was glad she was my homegirl. I figured Smokey hipped her on to a lot of shit. His years in the pen had Bloods from different parts of Los Angeles County coming to our neighborhood to see him.

Now that I was armed it was time for me to put in work. I decided that I wasn't going to bang anymore but some niggas won't learn until you show them. I was waiting for Kool Aid to meet up with me to handle the business at hand. He was finally released while I was in the hospital. It was good to see that stocky ass nigga. All I kept hearing was Kool Aid was kicking up dust in the juvenile jail system. They almost shipped him to the penitentiary but he was able to get a release before they could. He had also changed throughout the years. He was a much more charismatic gangster like Smokey. He was one of those type of niggas that frightened the enemy once they saw him. I appreciated his temperament and was glad to see him free and healthy.

Kool Aid had come to the hospital to visit me. I felt bad about it because I never got around to visiting him when he got shot up. He wasn't tripping about that. In fact he brought up the day we got caught by the Lynwood Sheriffs.

"I'm telling you Blood, if you wouldn't have told me not to shoot that crab nigga I would have caught a murder charge or got my capped peeled from the pigs."

"Yeah them muthafuckas pulled up on us right when you put the gun away. I was tripping off that shit too, Blood."

"Yeah instead of a gun charge we would have been sitting on a murder charge. Everything happens for a reason. Did you really know that crab nigga or you told me that so I wouldn't shoot?"

"Nah I knew the nigga. I used to play Pop Warner football back in the day with that nigga. I know him as Lorenzo but I don't know what they call him in his hood." I shrugged.

"Well I'm glad now that you knew that nigga or we would still be doing time. I was about to let that nigga have it in broad daylight."

That was an inside joke between us. We had a Piru's dream to catch a Crip slipping and we were glad that we didn't go as far as we wanted to go.

Tonight was much different for us. Kool Aid had stolen a car and came back to Holly to pick me up. I was hoping that we wouldn't have to do a drive-by. I wanted to walk up on Roccy and peel his cap. We had roamed the streets several nights ago but we couldn't find him. At this point I felt like it was either him or me. My mom was worried that I was thinking about retaliating. She didn't understand the streets but I had to do what I had to do. She told me in the hospital that she was thinking about moving out of Compton. The thought of moving outside of the hood kind of pissed me off. She was tired and worried that my brother would get out and be in the same mix again. I couldn't worry about the things she was telling me. We decided to go on his street and park down the street in his neighborhood where most of his homeboys hung out. We got a glimpse of his homeboys while driving down the street but I didn't want to get at them. They were slipping big time but that didn't matter to me. Kool Aid didn't give me a hard time about it either. We parked down the street hoping that Roccy would show up. We heard some of his homeboys making noise and talking loud. I had my hand on the pistol ready to let go of some fire.

It would be another hour before we seen Roccy. He walked right past us and didn't notice us in the car. Kool Aid found a small Toyota Tercel that he stole for us to prowl the East Side streets of the Hub City. It was one of those cars that would be overlooked by everyone, including gangsters. We weren't really talking too much when he walked by. That was what probably saved us from being detected. He walked past the car like he didn't have a worry in the world. I hopped out the car once he was a little distant away. I looked around to see if he was followed or had some lingering homeboys around. I climbed out of the car without shutting it all the way behind me. I slid the brown handkerchief a little bit above the nose. I hid behind a tree then walked up on him quickly. My Pumas were quiet enough for me to not to get detected. I picked up the pace as I got closer to him. When I was within yards I whispered.

"What's up Roccy?"

He quickly turned around thinking it was one of his homeboys. I let off two shots in the leg area and he collapsed on the sidewalk. He groaned in pain as I ran up on him. He glanced up at me damn near crying.

"What's happening Blood. Do you remember me?" I pulled the rag down to reveal my face.

He wasn't very surprised. I had the drop on him while he lied on the ground. He attempted to slide backwards while trying to pull the weapon from his waist band. There was a brief admiration for my enemy considering he was fighting till the very end. We made eye contact for about two seconds then I started firing into his torso. Then I walked up and shot him in the head. I stared at his body stretched out for a brief second then Kool Aid screeched up.

"Get in."

I hopped in on the passenger side and we sped off. We dropped the car off on Rosecrans and a side street called Mayo Avenue. It was in Elm Street Piru territory so we felt safe. We were okay from anyone creeping on a major street. We still had to be careful about the Sheriffs. So we walked down Rosecrans until we made it up to Leuders Park. We cut through Leuders Park and made our way back to Roosevelt Elementary. On the other side of the school was Holly Street. We were panting when we were walking but we still talked.

"Blood, you know you gon' have to get rid of that gun that Reddy gave you." Kool Aid started in.

"Come on Blood, I know I have to get rid of this shit. I just want to know where I'm going to get another gun."

"Tell Reddy you had to put in some work and she will let you get another. You know you're her favorite." Kool Aid smirked.

"If I was her favorite she would have been gave up the ass."

"Reddy is in love with the big homie Smokey. She's been that way since we were thirteen and fourteen years old." Kool Aid shrugged.

"Yeah I know. She's still the finest female I know that is willing to put in work like a nigga will."

"I know, she's like the perfect Bonnie type bitch. Smokey-Ru made her that way, Blood. He doesn't hang around a broad too long unless she can catch a case like him. I heard him tell me that shit before and that's on Piru. He'll fuck but that's about it."

"Honestly only a nigga like Smokey could really handle a female like Reddy...give me your red flag so I can wipe this gun off. I'm about to throw it in this sewer drain."

We were on Holly street close to Compton Blvd. when I spotted the drain. After a thorough cleaning I tossed the gun in the drain and we cautiously strolled back to the hood to call it a night.

12
P-FONK PARADISE

Nah, I can handle that shit by myself!
Smokey-Ru

After Roccy was dead it seemed as though a weight was lifted off my back. I wouldn't call myself a killer but I did what I had to. Roccy would continue to come after me as long as he was alive. One of us had to go. I respected him as a soldier for his cause but a man has to do what he has to do to survive. Kool Aid was the obvious choice for me to put in work with because of his disposition about things. I didn't want to get out and gangbang but I had to handle one enemy and he understood that. If I would have rolled with Pookie it would have been a different thing. He would have wanted to scream out the set and all kinds of shit. Roccy and I both know who got him and that was good enough for me. So once again I was back on the block hustling for the car I was trying to get.

This particular Saturday I wanted to close shop for a few hours so that I could go to a barbecue. I was picking up Tamara a little later in Reddy's Monte Carlo. Everybody was going over Ronnie-Ru's house because he had been released from the pen. Smokey was paying for everything. It was gon' be crackin' all day and late into the night. Reddy was even telling me that I didn't need to hustle today. I had saved up enough to start going in with her but I wanted a car first. I found this Buick Regal for eight grand that was fresh off a small lot. Smokey-Ru told me to get a car for less than ten thousand and it won't be reported to the IRS. I don't know how he found that out but I had to listen. My plan was to pick it up this weekend on Sunday. I knew I would have fun for the day celebrating at the barbecue.

I decided to roll by myself to pick up Tamara. She told me to pick her up over her friend Nichole's house that lived in South Side. I told her I had access to a car and could come to Carson but she insisted we meet over there. When I went to pick her up she was standing a couple of houses down from the house and Nichole wasn't with her. At the time it was a little off to me but I was glad to see her fine ass. She smiled as she got into the car. We did the little routine of a peck on the lips then I rolled out. Tamara was classy about how she carried herself. You could tell that she was taught how to take care of herself. I mean as far as hygiene. She didn't depend on a nail shop to keep her nails done. She didn't depend on a beauty salon to keep her hair up to par. She was the first female that I was dating that knew the maintenance of a woman. She told me once over the phone that her mother and father were still together. That tripped me out because you didn't see that too much in Compton. She had on a yellow and blue flower dress that went down to her ankles. Somehow she managed to still make it sexy even though it was loose on the lower part. I knew that I was going to turn heads when all the homies seen her. At that moment I wished my brother Flintstone was out of jail.

When we made it to the party the homeboys were hanging out in the back deep. It was even a few Pirus from other sets. Some of the homies from Lime Hood came through as well as some of the homies from Leuders Park. Ronnie-Ru had comrades he was locked up with so when he touched down niggas wanted to see him. Everybody turned around and stared at Tamara and me when we walked into the backyard. Even Smokey who was in the middle of playing spades glanced at us and gave a nod of approval. Reddy was sitting on the passenger seat of Smokey's Chevy Impala watching the card game when she glanced up. She took a drag of her cigarette and gave a slight smile like she was impressed. Pookie was dancing with this female from MOB Piru when he seen us walk in. He stopped his dancing to walk over there and whispered in my ear.

"You just showing off bringing that fine ass bitch."

I didn't even respond. My facial expression had my answer. I had the baddest bitch in the whole party. We went straight to the dance floor and some of the finest females on the East Side had to acknowledge that Tamara was the truth. She danced with the latest dance steps but I kept it gangster and did the basic two-step. We partied hard as the alcohol and weed was spread throughout the party. I ain't talking about any bullshit stress weed either. It was that bomb Kush-Chronic California marijuana that would have you feeling good for hours. Tamara didn't smoke any weed but she got her drink on. A couple of the homegirls kept her preoccupied by asking her questions about her clothes. She had on sandals that I had never seen before. A few of the homegirls wanted to prick her brain about fashion tips. I went over there near Reddy so that Tamara could get acquainted with the hood bitches. Her and Smokey were talking when I walked up on them.

"You want me to roll with you?" Reddy asked.

"Nah, I can handle that shit by myself." Smokey replied.

"What's happening Blood?"

"That's a bad little broad you done pulled Grumpy." Smokey commented.

"Good looking big homie."

"Where you find her at?" He asked.

"She's from Carson."

"Okay, you done pulled you a high maintenance female. That's what I'm talking about Blood."

It was like Smokey was congratulating me. Carson was a city next to Compton with some pretty good neighborhoods. They had a few parts that were grimy just like Compton but a lot of it was upper-middle class black folks. There were a lot of two parent households in Carson. That meant in many cases that the women were well kept and knew how to be pampered but also knew how to pamper themselves. When me and her had sex I appreciated how her pubic hairs were trimmed and groomed. She didn't have any odor or anything like that coming from between her legs. She wore nice expensive perfume that wasn't over imposing but smelled as though it was her natural body odor. I've been to plenty of parties where females would be musty with perfume on. They wore sandals and their feet were dirty or their toes was unkempt. Tamara was a relief from all of that not only because of the obvious but also the delicate things a woman might neglect or overlook. I was digging this girl a lot but I didn't want to show it too much. I already knew she was the business but once Smokey signed off on her, no one could tell me shit.

"Yeah Grumpy she's a keeper." Smokey added.

I nodded with a slight grin on my face. I looked at Reddy and she seemed pleased for me as well. I could tell something else was troubling her but I left it alone. Reddy wasn't too big on questions. Besides she was still having a good time at the barbecue/party. When I looked around at the party and seen everyone dancing and laughing I knew that it was P-Fonk paradise. We didn't have to worry about the Sheriffs rolling up on us because we were in the back of private property. If an enemy decided to creep up in that party he was going to get weapons drawn on him from all kinds of people.

"This was a bomb ass all day party. This is the type of shit the homies should have all the time. If it was up to me, we would have this shit every weekend." Smokey said enthusiastically.

"Yeah this muthafuckin' party been popping all day. Niggas got they grub on, they drink on and their smoke on and got to dance to some jams." Reddy added.

"Come on Reddy let's get out there and dance." Smokey headed for the crowd.

We were in Ronnie-Ru's backyard and his driveway went all the way to the back where there was a garage. Everyone was dancing on the concrete and inside the garage with the entrance lifted up. Two cars could fit inside the garage but it was serving as a dance floor and the DJ was also set up on the inside. I watched Smokey and Reddy hit the dance floor and they both were doing the two-step. I laughed to myself as Pookie walked up.

"You want to hit this weed with me, Blood?"

He passed me some rolled up weed and I hit it a couple of times. It smelled like weed but it also smelled of something else familiar.

"Blood what is in this weed?"

"This is a primo." Pookie laughed.

"Why the fuck you giving me dope to smoke you dumb muthafucka?"

I took off on him. I threw a two-punch combo on him and he stumbled back. He came back with two of his own and we locked up.

"Ah Blood them niggas is scrapping." Someone yelled.

Before someone could get the upper hand the homies had pulled us apart. We both tried to break loose to finish our squabble but the homies had us both hemmed up. Smokey and Ronnie-Ru came over to see what was going on.

"What the fuck ya'll niggas tripping about, Blood?" Smokey demanded.

"This nigga gave me some weed with dope in it." I yelled.

"What?" Smokey looked puzzled.

"He gave you some weed with dope in it? What the fuck are you talking about?" Ronnie-Ru added.

"I passed that nigga a primo and he hit the shit once and started tripping. I was just trying to celebrate you getting out of jail. I didn't think he was gon' trip off that shit, Blood." Pookie replied viciously.

"Blood, did you tell him that it was dope in this joint before you gave it to him?" Smokey asked.

"Nah, but I wasn't gon give…"

"Well then Blood you was wrong for that punk shit. You let a man decide what he want to partake in, my nigga."

"That's what the fuck I'm saying." I replied.

I was fired up and wanted to finish our fight but Smokey called a shot on the shit. He walked over to Pookie and got up close to him. He leaned in but he spoke loud enough for everyone to hear.

"Blood, we should fuck you up behind doing that shit to your own homie. But both of ya'll niggas making our hood look bad when ya'll set tripping with each other. Consider this shit squashed but Pookie I better not hear you doing some shit like that to any of the homies again."

Just like that everyone let us go. It was kind of like they dared us to continue our scrap. I was still mad than a muthafucka while my bottom lip felt numb from the cocaine on my lips. My temper calmed a little when Tamara came over to me and started rubbing on my chest. Pookie and I were mean mugging each other for a minute. Some of the homies started gathering around him by the wall. Tamara and I were left alone in the grass near Smokey's impala.

"Are you okay?" Tamara asked.

"Nah that nigga pissed me off. And that's supposed to be my road dog."

"You ready to go?"

"You ready to get up out of here?"

"Yeah but you gon' have to get a room for the night. My parents think that I'm spending the night over Nichole's house." She smiled.

"That's straight; I'll get a room at the Ramada Hotel off the 91 Freeway."

"Okay, well let's go then."

We began walking over towards the driveway when Pookie pulled my arm. I almost fired on him again but I seen the look on his face.

"Let me get at you for a minute, Blood."

I told Tamara to hold up a minute while I walked closer to the brick wall with Pookie. He leaned in and spoke close to a whisper tone.

"That's my bad, my nigga. You know I got nothing but love for you Grumpy. I just got caught up in the moment." Pookie explained.

"Yeah Blood everything straight I just don't fuck with the dope. You know how I get down homie. You and I go back to elementary in the sandbox and shit."

"I'm knowing Blood. That type of shit won't happen again."

We shook hands and embraced. Everyone else was partying so only a few observers noticed us reconciling.

"I would have fired on yo ass too, Blood." Reddy snuck up on us.

"Hey Reddy, I was gon' put Tamara up in a hotel." I turned to her.

"That's straight. Go ahead and take the ride and give it back to me in the morning. Smokey wants me to drop him off at the house so that he could roll his jeep."

"Good Looking."

She nodded and turned around and got into the fray of the party. Tamara and I stepped out onto Holly Street and drove off in the Monte Carlo. Once we were up in the hotel room we took a shower together. We had sex at least three or four times that night. The next morning we got up before wake up time. We decided to stop and get breakfast from IHOP before she went back to Carson. We talked about different things but she was schooling me on things I didn't know about. I was really falling for this female and at times I had to check my gangster. We didn't leave the restaurant until a little past noon. I was on cloud nine until we got to Carson.

"Drop me off over here by the park."

"Why what's up? You ain't going straight home."

"Nah my friend owes me money and I want to pick it up from her and she's at the park."

"Well I'll let you get your money and wait on you so you don't have to walk home." I replied.

"That's okay Dwayne, I'll be fine. I might decide to talk with her for awhile. You get back to Compton and I'll call you."

"Okay."

We kissed then she hopped out the car. I leaned back in Reddy's Monte Carlo and cruised all the way home. When I made it back to the hood I decided to stop at home first before I returned the car back to Reddy. My mom was watching television in the living room. She glanced at me walking by.

"What happened around the corner last night?"

"What are you talking about?"

I didn't give her a chance to reply because I was walking in my bedroom. I wanted to change my clothes before I went back around the corner. Tamara had brought a change of clothes but I didn't think about it. Once I was dressed and ready to hit the streets I came back into the living room.

"What do you mean what happened last night? One of the homies had a barbecue and party until the late night."

"Yeah well someone got killed around the corner last night."

"How do you know all of that?"

"I heard all the paramedics and police around the corner. Then I got a phone call from one of the nosy neighbors saying some young guy named Ronald was killed on Bradfield Street."

"Ronald?" I shrugged.

Bradfield Street was two blocks west of Holly Street. None of the homies ever hung out over there so I didn't pay it any mind. When I hopped into the Monte Carlo it dawned on me who she might be talking about. But that was too hard to believe. I hit the corner off of Locust Circle onto Holly but before I could go that far I heard my name.

"Grumpy...Grumpy-Ru!" Someone shouted.

I hit the brakes, turned to look behind me and through my rearview mirror. Running up behind the car was Kool Aid. I waited until he got up on the passenger side window.

"What's happening, Blood?" He panted.

"Shit! I'm on my way to Reddy's house to drop off her car."

"You ain't heard what happened last night?"

"Nah, my mom was talking about somebody getting killed but she didn't know who."

"Smokey got killed last night."

"Nah Blood; don't play with me like that. My mom said Ronald but I didn't think she was talking about him. I can't believe any shit like that." I said vehemently.

"Yeah Ronald Polk is his government name. The fucked up thing about it is he was killed by a nigga he grew up with his whole life." Kool Aid sadly sighed.

"Somebody from the hood killed Smokey?" I asked in disbelief.

"Nah, that nigga Carl. Tierra with the big ole titties, her brother."

"You got to be bullshitting me, Blood. Hop in and roll with me around to Reddy's house. She's probably taking that shit real hard. I won't believe that shit until I know for sure with my own eyes he's dead."

Kool Aid hopped in on the passenger side and I rolled around to Reddy's house that stayed on Pannez. I could tell that Kool Aid hadn't fully accepted it yet either.

"When did you find out he was dead?" I asked.

"Timmy-Ru called me at the house this morning. He lives on Pannez so he was over there when they rolled on Bradfield. He told me he walked over to Bradfield in a robe and house shoes. He even heard the gunshots when they first went off."

We rolled around to Reddy's house and it seemed empty. I decided to walk around to the back house to only find Reddy's Mother Sharon answering the door.

"Hey Dwayne."

"Hey Sharon, I wanted to talk to Red…Sheila."

"She at Ronald's house. You didn't hear that he got killed last night?"

"Okay, I'll go over there."

"Hey Dwayne, you got ten dollars you can loan me?"

I pulled out a twenty and handed it to her knowing I wasn't getting it back. Reddy's mom was a serious alcoholic. It had taken a toll on her small frame. Reddy was only a young version of Sharon and it was a time that Sharon was a head turner. Now she was only a shell of what she used to be. It made me reflect that was why Reddy only smoked cigarettes. She never really drunk alcohol and she smoked weed socially. As I walked from the porch into the street I contemplated having to go to Smokey's house. He had an older brother that didn't bang but wasn't anyone to play with and an older sister. It was something that I wasn't looking forward to. By the time I got inside the car my mind was made up that I should go. When I rolled over to his house a bunch of homies was hanging out in front. It was most of the big homies. In fact, Kool Aid and I were the only ones from our generation there when we pulled up. Reddy was sitting on his porch smoking on a cigarette quietly. I felt bad for her and I felt bad for Smokey.

After making my way through all the homies I finally reached the porch to talk to Reddy. She was so zoned out she didn't realize that I was standing in front of her. Her mind was somewhere else and I had never seen her like that.

"Reddy!"

Her eyes slowly raised but they were hazy. It took her a few seconds to recognize or acknowledge me even though she was looking right in my face.

"What's up Blood?"

"I'm fucked up over Smokey. We lost a real good dude." I replied.

Her eyes were glossy and she seemed frail for the first time. She stood up and stared at me for a moment longer then hugged me. That was the first time I seen her give me a real emotion. I always knew her to be as hard as concrete. That was one of the few times I seen Reddy as a real woman. I hugged her and rubbed her back gently. It was a sad occasion and I knew she was taking it the hardest. When we finally broke our embrace I handed her the keys to her car.

"Hold on to them until you get you a ride." She waved me off.

I didn't see Reddy until the funeral. It was gangsters from all over the East Side and Damus from all over Los Angeles. Smokey was a well respected gangster. To my surprise there were Pirus represented from every set on the East Side. There was Lime Hood, Cross Atlantic, Elm Street, Leuders Park, MOB Piru and a few gangsters from Fruit Town littering the church pews. It was P-Fonk gangsters from everywhere even though the funeral was in Crip territory. Burgundy floated through the crowd like an ocean. Some of the homies were wearing Beige flags which were Holly colors while others wore Burgundy flags. The ones that wore

Burgundy flags on their head wore them Aunt Jemima style. I saw Reddy sitting up front in the second row behind the immediate family. She would glance back every now and then at me with a look of disapproval. She didn't think he should have had all those colors flashing at his funeral. It was bizarre to me because I seen Smokey loving something like this for his funeral. Many people probably would have expected Smokey to be glad we were representing in force. Reddy knew him better than all of us so I considered that. I wouldn't put my Burgundy flag on my head until I paid my respects.

When the funeral finally ended at the church I walked to the front to see my big homie laid out in a mahogany coffin. He didn't look the same. Smokey looked bloated and he had a bunch of make-up on his face. Someone had already slipped a Burgundy flag into his right side suit pocket. His haircut was close and lined up right. I stared at him for a minute holding up the line that was behind me waiting to see him. It was just hard to believe that he was now dead. He was like a superhero to me. That was the first time I realized that anyone can get killed in the streets of Compton. I threw up the Piru gang sign and prayed that he was on his way to P-Fonk paradise.

"You were the realest gangster I've ever known Smokey. Holly in Peace!" I whispered then walked out the door.

13
SET TRIPPIN

Let me go Grumpy, this nigga set tripping over a female!
Pookie-Ru

Three days after Smokey's funeral Reddy came knocking on my door early in the morning. It wasn't necessarily early but I hadn't got in the night before until two-something in the morning. When I glanced at the clock it was around nine in the morning. My mother had already gone to work by then. I peeked out the window to see Reddy with one foot on the bottom step smoking on a cigarette. Her eyes were blood shot red and she looked as though she hadn't slept in days. She still smelled good when I hugged her on the porch. I was in basketball shorts and a tank top when I stepped outside.

"I needed to holler at you." She said.

"Come on in."

She put out the cigarette then followed me inside. She didn't sit down right away but in fact began to pace as though she was trying to think of something to say. I sat down in a living room chair and waited for her to settle in. Frightened wasn't the word to describe how I was feeling but more like nervous. I didn't know if she was about to blow a gasket or what. I wasn't afraid for my safety or anything like that but I was worried for her. She wasn't the same confident but sullen woman I've known her to be. It was obvious signs of her being fragile and weak. You got to understand that this is a female I've known since I was a young boy and she's always been tough. She always kept her femininity but I've put in work with her. Reddy could catch a case with the best of us and stand tall. She once beat a murder charge because she kept her mouth shut. She was solid since I've known her now she was…different.

"I'm a real muthafucka Grumpy. I-I mean I've stayed true to the code. I ain't ever ran out on a nigga, I ain't ever been a snitch, I've did time for the hood and I've shed blood for the hood, you bee what I'm saying?" She asked passionately.

"Yeah Blood, you are stand-up homegirl like a muthafucka."

"So it's times when a bitch can't really handle some shit…I mean, I'm a woman and shit. I ain't ever gone dike or butch but I've had to be strong for a lot of reasons. But…But that was my nigga for real." She whimpered.

It was nothing I could do at this point. I was frozen in my chair damn near paralyzed so I couldn't move. When I lowered my head she came over to the chair and got on one knee. She looked me in my eyes.

"That was my muthafucka nigga, Blood. Why the fuck did it have to go down like that? And I asked him at Ronnie-Ru's party if he wanted me to roll and he was like Nah. I wouldn't have let that shit go down if I was there…do you bee what the fuck I'm saying?"

Reddy practically screamed the last question. Then suddenly she began sobbing uncontrollably. All I could do was wrap my arms around her to console her. She welcomed it and let out tons of tears in my lap. It was a messed up situation because we couldn't retaliate on anybody because it wasn't a gang enemy. We could maybe shoot up Carl's parents' house but people were still cool with Tierra. Tierra was even upset with her brother behind the shit and came to the funeral. Carl was locked up and awaiting trial but no one really knew what happened to make him shoot the homie like that. More than likely he wouldn't last too long in the pen because everyone belonged to a car. You had the

Crip car, Damu car, Piru car, Hoover car, Peckerwood car and the Mexican car. Once some homies from the Piru car find out he was locked up for killing a P-Fonk and he didn't belong to a car they was gon' kill him. Right at this moment though, Penitentiary politics wasn't the issue.

"I'm telling you Grumpy, shit ain't the same anymore. I really miss that nigga." She continued crying.

"We all gon' miss him."

"Nah fuck that."

She jumped from the floor and began pacing back and forth. She was doing something with her hands like pulling on them.

"Niggas is gon' be on some passive shit. This wasn't just another homie getting killed. That nigga was a real muthafuckin' Gangster that handled his business and took care of his homeboys. That nigga believed in what he was doing with all his heart."

The tears were still falling down her face. Watching this pretty woman break down was a difference experience for me. Reddy was like Wonder Woman to me but Smokey-Ru was like Superman.

"I ain't ever met a nigga like him and I don't think I ever will." I replied.

"He taught me how to shoot a pistol. He had faith in a bitch when most niggas was looking at me as some female they could fuck. I wasn't considered a rider until he put me on then niggas accepted me Blood."

"Damn Reddy I thought you were born shooting a gun." I said lightheartedly.

She smirked and finally collapsed on the couch. Both of her legs were spread open with her arms hanging over her knees while she hunched over. I gave her time to contemplate on her thoughts. The uncomfortable silence had me on pins and needles even though the air had lightened up.

"I was pregnant by Smokey but I had a miscarriage." She blurted out.

"Whoa, are you serious?"

"Do it look like I'm serious?"

Her face was stone and sullen like she had just pulled a trigger. I shook my head because I knew where she was going with this. Now I was the one that stood up and began pacing.

"And I'm fucked up about it because if I would have had the baby a piece of him would still be here with me."

She began sobbing again. I walked in the kitchen because I didn't know where else to go. I went into the refrigerator and grabbed the cold water. After getting two glasses from the cupboard I poured her and I a glass then walked back into the living room.

"Here Reddy, drink some of this."

She grabbed the glass of water while the tears were still flowing. At that moment I tried to picture Reddy as a Mama. It was a little difficult at first but then I realized she would be a disciplinarian type parent but in a gangster way. Reddy looked up at me with her wet pretty face as if she was reading my mind. That's when she sipped the drink of water. That is when it dawned on me that I loved this woman. Not the type of love a man has for a woman that is in an intimate relationship. More like understanding this person and a human being and being empathic to their plight. She was true to everything she stood for so it was natural for her to deeply mourn the loss of a loved one. Reddy would walk through the depths of hell for a friend because they were a friend. She wouldn't need any other reason. That was what made her special. My own maturity made me look past her sporadic behavior, her low tolerance for most things and her icy disposition. I was able to look at all of her facets. As these thoughts ran through my head she began wiping the tears from her face. She stood and swigged the water in one lift of her glass. She passed me the glass and straightened herself out.

"I'm about to be out."

"Much love, my nigga." I replied.

Reddy smiled then walked to the front door. She opened it still with her head down. Her ponytail was pointing upward as she unlocked the chains on the door.

"Reddy, I got to ask you this. Did Smokey take your virginity?"

"Nah, yo brother Flintstone did."

With that being said she walked out the door. That didn't surprise me as much as I thought it would. I had heard many people say that a woman never forgets the man that took her virginity. That reaffirmed for me that what her and Smokey-Ru had was more than sexual. I locked the door behind her then peaked out the window. Maybe a moment later the phone began to ring.

"Hello?"

"Dwayne, what time are you going to pick up your daughter today?" Neicy echoed through the phone.

"I'll come pick her up in about an hour." I said sharply.

"So how have you been? You've been acting funny ever since you bought that Cadillac."

"Whatever...I have to go. I'll be through to pick her up."

Neicy was referring to my new Fleetwood Cadillac. It made me feel good to be rolling in a righteous ride. I was lucky enough to catch a deal for seventy-five hundred with a new engine. I was planning to slap paint on it just to touch it up a little better but I was already flossing. Once I put rims on the ride and some beat in the sound system it would be over. After getting dressed and eating lunch/breakfast I hopped in the Cadillac and dipped off Locust Circle to Holly Street. That's when I spotted Timmy-Ru and Kool Aid talking on the block. I pulled up in front of them and we embraced.

"What's up with you Grumpy?" Timmy-Ru yawned.

"I'm about to roll to Fruit Town to pick up my daughter."

"Oh yeah." Kool Aid nodded.

"I'll probably let her play at the park then get her some Ice cream. Do some shit like that then my mom will be at the house and she can chill with her grandma."

"Reddy just left from off the circle about an hour ago. She said what's up then kept it pushing. She ain't the same since Smokey got killed." Kool Aid mentioned.

"Yeah I spoke to her earlier. She's a soldier..."

Gunshots suddenly went off on Holly Street. I heard someone yelling 'Holly Hood' while bullets flew down the street. OG Tank from the enemy hood came rolling by in an all blue glasshouse. On his heels was Loko running down the middle of Holly Street screaming at the top of his lungs. He's letting off so many times I almost ran for cover. I slightly ducked for a minute when I turned around Timmy-Ru had his pistol drawn. I couldn't tell what Kool Aid was doing. My gun was tucked under my driver's seat but my door was closed. We just watched the spectacle when we realized that it was friendly fire. OG Tank was ducking down but gave a glance at us and tried to throw up the Crip sign but almost lost control when he seen me.

"Get the fuck out of our hood Blood." Loko shouted.

OG Tank didn't even stop at the Stop sign. He ran right through the sign and picked up speed by the next block. It didn't matter at that point because Loko had run out of bullets. He walked back towards us loading up his pistol talking to himself.

"This crazy ass nigga gon' make it hot around here in the middle of the day." Kool Aid commented.

"Yeah I'm about to pick up my daughter anyway."

"Alright Blood, I'm out this bitch too." Timmy-Ru walked off with Kool Aid.

I hopped into the Cadillac and made my way to Fruit Town territory. It was the middle of the day so I was hoping everything was cool. My car wasn't that familiar since I had only been over Neicy's house once before in it. My mind wandered to the incident on Holly Street and I just shook my head. OG Tank was one of Roccy's big homies. I think he heard through the grapevine that Smokey was killed so he thought he could roll in our neighborhood. He wouldn't have dared done that shit if he knew Smokey was around. He wouldn't have done it if he would have known my brother Flintstone was out of jail. That's when it dawned on me why he was nervous when he seen me. In my later years I looked more and more like my brother. The time I did in jail had bulked me up some so my face resembled Flintstone's. OG Tank was of their generation and knew firsthand how people like Flintstone, Sly, Smokey and other big homies got down. My mind was on that until I reached Piru Street in Fruit Town. When I pulled up to the house Neicy and Jada were already outside in the yard. Neicy had Jada in a cute outfit that made me smile. No matter how I viewed her I had to admit she took care of my daughter. Instead of letting her run and jump in the car on her own she walked her down. We hadn't been spending any time as a couple and I was pretty sure she was fucking someone else. I didn't waste my time accusing her. Besides, ever since Tamara came into the picture I had been alright. Tamara still hadn't seen the Fleetwood yet.

Neicy opened the door and let Jada climb inside then slid in on the passenger side. I thought she was about to ask me for money.

"How are you doing Dwayne?"

"I'm living the good life and trying not to get caught slipping." I nodded.

"Well you and I haven't spent any time together."

"We're spending time together now."

"I mean alone."

"Daddy are we getting Ice cream today?" Jada interrupted.

"Yeah, if you want to." I replied.

"So let's hook up this weekend or something." She smiled.

Neicy was still a pretty bitch and I still wanted to tap that ass. I had to pass this weekend because I was planning to chill with Tamara. Then the next day Reddy was planning to hook me up with her connect. The same Mexicans that supplied Smokey. She was letting me put in on a whole bird (Kilo). Life was good right now for me. Now my baby mama wanted to give me the ass again.

"This weekend ain't that good for me."

"Okay well let me know when it's good for you and we can get a room and everything just for you and me."

"Damn, okay."

She hopped out the car after kissing Jada. I wasn't in a rush to hit that ass when I had Tamara but it was in the back of my mind. I figured Neicy must have gotten into it or broke up with the nigga she was fucking with before. I drove off with her suggestion in my head but honestly I was waiting on the next time I was seeing Tamara. Don't get me wrong, I keeps it gangster and would fuck both of them but Neicy was like a downgrade from Tamara. My daughter took my mind away from all that sex on the brain by talking my head off. She talked about everything under the sun that she knew about. And whatever she didn't know about she asked me about. After we left the park I was burnt out on answering questions. My daughter didn't slow down from talking until I bought her Ice cream. It was still fun in an innocent way. She had those bright eyes and hadn't dealt with the harsh realities of the world. Even though she lived in rough ass Compton, California.

After getting Ice cream I took her to my mother's house so that they could bond. When I walked in the house my mother was in the kitchen. She peeked out of the kitchen when she heard us come inside.

"Grandma!" Jada shouted.

She ran to her grandmother as fast as she could. My mother spoiled her to death because she only had boys. This was the little girl in the family so she could ask for the world and get it from my mom.

"I gotta go potty, Grandma."

"You know where the bathroom is child." My mother laughed.

Jada ran off into the bathroom and shut the door behind her. My mother lowered her glasses and glared at me.

"What!?!" I asked.

"Who was the fool that was running down the street shooting at people earlier today?"

"I don't know." I lied.

"Someone told me you were outside when it happened. Dwayne what did I tell you about gangbanging?"

"Mama I wasn't outside gangbanging. I stopped to talk to a couple of homies then went to pick up Jada. It must have happened after I left."

"Daddy I washed my hands by myself." Jada said proudly.

"That's beautiful." I replied.

"Jada there is some candy on my dresser in the bedroom. Get the piece of candy then turn on the television. You can watch what you want to watch and I'll be in there in a moment." Mama said softly.

After Jada took off running to the bedroom Mama glared at me again. She sat her glasses on the counter and sighed.

"Dwayne I was waiting until yo brother got home before I told you this but I might as well tell you now. I'm about to move out of Compton. It's been too crazy around here for me and apparently my children are contributing to this. At least that's what I've been hearing."

"Aw Mama, you can't believe everything some people say. Some people don't have a life so they put extras on what we're doing." I shrugged.

"Well you two are in and out of jail so you haven't convinced me that they are lying. I'm just tired Dwayne and I don't know what I'll do if I hear about you or Dion getting killed like that boy Ronald or Dion's friend Chris."

She was talking about the homeboy Slow that was Flintstone's road dog. Flintstone went on the deep end after losing Slow. They did all their dirt together. I got locked up on a gun charge before he did but he was locked up only a month later. He and Smokey were the main ones pushing the war against our enemies. Smokey was sneaky about doing dirt when Flintstone was out in the open about his dirt. He just wasn't ticking the same when Slow fell.

"Do you understand where I'm coming from Dwayne?" She interrupted my thoughts.

"Yeah I hear you. When are you thinking about moving and where?"

"I don't know where just yet but I plan to leave in the next six months." Mama sighed.

It bothered me that she was leaving but I also knew that she had to do what was best for her. Mama did her job and provided us with food, shelter and clothing. My dad paid child support but that wasn't anything compared to what my mom sacrificed. I just had to prepare myself for her move.

I said my goodbyes to Jada then stepped outside. I called Tamara but she told me she couldn't talk right then. Sometimes I got the impression that Tamara was hiding something from me. I didn't know if she had a nigga in Carson she was dating behind my back. We wasn't official but it did run through my mind. At this point though I had been knocking the bottom out of her. So if it was someone else they wasn't getting it like I was. The sun was starting to set when I stepped on the block. Some of the homies were hanging out at Slim's house. When I pulled up I was greeted by Kool Aid, Loko, Timmy-Ru, Pookie and Boney-Ru. Boney-Ru had just missed Smokey's funeral by a couple of days. He was in the County Jail on warrants and shit like that.

"I heard the Lime Hood homies were having a party." Timmy-Ru mentioned.

We hadn't even made it to Slim's backyard. We were all hanging out in his front yard just watching our surroundings. I tapped Loko on the shoulder and whispered in his ear.

"My mom just was asking about that shit you did this morning."

"Yeah that crab nigga Tank been rolling on the set lately. I had to let that nigga know what time it was." Loko smiled.

"I say we roll up to that muthafucka and turn it out." Pookie suggested.

"There you go set tripping." Kool Aid chided.

"Yeah I got love for a lot of those niggas." Timmy-Ru remarked.

"Well we'll leave in a few hours so we won't show up too early." I replied.

We rolled five deep up to the Lime Hood party. I wasn't worried about anything because I was with the homies and we were going into a hood that we were cool with. Set tripping occurs when two people from different sets that get along start beefing with each other. When that happens it is usually over a female. We got into the party and it was cracking like we expected. It was females outnumbering men three to one. This was the type of vibe I had been looking for since the big homie was killed. We would have it in our hood when he was alive but now that he was dead we sought it elsewhere. A good forty-five minutes into the party I hear Pookie's voice going up an octave.

"Blood, this bitch was getting at me. So don't come up trying to check me Blood."

"You in my muthafuckin' hood, Blood."

"I don't give fuck where I'm at."

By the time I figured where the voice and the body was of Pookie he had taken a swing on Big Duke from Lime Hood. His punch landed true and it knocked Big Duke into a crowd of females bunched in a circle near a couch. One of them started screaming so naturally that escalated the situation. I ran over to break it up but I didn't want to grab Pookie and he wasn't able to defend himself. I was dancing with this cute caramel girl named Beverly when I was tapped on the shoulder. Even though I was on my way to try to put an end to it I turned around. It was Monk from Lime Hood.

"Those niggas is set tripping Grumpy, let's break this shit up. You grab Pookie and I'll grab Duke."

I respected Monk so I decided to roll with what he was saying. Besides, I didn't really want the party to end. We both grabbed our homies but then the music was cut off. Pookie was struggling for me to let him go.

"Let me go Grumpy, this nigga set tripping over a female." He yelled.

"Calm down and squash this shit so we can keep the party going." I said calmly.

Big Duke was seething inside but Monk must have said the right thing because he had let him go but he didn't attack. Pookie must have noticed that as well because he calmed down moments later. When I felt it was calm enough I finally let him go. I walked over to the window seal just to get a breath of fresh air. I sat there for a minute just to catch my breath. To my surprise a beautiful chocolate bombshell walked over next to me. She smiled at me then leaned on the wall.

"They call you Grumpy?"

"Yeah, you know me?"

"Nah I just heard yo homeboy say your name."

Her body was banging and everything she was wearing was fitting her tight. I did a quick scan of her from head to toe.

"Are you from Lime Hood too?"

"Nah, I'm from Holly Hood. Since you know my name what is yours?"

"My name is Pam. We should hook up. I thought you were cute when you were dancing with that one girl."

14
SET UP

Well let's see who this piece of shit is!
Shorty

We pulled up on the block with me driving. Reddy was on the passenger side while Pookie was in the backseat. Pookie just came along for the ride because I happened to be hanging out with him when Reddy pulled up. She looked at me a little strange when she realized he wasn't getting out of the car. It seemed as though she didn't really care after giving it a second thought.

"I'm going inside while ya'll post up out here. I will tell him that I'm going to introduce him to a new client. I'm vouching for you Grumpy so you need to be ready for this shit. These muthafuckas is connected to some real people that goes all the way to the pen. Be careful and don't be bullshitting with them."

I nodded without saying a word. Pookie was in the back seat seeming a little fired up and it didn't sit right with Reddy.

"Make this nigga stay in the car Blood." She climbed out.

I glared at Pookie and it looked as though he was salivating over what he was looking at. Turning sideways my eyes narrowed in on him.

"What the fuck is up with you, Blood?"

"If this is the spot we could rob these niggas and come the fuck up. That's what I'm talking about." He smiled.

"Blood, Reddy is giving me a connect and you on some stupid shit. You fucking up money for me with these people." I snapped.

"Aw nigga you tripping. If we were to rob these niggas they wouldn't know who hit them. All they would know is they were got. Two niggas with masks can rob their asses blind and that's on the set. They won't even know it was us. And you know they'll be able to get more dope so you will still be handling your business."

"You don't know what the fuck you talking about. Blood, I should have left yo ass in the hood." I sneered.

"Grumpy, come on in he wants to meet you."

"Bring the other guy in as well."

It was a fat Mexican cat with an East Los Angeles Latin accent. He breathed hard whenever he walked. It was subtle things that let me know he had paper. He was well groomed to be a big husky cat. I shook his hand and watched when he shook Pookie's hand. I was a little nervous because I didn't know if Pookie was gon' fuck this up for me. For the most part he mellowed out during our brief conversation. The Mexican cat that Reddy introduced me to went by the nickname of Poppy. He was probably in his late twenties or early thirties with only a thin mustache for facial hairs.

"Are you able to handle a whole bird, homes?"

I nodded without saying anything. He smiled and patted me on the shoulder. He sat on the steps of the porch and pulled out a cigar and lit it up.

"We will meet somewhere once the money is right and I will give you what you need. Did Reddy tell you how much you had to pay for a bird?"

"Yeah."

"I like this guy, homes. He doesn't talk too much and he stays serious. Okay I'll tell you what. If you have the money we can work together."

I handed him a brown paper bag with the money inside. There was nothing but hundred dollar bills inside the bag. He took the bag and handed it to a pretty Mexican girl. She ran up the porch stairs and went into the house. Poppy started walking us back down the walkway back to my car.

"You straight with me homes and I'll be straight with you. I've done a lot of business with Reddy and your homeboy Smokey. I was sad to hear about him being killed. Some people don't have any honor about their shit."

"Yeah that was a big loss." I frowned.

Reddy and I made brief eye contact. It was something that bothered me still to see her vulnerable like that. To me she covered it up pretty good in front of Poppy and Pookie.

"Well here is a pager number that you can contact me. Put in the number eighty-eight after the number so I will know it's you." Poppy explained.

"Why the number eighty-eight?" I asked.

"Because H is the eighth letter in the alphabet and you are from Double H." Poppy smiled.

"Okay."

Even Pookie could appreciate that. Poppy had a way of talking but studying us as well. He was observant about our gestures and our mannerisms. He was a real seasoned gangster and under that jovial demeanor was a serious man.

"Pop your trunk homes."

By that time we were standing next to my car. After popping my trunk someone came from what it seemed out of nowhere and stashed the package in the trunk. All three of us shook Poppy's hand then I drove back to the neighborhood. I dropped Reddy off at her car that was parked on Holly Street and Pookie got out with her. I already knew how to cook up the dope so I wanted to prepare to do it. After that was ready and packaged I was going to hook up with this girl Pam that I met at the Lime Hood party. Only way that wasn't going to happen was if Tamara called. We had been spending time together but I still hadn't met her family. I introduced her to my mom and they got along well. My problem with Tamara was that she would go days without speaking with me then call. At some point I asked her if she was messing with someone else and she told me no.

"I mean, we never made it official so I can't say shit if you fucking with another nigga."

"It ain't like that at all Dwayne. I just got some issues with my family.   I can't get into detail right now but try to understand…please."

After that conversation she made a lot of time for me then went missing for a couple of days. She spent another three days with me then she disappeared again. I was trying to understand but it was something not sitting right with me on the inside. That was what made me go ahead and see what was up with Pam. We hooked up once before and I took her to a cheap motel. We got it on; then I dropped her off over her cousin's house in north Long Beach. She was another female that didn't want me to drop her off at the house. I was supposed to pick her up at her cousin's house when we hooked up the second time. It didn't bother me like it did with Tamara. Tamara was a keeper in every sense of the word. Pam was fine as hell but you could tell that she was a hood bitch that I could pull anywhere in Compton or L.A. When I picked Pam up today she was all smiles. She had a pretty smile and her hair laid flat down her ebony skin. She had curls complimenting the ends of her hair. When I seen her walk up to the car I was like damn. She wore tight Levi jeans and a half shirt. Her knockers were pointing directly at me. I couldn't wait to suck on those big ole melons. She climbed in the car then leaned over and kissed me on the cheek.

"Are you ready?" I asked.

"Yeah but could you stop by my house so that I can pick up something?"

"Okay, show me where I'm going."

I figured she stayed in Compton but I never knew where. We rolled over past my neighborhood and into enemy territory. I thought about the area and I quickly grew uncomfortable. She directed me to what appeared to be a vacant house.

"You live here?" I asked suspiciously.

"Yeah, you want to come inside?"

"It looks vacant that's all."

"We are having some work done to the house so everything is in the back. You want to check it out?"

"Nah, you are coming in and out...right? I can stay in the car."

She let out a sigh then climbed out of the car. She walked to the back of the house while I kept the motor running. It seemed like she was back there longer than I wanted her to be. This made me a little paranoid beside the fact that I was in enemy territory. I glanced through my rearview mirror constantly. My eyes were moving to the side window mirrors and everywhere. It was relatively quiet on the block. It was the middle of the week mid-afternoon. Before I could swat a fly away I seen someone running from the house ducked down low with one hand behind his back. I turned around to see the pistol pointing right at me. I quickly put the car in drive and when I looked up two more shooters were coming at me from the front. Shaking like a muthafucka, I put the car in drive and punched on the gas. The screech of tires and the sound of gunshots firing off rapidly had my heart beating a mile a minute. Then the shatter of glass going everywhere made me yell out in pain. Both my front and back windshields were shattered as I sped past the two in front of me. They didn't stop letting off until I hit the corner. I could have easily run into another car but fortunately for me none were coming in my direction. I was leaning so low down into the car that I couldn't see what was in front of me. Finally I lifted my head up and made a quick right at the end of the block. When I glanced behind me I noticed they were chasing after me at top speed. It didn't matter because my car was still rolling so I hit the gas again. Then I dipped on two side streets until I found myself on Bradfield. Speeding down Bradfield to Alondra then I hit a left on the major boulevard. I quickly made another left on Holly Street then made a right turn on Locust Circle. I pulled into the driveway then glanced around to see if someone followed me to my house.

"Fuck!"

When I stepped out the car I finally felt the pain of my shoulder. Either glass or a bullet grazed my shoulder after all those shots. I glanced down at the rest of my body and I was okay. Someone would have to drive me to the hospital just to get mended up. My obvious choice was Reddy. I went inside and called an auto body shop to fix the windshield. They promptly sent out a tow truck to pick up my ride. When I called Reddy she didn't pick up and neither did her mom. Frustrated I sat on the porch after taking off my shirt and pouring some peroxide on the small wound. Only thing was I didn't have any bandages. Now the pain in my shoulder was throbbing and the gash had a piece of glass in it. I pulled the glass out slowly and a tear fell from my face.

"Blood, that punk bitch tried to set me up."

I sat on my porch seething and in pain when the tow truck came and picked up the Fleetwood. Once the car was gone I walked down to Slim's house and knocked on his door.

"What's happening Blood?"

"This punk bitch tried to set me up. Do you have a bandage so that I can cover this shit up?"

"Aw Blood, you need to go to the hospital. That might be infected and all kinds of shit. I'll roll you to the hospital. Where's your Fleetwood?"

"Those crab niggas shot out both my front and back windshields."

"Alright let me grab my keys and take you to the hospital." Slim went inside to grab his keys.

I told Slim everything that happened while he drove me to Kaiser Hospital in the city of Bellflower. He told me I should get in touch with Reddy to handle Pam but I wasn't tripping like that. I shouldn't have been fucking with her if I didn't know her like that anyway. Now if I ran into the bitch it was on and popping. It made me consider that they may have come up to Killer King Hospital to get me up there. It was a good thing I had a medical card with Kaiser. Once I was checked into the hospital and seen the doctor they decided to keep me there for a couple of nights for observation. I didn't mind because I needed the rest.

Kool Aid parked the stolen car several blocks from where they were headed. He climbed out of the driver's side and glanced over at Pookie-Ru. Pookie was glancing down at his piece he promptly stuffed into his waist band.

"We gon' wait until someone comes outside then we gon' rush in with guns drawn. That's the way it has to go down, Blood." Pookie glanced at Kool Aid.

"And you're sure that its money and dope inside this house? This ain't a dry muthafuckin run?"

"Kool Aid, my nigga, at the very least we gon' come up on some yayo. I know they got cocaine up in there and money gon' be the bonus. Mark my words on this lick; you gon' be glad you did it."

"How did you find out about this shit?"

"I know people Blood. Sometimes you get lucky and you gotta move on some shit when it happens. Make sure you ready we're coming up on the house."

They strolled up to the porch then slipped on their black ski masks. Pookie squatted down and Kool Aid followed his lead. They were on both sides of the door. It would be another twenty minutes before someone came to the door. Their porch light was off so Kool Aid wondered if anyone would ever come to the door. Just when the thoughts ran through his head he heard footsteps coming towards the door. A Latin girl with a slight accent was talking loudly as she approached.

"Let me check the mail and then I'll fix it."

When the door opened slightly an arm poked out reaching for the mailbox. Pookie and Kool Aid quickly went into action. Kool Aid swung the door all the way open while Pookie came into house the pushing the girl to the floor. Following behind him Kool Aid ran towards the fat man sitting on the couch.

"Where's the shit at?"

"What are you talking about?" The fat man yelled.

"The dope muthafucka." Pookie put the pistol to the girls head.

Kool Aid's eyes got big but then he turned to the fat man then the butt of the pistol crashed into his forehead. The fat man started screaming.

"Shut the fuck up and get us the shit." Kool Aid growled.

The fat man went into a compartment built under the floor, underneath the couch and came up with a bag of money and two kilos of cocaine. Kool Aid peaked inside the compartment to see that it was empty. He grabbed a hold of everything then backed up towards the door. Pookie threw the young girl to the ground then ran out the door. He had barely made it off the porch steps when they heard a cannon like shotgun go off after them. Kool Aid only glanced back once since he was a few feet outside of the yard. To his surprise Pookie was squirming on the ground in spasms. After a few fits his body went limp. Kool Aid was able to hide behind a car before a second shot came from the cannon. He shot back at the man with the saw-off pump but missed him. It was a younger and leaner Mexican man that was carrying the weapon. He hid behind one of the pillars supporting the porch. Kool Aid let off several more times then took off running down the street. Nervously running off he kept his mask on just in case someone could point him out. He reached the stolen car and sped off into the night.

Poppy walked outside as quickly as he possibly could. Breathing and panting hard he was able to reach his cousin Shorty. He leaned on the pillar of the porch and took a moment to catch his breath.

"Did you get those fuckers?"

"I got one of them but the other one got away. This piece of shit, whoever he is put a gun to Sandra's head." Shorty walked down the stairs.

"That scared the shit out of me homes." Poppy followed him into the yard.

"How much they get you for, vato?"

"Two birds and about ten grand. That ain't shit though. I keep a stash in the living room just in case something goes down and I have to get rid of my real stash." Poppy shrugged.

"Well let's see who this piece of shit is."

Shorty walked up to the corpse and pulled the mask off his face. He studied the face but couldn't put his finger on where he knew the face from. It was somewhat familiar but he couldn't name the man. Poppy slowly approached the body and took a minute to catch his breath. Leaning on Shorty he finally gained his footing.

"You know who that is Shorty? That's that pinche Mayate that was with Grumpy and Reddy that day. She made the introduction so he could buy from us. He was gon' stay in the car until I told them to all come up, remember essay."

"Oh yeah, they were rolling in a white Fleetwood Cadillac. I stashed the yayo in the trunk of their car."

"Yeah that's it. So if he was one of them then that other guy had to be Grumpy. I've been dealing with Reddy for years and I ain't ever had this problem. Besides, it was another man that was with him." Poppy kicked the corpse.

"Yeah but we have to keep in mind that she might have known it was going down. She has to be looked at too Poppy."

"I don't believe that she would do that. She knows me and my family. It was just Grumpy and this piece of shit...Pookie that was his name."

Seconds later they heard the sound of sirens pulling up. Poppy looked at Shorty and tapped him on the shoulder.

"Give me the pump; you got a felony on your jacket homes. I'll say that I was the one that let off the shots. The ski-mask is proof that he tried to rob me."

Shorty walked back in the house as the police cars drew closer. Neighbors began to walk into their yard to see if they could find out what was going on. A homicide detective followed shortly after the squad cars.

15
MY WORLD

What if I don't want to be anything but a hoodlum...a Hub City Hoodlum!
Grumpy-Ru

When I made it home from the hospital my car was ready for pick up. I asked my mom to pick me up from the hospital and I walked to the auto-body shop that was on Holly and Compton Blvd. Of course she was livid about the whole ordeal. It wasn't anything I could say to combat the fact that I was shot at again. The ride home from the hospital was quiet for the most part. Once home, I called Reddy several times but she hadn't been at her house for awhile. On my way to the shop I ran into Kool Aid rolling up in a Cutlass Supreme. The car was decked out with a burgundy paint and a pearl. He had gold rims with gold spokes on his wheels. I wondered if he had stolen the car. He pulled up on me on the corner of Holly Street and Myrrh Street. He was leaning back in the ride like he owned the world. I quickly hopped inside.

"Are you going to Pookie's funeral?"

"What the fuck are you talking about? Pookie was killed...by who?" I asked dreadfully.

"If I give you the run down on this shit you can't speak on this shit, Blood."

"Don't tell me some shit like you had to kill him because if that's what happened I don't want to hear it, Blood." I shook my head.

"Nah, I don't get down like that. Pookie and I did a lick the other night while you were in the hospital. Oh yeah, I heard about that bitch from the Lime Hood party tried to set you up."

"What happened at the lick?" I asked impatiently.

"Pookie knew about a lick at these Mexicans' house. He told me it was guaranteed either dope or money and I was able to get both. We made it out the house but they started blasting and Pookie got hit in the back. That muthafuckin gun had kick to it, Blood. I tried to shoot back but it was just enough to get me out of there." He shook his head.

I could tell he was reliving the whole experience. But I sat in the passenger damn near enraged when I realized what happened. My head dropped for more than one reason.

"Did Pookie tell you how he knew about that spot?"

"Nah, he just said he knew people."

"Was the house an off-green color with two pillars on the porch?"

"Yeah that sounds about right but it was dark. I know the two pillars were there on the porch."

"The Mexican that you robbed was he a real fat muthafucka?"

"Yeah, how do you know all that shit? That Mexican with the pump was a skinny muthafucka though."

"That was a connect that Reddy hooked me up with and I dragged Pookie along with me. He talked about robbing the spot but I told him that he was fucking with my money. Since I was in the hospital and Reddy is missing in action he asked you to do that shit."

"You mean that nigga crossed some Mexicans you knew?"

"Yeah." I somberly replied.

"Aw this is some fucked up shit. That was your connect too?"

"Yeah."

"I knew I should have questioned that nigga a little more. I mean, rest in peace but damn Pookie." Kool Aid let out a loud sigh.

"This is really bad and if Reddy gets wind of it I don't know what the fuck she might want to do. Just do me a favor and take me to the shop on Holly and Compton Boulevard."

Kool Aid pulled off as we both stumbled into our thoughts. Not only did I lose my road dog, I lost my connect and my means to make some real money. When we rolled past Ronnie-Ru's house he whistled trying to flag us down. Kool Aid put the car in reverse and rolled up next to him. Ronnie-Ru leaned in on the driver's side window.

"Aye Blood, have you talked to Grumpy? Oh shit there you are. Get out for a minute so that I can holler at you on some serious shit."

I climbed out the car expecting to hear more bad news. He was stone faced when I walked over to the sidewalk with him. His head was lowered and he had a frown on his face.

"Yo brother just called me from the pen. He said that word has spread that you tried to rob a connected Mexican with Pookie. Some nigga named Potty or some shit like that got a hit out on you. Word is that he got a cholo named Shorty to handle it for him." He explained.

"I was in the muthafuckin' hospital when that shit went down. Did he say if he tried to call the house first?"

"He said he tried to call but he didn't want to tell your mom. If she knew that someone had paid for you to be killed she would have a heart attack. So he hit me up about it and told me to tell you to not leave the hood unless you have to."

"I ain't about to be on lock down and I'm on the streets. This muthafucka got a gun and so do I."

"I knew you were going to say that. Well if you need some more heat just let me know because I got some guns for you.

Don't underestimate this cholo because Flintstone was telling me that he had a name for smoking fools. He reached out to the pen trying to get info on you so he's thorough." Ronnie-Ru looked me in the eye.

"I hear what you saying, big homie." I sighed.

He went back into the house while I walked over to the shop. Kool Aid waited for me to finish but I told him to pull up in the shop behind me. I paid for the amount to get my car out the shop but I winced when I heard the price. I had a kilo of dope already cooked up and waiting on me but after that I didn't have any other way to make money. If I could get in touch with Reddy she might be able to get me another connect. I climbed into my Fleetwood with my head racing. I parked on Holly Street so that I could get out and talk to Kool Aid.

"What was Ronnie-Ru talking about?"

"That lick ya'll done got a hit put out on me. I got to figure out a way to get this fool before he gets me." I rubbed my head.

"Aw my nigga, I wouldn't have done that shit if I would have known it ran this deep. I thought it was some unknown people. It gets deep when the big homies hear about." Kool Aid shook his head.

"Yeah and that shit came from the pen. My brother Flintstone called Ronnie-Ru to warn me. I played it cool with Ronnie-Ru but I got to figure out how I'm gon' smoke a nigga that knows what hood I'm from but I don't know where he's from or at."

"We can post up over there and maybe catch that fat muthafucka slipping. Hold him for ransom to call off the hit. I'm down since I got you in this shit, Blood."

"We can try to scope this fool and see what happens. I'll holler at you about it later. I'm going to park the car in the backyard so that it won't be out in the open."

My spirit was down and so was my world. I needed to hear some good news for a change. When I made it home the phone rang thirty to forty minutes after I got home. To my surprise it was Tamara on the line.

"What's up baby?" She cooed.

"What's up with you?"

"Did you miss me?"

"Come on Tamara, you are playing too many games. If you want to see me regularly then you need to act like it. This disappearing shit every few days is for the birds." I snapped.

"Well I was hoping to meet up with you today, handsome."

"What you want me to meet you around the corner from your house or at the park or are you at Nicole's house?" I asked scornfully.

"I'll tell you what; come pick me up in front of my house so you can meet my mom and dad."

"Are you serious?"

"I'm serious."

It was about time I heard some good news. Maybe she wasn't ashamed to introduce me to her family after all. My mood changed after she told me that. For a while all my worries wasn't that important even though I had a hit put out on me. I climbed into my car and made my way to Carson. Nervously driving on my every turn I peeped to see if someone was following me. I made a left off of Holly Street to Alondra Boulevard, stayed straight until I got to Atlantic and made a quick right. That was the quickest way for me to get to the 91 Freeway to Carson. I always liked rolling around in Carson because it seemed as though all the lawns were manicured and most houses were decent looking.

When I got over to her house it looked as though it was a mini mansion. Tamara was already outside wearing one of her long summer dresses that went down to her ankles. She always looked conservative even though she had a banging body. She looked more like a wife than girlfriend. That's at least how I perceived her. She wore leather open toe sandals that blended in with a dress that was assorted with various colors but mostly dominated by the color tan. She was always very color coordinated and classy. Since I was meeting her parents I decided to wear a button down shirt but I refused to tuck it in like a square.

"It is so nice to see you again Dwayne."

We hugged then she grabbed my hand and led me into her house. It was just as beautiful on the inside as it was on the outside. In fact, it was much better on the inside. Her parents had a mirror glass wall once you walked inside that led down a hallway decorated with pretty tile flooring. It also had a high ceiling and hanging from it was a chandelier. When you turned to your right there was either the living room or den. The white walls were covered with beautiful paintings of black art and ornaments. It was amazing to me how much they paid attention to detail.

"Have a seat and I'll get my family."

I sat down on a yellow couch that blended in perfectly with the décor of the room. It was a love seat as well that sat in front of a small book shelf. There was no television in the room but it was designed like someone lounged there every day. When Tamara came back into the room she was followed by three people. The man was middle-aged with a salt and pepper afro that was neatly cropped. His mustache was well groomed even with no beard. He wore one of those colorful Bill Cosby sweaters and a pair of blue slacks. The woman standing next to him was a slightly older version of Tamara. She was a gorgeous older woman. Then there was a little girl that had to be around ten or eleven years old. She was all smiles when she walked up. I quickly stood up to greet them. Tamara came over to stand next to me and make the introduction.

"Mom, Dad, this is Dwayne Pittman."

"It is nice to meet you Mr. and Mrs. Walker." I shook their hand.

"It is nice to meet you as well Dwayne. Welcome to our home." Mrs. Walker replied.

Her father didn't really say anything to me but I would catch him staring from time to time. He was definitely sizing me up. All of us stood there for a moment uncomfortably.

"Go ahead and have a seat Dwayne and I'll fix you something to drink." Mrs. Walker offered.

"Thank you."

I sat down with Tamara sitting next to me. Her mother brought in a glass of lemon tea that was the best I had tasted of date. Her father was glancing over at me even though his chair wasn't directly in front of me. In fact it was over to the side of the couch I was sitting on. It dawned on me at that moment that I really liked Tamara. Normally I wouldn't allow myself to feel so uncomfortable.

"So Dwayne, Tamara tells us that you are about to attend college." Her mother asked.

Tamara and I once had a conversation about me going to school to be an auto mechanic. I always had an interest in the building and fixing of cars so I told her that if I ever went back to school it would be for that. I thought it was best to go along with what she said.

"Yeah I planned on getting into being an auto-mechanic."

"Well auto mechanics can make pretty good money. Do you know what school you want to attend? Tamara may attend Cal State Long Beach or Dominguez Hills but we prefer that she gets into USC." Her mother explained.

"Oh well, I was thinking about going to Compton Community College. Once school was finished I could fix the people in my neighborhood's cars." I replied.

"Where do you live?" Her father finally asked.

"I stay on the East Side of Compton."

"Compton?"

"Yeah I've grown up there my whole life."

"Is that so?"

Mr. Walker leaned back in his chair after glaring at Tamara. I was even more uncomfortable than before. After making small talk for another twenty minutes Tamara found an exit strategy by saying that we were going to the movies. She ran upstairs to grab a sweater and freshen up for whatever we might get into. Her parents had left the living room and gathered somewhere near the kitchen. They were whispering but I could hear what they were saying.

"He's nothing but a hoodlum."

"You don't know that Errol."

"Our daughter is dating a hoodlum and she was probably introduced by that fast tale girl Nicole. I'm thinking about not letting her go with him tonight." Mr. Walker replied vehemently.

"If you do that then she's going to sneak around to see him. Let's just believe that we raised our daughter to make the right choices. He's probably just a phase she's going through."

When I heard Mrs. Walker say those words I was wounded. She sat up in the living room and smiled in my face. Where I come from when someone didn't like you they showed it. Most people I grew up with didn't smile in your face if they had a problem with you. This was a culture shock for me. I slumped on the couch and my face scrunched up. Tamara walked downstairs and noticed my facial expression. She usually kept a smile on her face and usually I was happy to see it.

"What's wrong with you Dwayne?"

"Never mind; are you ready to go?"

She shrugged and nodded so I quickly walked towards the front door. I heard her say her goodbyes to her parents then she came outside. I was already sitting in the car once she came outside. My mind wouldn't let rest what I heard from her parents. Glaring at Tamara I wondered if she felt the same way. Was I just some passing phase?

"Do you think I'm supposed to be with you? I mean do you think I deserve you?" I asked.

"I'm with you ain't I?"

"Yeah but it could be some passing phase or something. You could want someone else but just dealing with me to pass the time." I sharply replied.

"I mean...you are rough around the edges but what would I expect. I enjoy spending time with you and that is all that counts."

"Nah that ain't all that counts. If you trying to be with me then you need to be with me however I am. I'm a gangster and a hoodlum; are you cool with that?"

"You might not always want to be a hoodlum. You could really do something with your life that can be good." She sighed.

"What if I don't want to be anything but a hoodlum...a Hub City Hoodlum?"

"Well that's on you but one of these days you will have to grow up and be a real man. All of that street stuff will have to be something of the past."

"Grow up? What do you know about being a real man and having to grow up? I'm all grown up and I still keep it gangster. Oh so you saying since I rep my hood that I'm not grown up?"

"No Dwayne, that's what you are saying!"

"Nah I'm Grumpy-Ru from East Side Bompton Holly Hood Piru Gang." I snapped.

"Oh so now you're gangbanging on me? If you ain't feeling good or you are pissed off about something then you can turnaround and take me home." She calmly replied.

I sped up to the light to make a left. The first chance I was able to make a U-Turn I made it and headed back to her house. She was actually surprised that I took her home. In my heart I was already missing her but I wasn't about to let any broad turn me into bitch. I don't know if she was being condescending before she got out the car because she said something calmly.

"Whenever you've gotten over what you are upset about you can give me a call."

That just inflamed me more at the time. I watched her walk up the driveway and into the house. Even though it was hurting my heart I knew I had to let her go. She would have eventually tried to make me something that I wasn't. The last thing I needed was for some female to get me off my game when I was still dealing with some unfinished business. My world was getting more fucked up every day. Losing Tamara was painful but I had to bottle that shit in.

When I made it back to the hood it felt like I was in physical pain. I needed something to numb my senses for a minute. There weren't too many people hanging out at Turtle's house so I rolled down Holly Street to Ronnie-Ru's house. When I pulled up a few of the homies were hanging out drinking and smoking weed. Kool Aid and Timmy-Ru were chopping it up over near the brick wall so I eased over towards them.

"You want to hit this weed Grumpy?" Kool Aid asked.

"What is this shit?"

"This is that bomb ass Chronic."

When he passed me the weed I took a deep hit then held it in for a few seconds. I let it out with that California breeze and smiled.

"Let me take a hit of that Thunderbird, Timmy-Ru?"

He passed me the bottle and I took a couple of swigs to the head. I leaned on the wall trying to let the intoxicants take hold so I could escape my world for a moment. I looked up to see Ronnie-Ru in the middle of a dice game with Nuck, Slim, Turtle and a couple of niggas from Leuders Park. Nuck once again was winning and talking shit in the process. At least while I had a buzz

Nuck's crazy ass would make me laugh while he broke up the dice game.

"Ten-Foe back doe little Joe! I'm about to break all you niggas and send you home broke explaining shit to ya'll bitches." Nuck laughed.

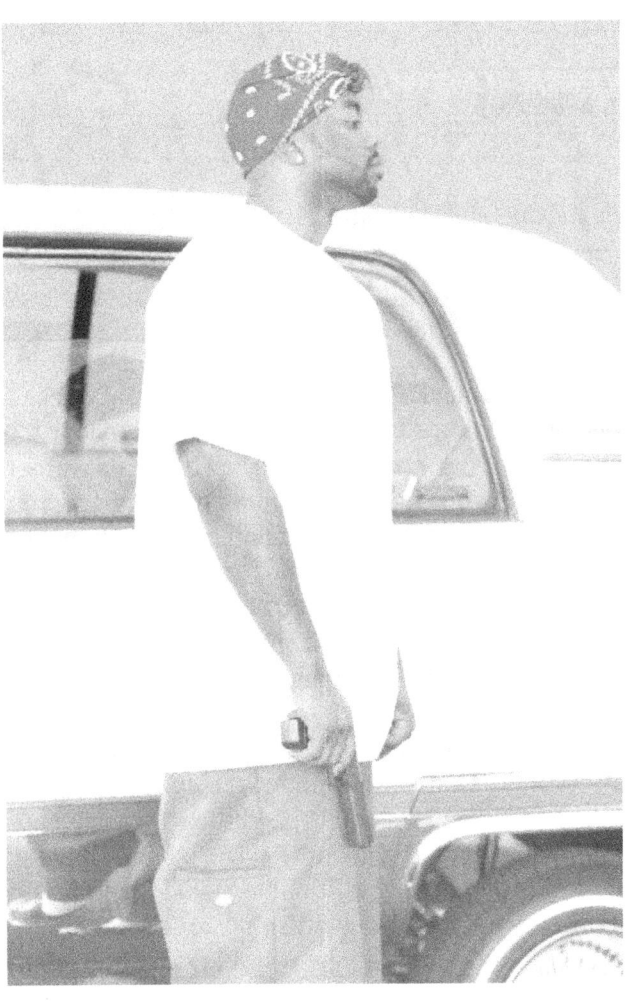

16
BLEEDING BURGUNDY

Get in the fucking car Dwayne!
Baby Blue

I moped around the house for at least a week. Tamara called a couple of times but I didn't answer the phone. Not only was I dwelling on my break-up with her but I also was trying to figure out how I would get at Poppy and Shorty. I couldn't be honest and tell them that it was another one of my homeboys because they would be coming after Kool Aid. Kool Aid and I scoped his house a few times but it wasn't safe. He had people posted up on the porch and the side of the house. It boiled down to me either getting at them or going through Reddy. She was still missing in action.

Pookie's funeral was scheduled a day after I decided to leave my house. That's when it hit me that Reddy could have gotten killed. If Smokey could get killed then anyone can get killed. I hadn't thought about Reddy being killed until that moment. It was time to get at Ronnie-Ru and load up. I could get a few homies to rally up but it wasn't like it used to be. Niggas had grown up and gangbanging was played out. Many of the homies that were still alive was willing to put in work but not over any ole bullshit. Smokey could rally the troops when he was alive but now that he was dead it wasn't the same. Some of the homies had families now and everything. If I had to handle some shit I might bring one other person but that was about it. As long as there was a source to get weapons and ammunition I had a fighting chance. I pulled the Fleetwood from out of the backyard and washed it up first. Then I rolled down Holly Street to Ronnie-Ru's house. He was in his backyard lifting weights with Jake-Ru when I walked back there.

"What's happening Grumpy?"

"I need to holler at you for a minute."

"Oh yeah…you can talk straight. It's just me, you and Jake."

"I'm gon' have to take you up on that offer. You know the heat you told me you had." I nodded.

"Alright let Jake finish this set then we can talk."

After Jake finished his set on the free weights he sat it on the bench press then stood up. Jake always held size in his arms. He had about eighteen to nineteen inch arms with skinny ass legs. That's how it was for cats that went to the pen.

"Are you going to the little homie Pookie's funeral, Blood?" Jake-Ru asked me.

"Yeah, I plan on going."

"You sure you want to do that?" Ronnie-Ru asked.

"I ain't letting anyone stop me from going to my road dog's funeral."

"You on some stupid shit Blood. These ain't crab niggas trying to get at you over some muthafuckin' gangbanging shit. These are connected muthafuckas that kill niggas because they think you did something wrong. They won't announce their set and all that shit. They gon' sneak up on you and start dumping. I thought you was laying low, that's why I ain't seen you in awhile." Ronnie-Ru put his finger in my chest.

"Blood I'm a grown muthafuckin' man. If I'm supposed to die let me at least go out the way I want to." I shrugged.

"Flintstone is getting at me too about this shit. That nigga is touching down later this year and he wants to see you alive, Blood."

"And I want to be alive. Hiding and all that shit ain't what I'm good at big homie. I got to come at these fools the way I know how."

"Alright then you young dumb muthafucka. Follow me upstairs."

Ronnie-Ru was growling like a grumpy old man. That was the one time I thought they should call him Grumpy. He grabbed his tank top from off the milk crate and walked towards his house. I followed him upstairs into his bedroom. He let Jake-Ru come in with us then he closed the bedroom door behind him. He went under his king sized bed then came out with an old school suitcase. When he opened it the suitcase was filled with different types of weaponry. First thing I needed was semi-automatic weapons. I picked out two handguns then grabbed a couple of boxes of bullets.

"What do I owe you?"

"If you get through this shit then you can take care of me."

"Good looking big homie."

My next step was to stop by Sharon's house to see if Reddy was there or had been there. When I knocked on the door no one answered after the third knock. As I walked down the stairs the door swung open.

"What's up Dwayne?"

It was Sharon. I could tell that she was drunk because she spoke with a slur. It also appeared as though the door was keeping her balanced. I reluctantly walked up the stairs and onto the porch.

"I'm looking for Sheila. I haven't seen her in awhile and I wanted to know if she was okay."

"She's been with her cousins up in Moreno Valley for the last month or so. After Ronald died she said she needed to get out of Compton for awhile. She's got people on her daddy's side of the family out there." She stammered.

"Could you tell her I need to get at her?"

"Yeah, she called today but we didn't talk too long. She needs to hurry up and come down here so she could take care of her mama."

"Okay well when the next time she calls let her know that Dwayne needs to holler at her as soon as possible." I walked down the stairs.

"If you want I can give you the number to where she's at?"

"Yeah that'll be cool."

She scrambled into the house half staggering before she found her way to a pen and pad. I began looking around to see if anyone was scoping me out. I hadn't been out in the open like this in awhile. She came rushing back to the door with a smile on her face.

"You know you look just like yo daddy." She remarked.

"You knew my daddy?" I asked surprisingly.

"Yeah, when he and yo mama first moved in that house on Locust Circle. When I was still with Sheila's dad Roy we used to come to your house and play spades and dominoes. Everything changed when yo dad got that other girl pregnant." Sharon frowned.

She began to tear off a piece of paper with a phone number on it. She was happy to slide me the number like she had done a good deed.

"Thank you Sharon."

"No problem. Do you have a twenty you can loan me Dwayne?"

I went into my pocket and handed her forty dollars. I needed the information she gave me. I probably gave her the extra twenty because I found out that Reddy was still alive. Walking to my car I thought about Sharon and what she said about my father. I hadn't talked to him in years. When he and my mom broke up we kind of broke up with him as well. I don't think that was good for any of us. It bothered me a little bit as I rolled to the house.

Once the car was secure in the backyard I rushed inside the house to make the phone call. No one picked up the phone until the third ring.

"Hello?" A woman's voice answered.

"Can I speak to Sheila?"

"Hold on."

I heard her sit the phone down. There was a lot of activity in the background but I tried to ignore it. The woman's voice whispered to someone.

"Go tell Sheila that someone is on the phone for her. She ain't been out here that long to have niggas calling here for her."

Footsteps in the background let me know someone went to get Reddy. I could hear her talking once she walked into the room.

"What nigga you got calling my house?"

"I don't know who the hell this is Auntie…Hello?"

"Ay Reddy, this is yo nigga Grumpy."

"What's happening Blood? My mama must have given you this number." She replied.

"Yeah I just got it from her ten minutes ago."

"I'm glad ain't no one trying to kill me. Her ass would have gave me up right away. Did you slide her some money?"

"Yeah!"

"She sold me out for twenty bucks. What's up with you my nigga?"

"I got some real bad news."

"What the fuck, one of the homies got killed? Who got killed now?"

"The homie Pookie got killed about a week ago."

"Are you serious? Somebody got to that turned up nigga? That's fucked up to hear. When is his funeral?"

"Tomorrow at noon."

"I won't make it in time. My relatives don't wake up until eleven or twelve and I didn't bring the Monte Carlo out here. Save an obituary for the rest of my collection."

"There is more to it than that."

"What's up?"

"He tried to rob some people we know and that's how he was killed."

"Some people we know? I know we on the phone but you got to explain that shit better than that, Blood."

"Fat Mexican Blood close to Compton." I sighed.

"You got to be bullshitting me? He didn't do that shit by himself, Grumpy. You must be on some stupid shit nigga."

"Think about it Reddy. Would I be that stupid?"

She must have thought about it for a moment because the phone was silent. There was still noise in the background wherever she was. My impatience was growing because I was ready to get past all that shit and get to the point.

"He got a nigga that didn't know who they were, to do it with him?"

"Bingo!"

"They know that Pookie was one of them?"

"Yep!"

"So they think you were the one that was with him."

"Now you know what the fuck I'm dealing with."

"That's an easy handle. I'll let him know that you wasn't the one and he should get at someone else. I'm coming back down to the Hub City tomorrow. My relatives are too crazy for me and my auntie be riding on me like my mama should." She chuckled.

"So it's an easy fix?"

"Yeah don't worry. I'll get at him face to face and give him the run down. He probably won't let you come back but you will be cool. I got you on this." Reddy replied with confidence.

"Alright then, I'll see you tomorrow."

"Can you manage to stay alive until tomorrow my nigga?"

"I'll be waiting for you in the hood after his funeral."

When I hung up the phone with Reddy it felt as though a load was lifted off my back. I was so relieved I wanted to lie down and go to sleep for hours because sleep had been difficult for the last week behind everything I was dealing with. I kicked off my shoes then the phone rang again. Reddy probably wanted me to give me the run down on something.

"Hello?"

"Hey Dwayne."

"Who is this?"

"You've already forgotten my voice?"

"Tamara?"

"Yeah I've been calling you but you haven't been picking up. I left several messages for you as well. If we are through you could at least give me closure and let me know."

"I got to be straight with you, Tamara."

"That's all I've been asking."

"I overheard yo moms and pops calling me a hoodlum and I was some passing phase that you were going through." I explained candidly.

"Are you serious?"

"As a heart attack."

"That's why you had an attitude when I came down the stairs that day. Look Dwayne, I like you and I think you like me too. I don't know anything about a passing phase but I like spending time with you."

"What about me being a hoodlum? I am what I am!"

"As long as you know how to treat me then we don't have a problem. I missed you. I wish you would have told me that day what you overheard."

"I missed you too." I admitted.

We made small talk for another thirty minutes then I went to sleep. I didn't wake up until about three in the morning then I went back to sleep. The next morning my eyes finally opened at thirteen minutes past nine. I really needed the sleep. I felt really good when I hopped out of my bed. When I looked in the mirror my face looked refreshed and my eyes were clear. Taking a deep breath I jumped into the shower and was there almost an hour. After fixing breakfast I decided to drive to the funeral that was in Los Angeles. Pookie's mother told me she wanted the funeral outside of Compton. She didn't want all the homies to come to the funeral. She expected me to be there but other East Side homies might come up there wearing their colors.

I drove up to the funeral around eleven in the morning. It was one of those gloomy California days. Clouds were out but it didn't mean it would rain. I cruised down Compton Blvd. to the funeral home going west to Los Angeles. Once I reached Avalon I made a right turn and kept it pushing. I was in a black suit with a burgundy shirt and tie. I picked it out just for Pookie's funeral. The moment I arrived I realized that it didn't stop most of the homies from the East Side who had love for him from coming. It was packed with a bunch of niggas that didn't want to buy a suit for a funeral or didn't have the money to. It was a few Damus from LA that must have known him when he was locked up. I sat in the back once I realized that I couldn't find a place up close. Pookie had a young brother we called Lil Pookie who was much more reserved than his older brother. He had a look on his face of pure fury. Pookie's baby-mama was sitting in the front row with the family. They had a son together but it didn't look like she was letting him come to the funeral. His mother was sitting up front with a few relatives that were familiar but I didn't know them very well. A man on the front row on the other side of the pew was sitting there and he looked just like Pookie. He seemed as though he was an older version of him. It must have been his father but we didn't have too many of those in the neighborhood so I wasn't for sure. The funeral was mostly reserved and mournful until a few Pirus came barging in stumbling over each other. We were in the heart of Crip territory from the writing on the wall. Too many homies from the East Side were flamed up with flags on their head Aunt Jemima style. A pack of three stumbled into the main hall tripping over each other in the back of the church.

"They got guns Blood."

I heard a woman scream then a few of the people in the pews began to stand up. I made my way to the back of the church to peak outside. If I could get a chance to pull my gun from out of the trunk then I would be straight. I would have had it under the seat but I was worried about getting pulled over in the city. When I glanced outside there was no one around so I went back inside. There was no more commotion after the incident. I gave Pookie a burgundy handkerchief when I passed by his casket. He looked much darker than usual and his lips looked chapped. Tears welled up in my eyes but I had to keep it pushing.

"Rest in Peace my nigga."

I didn't leave right after the funeral. I watched them put my former road dog in the hearse. His family were the pallbearers. Lil Pookie came up to me as I leaned on the church wall outside.

"Was it some crab niggas that got my brother, Blood?"

"Nah it was behind some robbery shit."

"Were you with him?"

"Nah I didn't know he did it until he was already dead."

I embraced him then walked back to my Fleetwood. Once in my car I turned up the music I was playing in the car. Pookie was a big fan of the Stylistics so that was what I played. He was also feeling a young rapper by the name of 2Pac. All I remembered him playing was the new album 'Me against the World' but I hadn't bought a copy for myself yet. The Stylistics mellowed me out so much that I vowed to buy some weed once I made it back to the neighborhood. The car in front of me was driving too slowly; so I dipped over in another lane. Glancing at my rearview I noticed a car changing lanes with me. It didn't bother me at first until I dipped over in the gutter lane again and they followed. I thought it was a little strange then it dawned on me that some Crips could have followed me from the church. This time I dipped onto another street and they followed behind me. That sealed it for me but I was cursing under my breath because my gun was in the trunk of my car. From the side view window it looked as though they were loading up. There was nothing I could do unless I got to my car trunk. I hit a few corners and they were right behind me. They didn't give a damn if I knew they were on my tale. My nerves started bothering me because there was nothing I could do. They began to speed up to catch up with me so I pushed on the gas. The Cadillac was a blessing because it started taking off while I'm stuck in the middle of the West Side of Compton. There was no time to find out if I was in friend or enemy territory. Some West Side Pirus will set trip if they are young muthafuckas. The Crip sets would try to kill me as much as this fool chasing me. With a quick turn I dipped into an alleyway. I put the car in park and jumped out and popped the trunk. Digging for the gun I had to be fast because whoever this was wasn't far behind. I grabbed the pistol right before I heard the skidding of tires. The next thing I knew I was dodging bullets from a sub-machine Uzi. I ducked under the car on the other side but it felt like I was hit. Then I felt the warm liquid leaking down the same shoulder I was shot in before.

"Blood!"

Not only was I hit but my car took another shooting. The back window was busted out yet again. Glass was littered all over my suit jacket lying in the back seat. I figured he was going to come around for a second pass so I had to leave the car parked for awhile and come back to get it. I thought it was best to run to the other end of the alley to avoid him. He must have sped around the corner and expected me to run that way. When I reached the end of the alley the same car screeched it's tires about three yards away from me. I pulled out my gun and started dumping into the car. The pain in my shoulder was ignored as I let off as many shots that I could while running in another direction. He took cover and when he lifted up he let the bullets from his Uzi fly. I hid behind a building and took off running back down Compton Blvd but I heard him screeching off towards me.

"I got to get away from this muthafucka." I said while panting.

He rolled up on me while I ran down the major Blvd. even though he was going in the wrong direction. He was trying to catch up with me. Suddenly I stopped and turned toward the car and let off the rest of the shots in my clip. His car got most of the damage and it halted his pursuit. Once I realized I was out of bullets I took off running at top speed. When I looked behind me he had began running after me. He left his car abandoned in the middle of a major boulevard.

"Yeah he wants me bad."

I could tell that he was Mexican from that second attempt on the major street. Reddy hadn't straightened out the situation yet. I looked back and he was running after me while loading up another clip. My small reprieve was because he had finished a clip. He had let off a lot more bullets than me but he had already reloaded. His plans was to mow me down in the middle of the street. He let off a round but I had ducked behind a car after seeing him reload. I knew he was creeping to finish me off but I didn't know what to do. In a matter of seconds I decided to take off in the middle of the street and dodge cars. When I took off he pointed the gun at me but was hesitant. There were cars driving by on both sides. A chill ran down my spine as I felt the end coming. Once I was across the street I was running in the same direction of traffic on that side of the street. I tossed the gun in a large dumpster in a side alley and kept running. When I glance at the alley I quickly realized it was a dead end. Pushing East my body was fatigued and losing its strength.

Suddenly a car pulled up next to me. It was rolling at a slow enough speed to be riding next to me. My upper body was soaking wet with sweat while blood soaked my burgundy shirt. Anticipating a gun to be pulled to finish me off was excruciatingly nerve racking.

"Get in the fucking car Dwayne."

I reluctantly leaned down to see who it was that new my government name. To my surprise it was someone I wasn't expecting to see in a million years.

"Lorenzo?"

"Yeah you need to get into this car before that Mexican fool light yo ass up."

I opened the car door while it was still rolling and hopped inside. Turning around the Mexican had stopped running once he seen me jump inside of a car. He was too far away from his car to go back and chase me. I took a deep breath as Lorenzo a.k.a. Baby Blue made a quick right and sped off down the street.

17
NO COMPROMISE

I'm killing that pinche Puto if it's the last thing I do!
Shorty

Baby Blue drove at top speed down Wilmington Blvd. until he reached Alondra. He made a left on Alondra Blvd. heading east until he reached Holly Street. He glanced over at me a few times as I caught my breath.

"Why in the fuck you got Shorty on yo ass?"

"You knew that Mexican that was trying to kill me?" I asked in disbelief.

"I know of him. He does killings for top muthafuckas in the dope game. I've seen him here and there but you must have fucked up big to have him after you." Baby Blue shook his head.

"Not really; he thinks I did some shit I didn't do but my nigga that did the shit I can't give up. So I'm stuck dealing with this shit." I sighed deeply.

"Yeah because it seemed like you were smarter than that. A muthafucka that crossed Shorty was either stupid or new to the game and you ain't either. Well here is Holly Street so you should be good in your own hood."

He pulled over on the side of Alondra Blvd. that was closer to his hood. That's when the pain in my shoulder kicked in because I made a sudden move. I moaned in pain while opening the passenger side of the door.

"Good looking Lorenzo. I know you didn't have to get in the middle of this shit."

"No problem. You better be glad Shorty only got yo shoulder. He's good at what he does so you need to load up."

"Yeah I heard. Ay Lorenzo what happened to you and me? We used to be cool back in the day when we played Pop Warner and everything."

"I think because you were Blood and I was Crip we let that shit come between us. We older niggas now so we can handle shit differently now."

"To be honest with you, I never gave a fuck about you being a Crip. I just had to represent where I was from, that's all." I replied.

"I know homeboy; I was on some dumb shit. Me and you straight." He offered his hand.

We shook hands then I stepped out of his car. I ran across Alondra Blvd. to Holly Street. Every five or six steps I would look behind me to see if anyone was following. I doubted if Shorty would come to my hood and try to start something because he wouldn't know what to expect. I was safer in my hood than anywhere else. Especially since it was broad daylight things were calmer. When I got down to Turtle's house he was already posted up in the backyard. They didn't go to Pookie's gravesite either. When I unlatched the backyard gate the first person I saw was Reddy. She was sitting down playing dominoes with Turtle, Nuck and Slim. Slim saw me first.

"What the fuck happened to you young Blood?"

Everyone turned to look at me while I held onto my shoulder. Reddy jumped up knocking over the chair she was sitting in.

"They tried to get at you?" She asked already knowing the answer.

I nodded but needed to sit down. I rushed over to the backyard bench near the fence and collapsed.

"Come on Grumpy, I'm taking yo ass to the hospital."

"Nah Reddy, I got to get my car over on the West Side. Then I can go to the hospital." I replied stubbornly.

"Okay, we'll get your ride then you going to the hospital. Ay Nuck, roll with us so you can drive Grumpy's Cadillac back to the hood." Reddy said.

Nuck quickly stood up and followed us to Reddy's car. It sort of surprised me that Nuck followed her instructions so easily. He was one of the founders of my hood. He must have understood the urgency of everything. That was one of the few times he didn't have that devious smirk on his face. They threw me in the back seat of Reddy's Monte Carlo and we rolled out. When they needed directions to where the car might be I would peek my head up to tell them where to go. Fortunately for me my car was still where I left it.

"Damn Grumpy, yo windshield got shot out again?" Nuck said.

"When did it get shot out the first time?" Reddy asked.

"I'll tell you about that shit on the way to the hospital."

I handed Nuck the keys and told him to take it back to the shop on Holly Street and Compton Blvd. Reddy glanced around then punched out to the hospital.

"I need you to take me to Kaiser Hospital in Bellflower. That muthafucka Shorty might be looking for me at Killer King and I got a Kaiser card anyway."

"So it was Shorty that was going after you? Where did he spot you at?"

"I think he waited until I left the funeral then went after me."

"How do you know it was Shorty? Did you see his face?"

"I seen his face but I didn't know who he was. I found out who he was from the most unlikely of people. You know that Crip nigga Baby Blue? He told me."

"Where the fuck you seen him at? He was trying to blast on you too."

"Nah Reddy he was the one that saved my life. He pulled up next to me while I was running from Shorty's sub-machine Uzi. He and I used to play Pop Warner football back in the day. When I got inside the car he told me that it was Shorty."

"Bwahahahaha!" Reddy laughed loudly.

"What's so fucking funny?"

"A nigga that you would think would be out to kill you saves yo life. You got some kind of guardian angel looking after yo crazy ass Blood." Reddy smiled.

That made me look her in the face. She looked younger and well rested. The pretty Reddy from high school was in the car with me. Her trip to Moreno Valley was well needed.

"I guess I do but it ain't over with yet."

"Well I will talk to Poppy today so don't trip. Once I leave the hospital I will go by the house and holler at him. Shorty's crazy ass will probably be there. He was the one that put the dope in yo trunk that day we went over Poppy's house."

"I didn't get to see him but he must have remembered my car. It felt like Blood wasn't gon' stop. I thought I was dodging Robocop or some crazy shit like that." I sighed.

"Well it should be okay after this. Let Pookie Holly in Peace but he was a knucklehead for real. It was Kool Aid that did that shit with him huh?"

"What makes you think that?"

"Come on now, he all of a sudden is pushing a fresh ass ride with rims and everything. I've already heard he got dope on the street. Does he know the shit that you are in behind that lick he did?"

"Yeah he peeped out Poppy's house with me for a few days but they had that muthafucka secured like an army fortress."

We rolled into the hospital parking lot by then. She parked the car and sat inside for a minute.

"What's this shit about you getting your windshield shot before?"

"This crab bitch named Pam tried to set me up. I met her at a Lime Hood party and she had me take her to her hood and while I waited in the car niggas came out shooting. She tried to get me to come inside with her but I didn't fall for that shit. I was in the hospital from that shit when Pookie did that dumb ass lick."

"Damn you do got somebody watching out for you. Were you able to get at that bitch Pam for trying to set you up?"

"Nah Reddy, I got bigger fish to fry."

With that said I climbed out of the back seat wincing in pain. This time the bullet must have hit a bone but I had grown accustomed to the pain. She followed me into the emergency entrance then waited until the nurse came to get me. I was admitted a lot faster because I had a medical card. She gave me a hug then watched them take me away on the gurney.

Once the double doors were closed and Grumpy was out of sight, Reddy rushed back to her car. She needed to get at Poppy as soon as possible. She jumped on the 91 Freeway and made her way to Los Angeles and got off on Avalon. She rolled through the city of Carson to get to LA.

"I wonder if Grumpy still fucking with that Tamara girl from Carson." She thought out loud.

When she pulled up in front of Poppy's house she understood quickly what Grumpy meant. There were Mexican gangsters posted up in the front yard and on the side of the house. If you were trying to get in this house you were going up against a small hit squad. Reddy had just bought a three-eighty that didn't have any murders on it. She wouldn't last long against what they were carrying but she still tucked it in her pocket. She didn't know what to expect from Poppy after everything hit the fan. When she walked in the yard two of the Cholos walked up to her with tight jaws and wrinkled foreheads. One of them lifted their T-shirt to let her know that he was ready to pull out on her. She mean-mugged him before saying anything.

"Tell Poppy that his homegirl Reddy came to see him." She announced.

One of the Cholos standing on the porch ran inside the house. He was back outside in less than two minutes. He nodded for her to come upstairs.

"You want me to search her first, homes?"

"You ain't searching that female, essay."

"I wouldn't let you search me anyway, Blood."

Reddy walked up the walkway with her eyes focused on the front door. She could see everyone through her peripheral. If anyone was to make a sudden move she would pull out the gun and have a shootout. She made it to the front door without incident. When she made it to the living room Poppy was sitting on the couch eating a massive T-bone steak. He smiled at her with food in his mouth.

"Have a seat homegirl. Are you ready to do business again?"

"Nah, I'm here to talk to you about my homeboy Grumpy."

"That pinche Mayate is dead, Reddy. Your other friend put a gun to my daughter's head and he robbed me of my money and goods. There has to be consequences for that shit...he's fucking dead." Poppy angrily replied.

"Even if he wasn't the one to do that shit? Grumpy was in the hospital when that shit went down. If you want hospital records I will get them for you. But you need to call off ya dog because he tried to get at him earlier today."

"I ain't seen Shorty all day. I know if I don't see him he's taking care of business. So you say your man was in the hospital? Does he know who was with him when the shit went down?"

"He told me he didn't know the shit went down until he got out the hospital."

"Why didn't he get at me? If he would have told me instead of staying away I wouldn't think he got something to hide."

"He was trying to get at you through me Poppy. I needed time away from Compton after Smokey died so I got away from the hood for awhile. He didn't know how to contact me so he stayed away."

"Shorty did tell me that he was driving that same Fleetwood but he could be smart and just wait awhile to spend my money. At the very least he knows who the other Puto that robbed me was."

"I think he got somebody from another hood to do that dumb shit. Think about it, Grumpy just came up on buying a key from you. Why would he fuck up his money and rob you on a one time deal and he didn't know if he was gon' get anything? My young homeboy ain't that stupid. I need you to give him a pass, Poppy...for me."

"Okay Reddy, but I can't do business with him anymore. Just in case he was with that piece of shit and he probably knows who was with him."

"I appreciate you Poppy."

"Yeah, yeah, yeah...next time make sure you don't bring any dumb people to my door. You owe me one Reddy; now get the fuck on so I can finish my steak."

"Alright I'm gone; but make sure Shorty knows that he needs to back off of Grumpy." She stood up.

"I'll tell him the moment he gets in."

Reddy walked out the door with no problems. Poppy laid back and continued to enjoy his steak. One of his homeboys came in to check on him.

"Who is the Mayate bitch, homes?"

"That Mayate bitch got more heart than you would ever know. She's a bitch that keeps her word and will die by it so show her some fucking respect."

"I was just asking essay damn."

"Shut my fucking door, homes."

Poppy began choking on his food after yelling at his homeboy. He attempted to stand up but his weight was making it difficult. He coughed several more times then collapsed on the floor. The homeboys outside ran inside once they heard the thud of his body hitting the ground. Several of his homies came to his aid while he was squirming on the floor.

"Let's try to pick him up."

"Does anyone know CPR essay?"

"I ain't about to give him CPR even if I knew it. Try to roll him over and see if we can get him to spit it out while he's on his stomach."

They rolled him over and he began to squirm more than before. His body went into convulsions while one of them tried to pat his back. He continued to shake until finally his body went into one more spasm. After a few seconds of that his body went into shock and he went stiff. His homeboys stared at him for a moment not really believing what they were seeing. Two of his homeboys together was able to roll him over on his back. After pushing his stomach in and out a few times they realized he wasn't breathing. The body laid on the carpet limp and no air was coming from his mouth or nose. He was dead.

"Fuck homes! He's dead then a doorknob."

The room was extremely quiet. Even though there were men posted outside in the yard the door was wide open. No one noticed a dark figure walking into the house. The person was so quiet that when they looked up everyone was startled.

"What the fuck Shorty?"

"What's wrong with my cousin essay? Why is he laid out on the floor and why haven't you sorry fuckers picked him up?"

"He was eating on a steak and choked on it. I think he's dead Shorty."

"What the fuck you mean he's dead?" Shorty snapped.

"I checked for breathing through his nose and mouth and nothing was coming out. We need to call the paramedics or something."

Shorty dropped to the floor and lifted the body of his cousin and wept. Tears fell down his face as he attempted to lean Poppy on the couch. He kissed him on the forehead before he looked up at his homeboys.

"What the fuck happened? How did he choke on his own food?"

"Some Mayate bitch came by to talk to him for a minute. After he finished talking to her she got up and left. He said something about her and then began choking on his meat. He coughed a few times then he passed out. We tried to get out what was lodged inside of him but it was too late. You walked in a little bit after he died homes."

"Call the fucking paramedics?" Shorty yelled.

One of his homeboys went into the kitchen to quickly make the call. Shorty rocked with his cousin.

"Was this Mayate bitch a light skinned girl with a nice petite body?"

"Yeah homes, she had ass but she was skinny."

"That was Reddy."

"Yeah that was the name Poppy called her."

"So do you think that bitch killed my primo?"

"I don't think so homes. He was saying good things about her before I closed the door and went back on the porch."

"Did you hear her say anything or did he say anything to let you know what they were talking about?"

"Nah Shorty she wasn't here that long. She was talking low but I remember Poppy saying she owed him. That was all that was said."

"Knowing Poppy she was able to talk him into letting up off the Mayate that helped rob the stash. I'm killing that pinche Puto if it's the last thing I do. No compromise. There ain't shit that Reddy or that piece of shit can tell me to stop me from going after him." Shorty vowed.

I was in a half nod when Reddy walked up on me in the hospital room. They had given me something for the pain. I drowsily tried to have a conversation but my words were slow and labored.

"What's up Reddy?"

"I talked to Poppy and he said you will get a pass. All you need to do is get some rest while you are in the hospital. Just make sure to call yo moms and tell her that you are at a girlfriend's house or some shit."

"She will know that I used the Kaiser card. Just come pick me up when they release me from here." I replied.

"Okay that's cool. Do you need me to take care of anything while you are up in this bitch?"

"Nah I'm good. I'll get my car out the shop when I get out of here. Did he say anything about getting work from him?"

"He told me that he ain't fucking with you. He's like if you wasn't there then you know who was there. He still doesn't trust you. It was just a bad move to bring Pookie's crazy ass. Rest in Peace." Reddy sighed.

"So I ain't got means or a connect to make any money."

"Don't trip I'll connect you to someone else. Be careful about how you get at him though because he is an old school Crip but he's got good product. You won't get to know where this nigga live."

"Will he fuck with Pirus?" I eagerly asked.

"Yeah as long as he don't have to worry about you snitching or cheating him out his money."

"What's his name?"

"I don't know his government name but he goes by Big Black. Don't fuck this one up Grumpy because this nigga has reach. He's the type of muthafucka that will catch you in your sleep. And he's strictly business."

"I didn't fuck up the first time. I just got blamed for that shit."

"Well I'm gon let you rest and I'll be up here tomorrow."

Reddy walked out the door and I dozed off.

18
SEASONED

This was the muthafuckin hand you were dealt so deal with it!
Reddy

I was in the hospital for a few days before Reddy came to pick me up. My shoulder was in a half cast and my arm was in a sling. The hospital prescribed painkillers to ease the pain. That helped a little but they left me drowsy a lot of times. I rolled out of the hospital in a wheelchair. Reddy pulled up in front of the hospital and took me back to the house. I thought it was best to hibernate so that I could fully recover but my money was running low. I had a little savings but it was depleting fast. Reddy was supposed to link me up with another connect but I wasn't ready to hit the block yet. After a month of sitting around the house and having Tamara come through it was beginning to get tired. We had rekindled our thing but it wasn't the same. It was one of those relationships that you let run its course because you know it wasn't going too far. The sex even wasn't the same. That could have played a part on my arm being in a sling. I was much grumpier than before. Glad to be alive but irritated that I had to go through all this shit. After a month sitting around I called Reddy and told her I was ready to hit the block.

"Okay, I got some bad news to tell you in person anyway."

When she got to my house I was sitting on the couch. She sat down in the same chair I was sitting in when she cried in my lap. It was still hard to believe at times that Smokey was actually dead. When we made eye contact I could tell that the stress of the streets was getting to her again. Her pretty face showed signs of stress. She was in need of another getaway.

"Ay Grumpy, I got to tell this to you straight. I found out through word on the street that Poppy is dead."

"Aw that's fucked up. How did he die?"

"He choked on some food."

I had to hold in my laughter. He was fat as hell but I didn't expect to hear her say that to me. I yawned so that I could hide me wanting to laugh.

"Well he told Shorty to back up off me, right?"

"I don't know if he got a chance to." Reddy slightly winced.

"So this muthafucka might still be on the hunt for me? Are you serious?"

"Yeah it's real fucked up. I rolled past there to peep out the scene and it didn't look good. Shorty is a hot head so he is quick to kill where Poppy was about his business so he used violence only when necessary. Things are different now. I'm worried about going over there."

"How are we gon' get at this fool? Fuck Reddy, I don't need to hear this shit right now."

"Would you have preferred I didn't tell you?"

"Shorty is a veteran at killing people. Lorenzo was telling me that he makes big money doing hits for shot callers. How am I gon' go against this fool, Reddy?"

"You sounding weak then a muthafucka my nigga. This was the muthafuckin hand you were dealt; so deal with it. You a seasoned vet like Shorty is and the question is if you want to live more than he does. That's how the streets are Grumpy. I shouldn't have to explain this shit to you. Some niggas want to live more than others."

"Smokey was a real gangster and he still got dealt a bad hand and was killed." I replied.

"That's some different shit. Smokey was betrayed by a nigga he had love for. You know that Shorty is an open enemy and you hoping that you can slide through some shit without getting caught up. If that nigga is on the hunt then you be on the muthafuckin' hunt." She said the last sentence viciously.

"Okay, then I'm about to go hard after this nigga."

"That's the Grumpy I've grown up to know and love. I've got a plan anyway."

She walked me through the plan then told me she would hook me up with the new connect at the end of the week. I was willing to leave the house but I mostly stayed in the hood. I didn't want to take the chance of getting into a shootout before I was one hundred percent. I was considering painting the Fleetwood a different color. After long consideration I realized I was only doing it to avoid Shorty. Fuck Shorty. He's got guns and I got guns. He's got homies and I got homies. His loyalty wasn't really to anyone except to Poppy. So it wasn't like he could rain down on my hood without repercussions. If it was a shot called from the pen or something I might get into some shit but other than that it was him against me. This was a personal matter so it was a matter of who got who first.

I hadn't really been out the house or the hood as of lately but I planned on getting out. My first stop was to buy me some gear at the Compton Swap meet. Back in the day the building that was used for the swap meet was once Sears. I didn't know what to expect whenever I went up there because the Mob Piru gang would still have to fight to claim that territory. I had to consider that since I wasn't banging it was still niggas doing that shit. Of course I still represented Piru but I wasn't set tripping anymore. So I rolled up there with Kool Aid because I knew he wasn't on that bullshit either. If someone wanted to trip we was gon' handle they ass because they wanted to trip. It's certain things that still the same about a hoodlum. We still keep that swagger and we still have that thousand-yard-stare. The look in our eyes that lets you know that if you come with some bullshit its coming right back at you. I had a big target on my back anyway so I wasn't tolerating anybody crossing me the wrong way. We rolled up to the swap meet in Kool Aid's car. We weren't in there two minutes before he was led somewhere else.

"Blood, check out that broad with the big ole ass. I'm about to push up on her fine ass."

"You better make sure she's cool with P-Fonk." I smirked.

"I know huh."

While he was talking to the caramel brick house I was looking at some shoes. I liked the Air Jordan Nike shoes that had red in it because he played for the Chicago Bulls. I was tired of wearing Chuck Taylor's even though I grew up wearing them. I picked out a couple of shoes and before I was done Kool Aid came back smiling from ear to ear. He must have gotten the phone number, I thought. That was why we called him Kool Aid because when he smiled it was a big Kool Aid smile. He had grown into his big smile now that we were older. We had grown close in recent years and we hung together if I wasn't with Reddy. A new generation of Holly Hoods were coming up and we were now the big homies.

"Yeah Blood, she slid me the number. She's a square broad that lives right outside the Mob hood. She ain't tripping about banging or anything. I'm trying to see what's up with that ASAP." He chuckled.

"Yeah she had a banging little body and a cute face. If her head is on straight you can sport her."

"I'm saying…"

As we were talking some young Crips came up talking loud and laughing. They were a few years younger than us. We wouldn't have paid them any mind but they were saying the word Cuz like it was going out of style. Any Blood or Piru even if he's slowed down from gangbanging still is irritated by the word Cuz. It's like a dagger being stabbed into your eardrum. Especially if you hear it a lot. I don't think they knew we were Bloods until they looked at our attire. We weren't flamed up but I had on a burgundy belt with black khakis, black Nike sneakers with burgundy shoe strings. I had on a white T-shirt covering the belt but it stuck out a little bit because I let it hang to the side. Kool Aid had on Beige which is Holly Hood colors but everyone doesn't know that. What gave him away was his all white Reeboks with red trimming and thin red shoelaces. They stopped in their tracks the moment they seen our dress attire. They decided to walk away and find another shoe spot. I was trying on the shoes to make sure they were comfortable. When we were almost done wrapping up the sale the same two Crips came back to the shoe store. This time they had two other Crips rolling with them when they walked up. One of the original two Crips walked up to the shelf and started going in hard.

"Aw Cuz, I'm love these B/K shoes. These are some real Crip shoes right here. I got to get these in all blue."

I glanced over at Kool Aid and he shook his head. Even though they had two more homies with them what made them think this was going to be easy? I decided to ignore them and continue the sell with the Asian man.

"This is Neighborhood Compton Crip on mine Cuz."

That's when I stepped away from the cash register and stepped outside the shoe store's small booth. This young nigga didn't know what he was getting himself into. Kool Aid was already outside of the booth and the young nigga got in arm's distance.

"Fuck Holly…"

Kool Aid threw one punch to his jaw that landed pinpoint on its target. The young Crip found himself on his back in a daze. His homeboy stood there in shock. That's how I knew they wasn't seasoned about this street shit. I quickly smacked the shit out of him with an open hand. He held his mouth and whimpered.

"Quit being so muthafuckin' disrespectful." Kool Aid snapped.

The other two Crips backed away as though they didn't really want anything to do with it. I shook my head and laughed as both of the youngsters got up and walked away as fast as possible. We were too old for this shit. Kool Aid and I both shook hands as I received change from the Asian man. He came outside of the booth to give me my money. When we looked up there was a crowd gathered around staring at us. I grabbed my bags and was walking off until I spotted her. She was one of the onlookers.

"Hey why do I keep running into you up at the swap meet?" I playfully asked.

"Because you live up here starting trouble." She replied.

"You always got a quick comeback. So how have you been doing Linda or should I just call you Redbone?"

"Oh so you remember my name. I didn't think you would remember my name since you never remembered my phone number."

"If you only knew the things I've been dealing with. We can always pick up where we left off."

"I didn't know we started up. You got to call me in order for us to even get started Mr. Trouble maker."

"Nah it ain't like that. We just had to teach those young niggas a lesson. I'm gon' take your number down again but this time I'm writing it on my arm. How about you write on my arm." Kool Aid handed me a pen.

She wrote her number on my forearm in big bold numbers. She didn't bother putting her name on my forearm.

"I bet you don't even remember my name?"

"Dwayne...right?"

"Yep so don't forget when I call you."

"If you call me. I see how you get down. You'd rather gang bang then call and talk to me."

"You got a smart mouth with yo fine ass."

"Would you like it any other way?"

"Probably not but…"

"HE'S GOT A GUN!"

I heard a woman scream and to my surprise it was the young Crip that Kool Aid had knocked to the ground. It looked like he had a twenty-two or something small like that. I pushed Linda into the booth and grabbed Kool Aid by the shirt. We took off running. To my surprise the young Crip started shooting in the middle of the swap meet. He wasn't that good at shooting because he let off six shots but not one hit us. I did hear the bullets wiz by as we dipped around a corner and into the side of the parking lot where Kool Aid parked. We reached his car in less than a minute.

"Blood I need to get my strap from under the seat and serve that little crab nigga." Kool Aid snapped.

"Nah, don't even trip off that dumb ass nigga. He couldn't even shoot. If you want to get at him later we can but the Sheriffs is on their way by now."

He nodded and climbed into his car and we drove off. When we got back to the hood one of the homegirls was barbecuing. When we walked in the homegirl Angie-Ru's backyard a bunch of homies were already there. To my surprise Reddy was there with Nuck whispering in her ear. She was listening like she was feeling what he had to say. I didn't know how to feel about that. I wasn't jealous in a boyfriend or girlfriend way but I didn't like her getting at Nuck of all people. That was why he was so cooperative when I had to go to the hospital that day. He probably was eyeing Reddy for awhile. I gave her a slight nod and she returned it to acknowledge me. I decided to go over by the grill where Angie-Ru was cooking because she knew how to burn. Everything Angie-Ru cooked was delicious. She was one of those homegirls that had a baby real young but she was always from the hood. She didn't hang out that much but when she gave a party at her mom's house everyone came. She was a big girl with big titties and a big ole ass with a pretty chocolate complexion. She was about four or five years older than me but she always was cool with me.

"Hey Angie-Ru let me get one of those hotlinks."

"Grab one of those buns."

I grabbed a bun and I was munching into a barbecue hotlink a minute later. I sat down at one of the tables and enjoyed my appetizers. Kool Aid came over to the table.

"Angie-Ru is giving out the food?"

"I asked her for a link and she gave me one."

Before I knew it Kool Aid was back at the table with a hotlink in his hand. I was damn near finished by the time he sat down. Reddy pulled up a chair and sat at the table with us.

"What's up with ya'll?"

"We just got back from the Compton Swap meet. This young crab nigga tried to blast on us."

"Damn Grumpy, you can't stay out of trouble."

"Yeah it tends to find me for some reason."

"I guess so. You ready to hit Skateland tonight?"

"I just told you I got shot at earlier today and that's all you got to say. You ready for Skateland tonight?" I mocked her on the last sentence.

"You ain't shot so I'm assuming you are fine. Why the fuck you got an attitude, Blood?"

"I ain't got an attitude."

"Well are you going tonight or what?"

"Yeah I'm going."

Kool Aid munched on his hotlink while watching the exchange between us. He was obviously getting a kick out of it.

"What the fuck you staring at?" Reddy asked.

"You two muthafuckas acting like ya'll married." Kool Aid laughed.

"Fuck you Blood!" Reddy and I said simultaneously.

"Ya'll even say the same thing at the same time. That's cute."

"Nah she got other niggas whispering in her ear." I curtly added.

"Oh that's why you acting all funky and shit."

I didn't take the time to respond. But we made eye contact and that was the end of that. Who was I to tell her who to fuck with and I wasn't going to cock block. But I knew she was settling for less because she thought she had to. Nuck wasn't anywhere a gangster like Smokey from my vantage point. I didn't have to say it but she knew it. We didn't talk about it the entire time at Angie-Ru's barbecue. Around eight in the evening we stepped out the barbecue and prepared to go up to Skateland USA on the West Side. Everybody rolled in separate cars so I pulled out the Fleetwood. I was sporting the Air Jordan's that I had bought at the swap meet. My wardrobe was black khakis, with a red belt, a black with red writing Nike shirt. I had a fresh diamond earring on my right ear. My daughter was spending the night at my house so I kissed her before I left. She was already asleep by the time I walked out the door.

We made it up to Skateland a little after ten. It was cracking with females all over the place. I spotted some of the homies so I hung out over near that area. The Holly Hood homeboys were up there about ten deep with a few young homies hanging too. Most of the homeboys were drunk before they came up to the spot. Skateland didn't serve alcohol so you had to get it on your own before you got up there. As the party went on the occasional fight jumped off over a broad more or less. It wasn't over near us so we didn't trip. It was amazing how the Bloods could all get together and still find a reason to beef with each other.

It was a time in my years when Bloods never fought against each other because we were outnumbered by the Crips two to one. We had to stick together. Nowadays it was different than before. There was always personal beefs because one nigga didn't like another nigga but it was never whole neighborhood beefing with each other. After three hours at the spot I decided to make my way to Los Angeles.

I walked out of Skateland with a clear head. I hopped into my Fleetwood and rolled out. I wasn't really tired even though it was late at night. It was a female that I wanted to link up with that lived out in LA. Reddy always told me that I shouldn't fuck with a female that I didn't know too well. This girl was on the up and up to me though. When I got deep into Los Angeles on Central Blvd a car rolled up on me that didn't look familiar. I turned down a side street but it went straight ahead so I relaxed for a minute. I wasn't trying to get caught up on another situation with Shorty. I couldn't tell who it was because the windows were tinted in a black Buick Regal. I rolled slowly down the street after taking a deep breath. There was no writing on the walls so I didn't know what hood I was in. I had passed the Nickerson Gardens but I was probably still in Watts. When I made a left on another side street I ran right into the same black Buick Regal.

A hand poked out of the window so the driver of the car was waiting on me with a nine millimeter pointed at my windshield. I instantly put the car in reverse and attempted to do a spin around. It was awkward but I made my full turn and pushed on the gas. The Regal followed behind me at top speed. This was getting crazy because every time I left the hood I was caught up in some shit. Maybe the Fleetwood was a trouble magnet. This time I pulled my glock from out between the seat cushions and made sure it was ready. I'm driving with one hand while the car is following my every move. It was definitely going to be another show down. My Cadillac dipped back on the major Blvd and took off top speed. I couldn't worry about police at this point because it was life or death. I didn't really know where I was going exactly. I couldn't bring heat to the girl's house I'd planned to visit so I decided to find a place to park the car. This time I came across a park so I rolled on the sidewalk and found myself on the grass in the middle of the park. This part of the park was totally empty so I hopped out with gun in hand.

The Regal Buick followed behind me and was parked on the grass as well. I took a couple of shots at the windshield and shattered it. I heard someone yell but he still was able to get out. I cut down a corner hoping to throw him off the scent but he was still coming. I ran down a dark alley hoping to duck behind some trash cans and catch him slipping. When he made it to the alley way he was a little more cautious before he walked in. He had his pistol drawn carefully making his way through the dark urine smelling pathway. The trash can smell carried a stench that would make someone vomit. Dogs had started barking once I was inside the alley. In fact I believe that's why he knew to come this way. I was halfway down the alley hidden behind a large trashcan. Something spoiled was filling up my nostrils that almost made me sneeze. I tried to clear it from my mind while watching him slowly approach. As he drew closer the plan was to light his ass up at close range. The anticipation was agonizing as he crept closer towards me. I heard something rumbling behind me but I was concentrating on him. When I glanced down to see what was going on it was a large rat only a couple of feet away from me.

I jumped out of the way of the rat giving up my position. He turned my way and I started dumping at him. I beat him to the draw but he was able to duck for cover. I was sure that I didn't hit him. If I walked up on him he would be waiting to light my ass up. My best bet was to take off running to the other end of the alley. In some places in Los Angeles the alley ways were longer than average. This was one of those alleys. I took off running wondering how many bullets I had in my gun. At least eight or nine shots went off in the alley. The gun had seventeen shots altogether. One in the chamber and sixteen in the clip. Even though the cold air was dominant I was in a hot sweat. I almost made it to the end of the alley before he started letting off. I ducked down behind another trash can, paused for a minute then rushed toward the end of the alley. Everything was okay once I made a quick once over of my body parts. There was no time to celebrate though. I was happy to be in one piece but I cursed that I didn't bring another clip with me. This was some wild-west shoot-out type of shit. My pistol was almost empty and I didn't know if I was going to lose the gunfight. Ducking behind a car I waited for him to surface from the alley. He took his sweet time and I knew the police would be called after all those gunshots.

When he finally surfaced from the alley he was extra careful. His pistol was leading the way then he would peak his head out to scope the scene. He seen what direction I ran because he turned his view left and focused on that direction. Like he was a trained police he inched out into the open with his weapon extended in front of him. The moment I saw an opening I lifted my head up and started dumping at him. He was quickly shot in the left shoulder even though I was aiming for the heart. Aggravated I let off the rest of the clip hoping I could finish him off. He let out a loud yell but pushed forward when he heard the click of my gun going empty. I cursed under my breath as I hid behind a Honda Civic. He released the clip he had and loaded another while we made brief eye contact. The smirk on Shorty's face was more painful than knowing the end was near.

19
DECISIONS

Nah you should stay here with me and cuddle!
Linda

Reddy waited for Kool Aid to pull up in his car before she climbed out. She stretched for a minute then waited for him to get out the car. She handed him the keys then made her way across the grass. Her direction was a little hazy but she was able to pick up a scent. This was the day she wore her all black Nike sneakers that matched the rest of her attire. Stopping for a moment to catch her breath the end of the greenery was near. If she went left she would find herself at the entry of a long alley. It would be best for her to run down the back street and come out on the other end. That way it would be a different direction and no one would feel like they were being followed. Walking at a slow run Reddy heard gunshots once she was halfway down the block. Her heart skipped because she was unaware of what was going on. She picked up her pace and continued forward to the end of the block. Squatting down and catching her breath became a priority as her heart was beating a mile a minute.

Once she was rejuvenated, she turned the corner to see someone hiding behind a car. Her eyes focused on what was coming out of the nearby alley. Hiding behind a wooden gate in the dark her figure could not be seen. To her surprise when she peaked out to see who she was looking for she realized he hadn't looked in her direction. Slowly she crept from her hiding place while the target loaded another clip. She waited until he was in the process of cocking back his weapon then she fired. She went low with her aim and made the man fall to the ground yelling loudly. She walked up on him and the person hiding behind the car emerged. It was her homeboy Grumpy. The man that she shot was squirming on the ground with his pistol only a few inches away from him. Tears welled up in his eyes as he tried to endure the pain.

"Why didn't you shoot him in the head?" Grumpy asked.

"Because he's yo kill not mine. You gon' have to decide right now if you want him to live or die. He's not after me like that."

Grumpy stared at her momentarily not seeing the sense in her logic. She picked up the gun of the man lying on the ground.

"You ain't got a lot of time to decide."

Grumpy grabbed the pistol and put two bullets in the head of who they knew as Shorty. Reddy tugged on his shirt then they took off running toward the end of the block. When they reached the corner a car was waiting for them. Grumpy quickly hopped in the backseat while Reddy sat in the front.

"How long did you have to wait Blood?" Reddy asked.

"I just pulled up a minute ago." Kool Aid replied.

"What did you do with Grumpy's car?"

"I parked it a few blocks away so he can hop in right away. We gon' dump this car around the corner from where he's parked and we can hop in my shit." Kool Aid replied.

"Grumpy hand me Shorty's piece." Reddy reached her hand toward the back seat.

She was already in the process of cleaning all of the guns while Kool Aid sped down a residential street. That's when the sound of sirens started filling their ears. After a thorough cleaning she put all the guns in a plastic bag. Kool Aid pulled up next to a white Fleetwood and stopped. Grumpy hopped out of the backseat and jumped into his car. The Fleetwood went down the street, turned right while Kool Aid turned left in the stolen car. The sounds of a helicopter filled the air.

"The ghetto bird is out, how far away are we from yo car?"

"We're pulling up on it now. You still gon' need to dump those guns."

"Pull over here and I can put them in this dumpster." Reddy pointed.

"We might as well dump the car here because the car is up the street."

"Nah if they find the stolen car here they might search around the area and look in the dumpster. Drive to the next block and we'll walk back to yo car."

She dumped the guns in the small dumpster then Kool Aid sped off to the next block. They hopped out after he parked and walked back to his car parked in front of a vacant house.

"Do you know what hood we in?" Kool Aid asked.

"Nah, not really."

They hit a few back streets then made a left on Central. When they finally made it back to Compton the Skateland parking lot was empty. Before Kool Aid finished making a left on Central and Rosecrans a Compton Sheriff squad car pulled up behind him. The quick sound of the siren and the flash of the lights startled both of them.

"Do you have anything dirty up in this muthafucka?" Reddy asked.

"Nah, we should be straight."

"DRIVER SLOWLY PUT YOUR HANDS OUT THE CAR AND DROP YOUR KEYS TO THE GROUND. OPEN YOUR CAR DOOR FROM THE OUTSIDE. AFTER THE DRIVER DOES THIS PASSENGER I WANT YOU TO FOLLOW AND DO THE SAME THING...SLOWLY NOW."

"This is going to be a long fucking night." Reddy remarked.

There I was cruising down Central Blvd. going south. A few police passed me by but never paid me any mind. I was probably too far away from the scene of the shooting to appear suspicious. I leaned back in my car and just played oldies from the radio 92.3 FM old school and new school. People were making dedications while the DJ allowed them to make shot outs. Now that Shorty was dead I had to map out the next stage of my life. What had me tripping was Reddy's decision to shoot him in the legs. She left it up to me if he should live or die. It's different when you kill a man. I've had to kill a man before but Shorty was different for me.   Roccy had to go because it was over gangbanging and he didn't know how to keep it moving without coming after me and my homeboys. Shorty on the other hand had a vendetta behind some shit I didn't do. His relative Poppy had given me a pass but that wasn't enough. This man would have hunted me down for the rest of my life. Shorty and I weren't meant to be enemies it just played out that way. That's what bothered me more than anything.

Before I knew it I was back on the west side of Compton. Skateland was damn near cleared out when I passed by. I made a left on Rosecrans and cruised down the Blvd. leaning to the side. As I moved closer to the East Side the oldies station played a block of three songs from the Stylistics. It was like a soundtrack to the mood I was feeling at the time. By the time I was rolling past Leuders Park they were playing the last song in rotation 'Break up to make up'. It felt good when I made it back to the neighborhood with that monkey off my back. I rolled by Ronnie-Ru's house but he had everything closed up and it was dark as fuck. I wasn't ready to go back inside but Reddy and Kool Aid hadn't made it back to the hood yet. So I decided to pull up in front of Turtle's house but he was asleep or gone as well. That was a hint and a half past my monkey ass that I should call it a night.

The next morning the first thing I did was call Linda. We had a conversation for at least an hour. We arranged a time for us to go out on a date the following weekend. I was hoping to see her before the week ended. I called Tamara but her little sister said she wasn't at home. After breakfast I hit the block to see what was going on. When I pulled up at Turtle's house a few of the homies were hanging out. I walked to the backyard and everyone was just hanging out. There wasn't anyone playing dominoes, shooting dice or playing spades. I walked up on Reddy smoking on a Newport.

"It took ya'll a long time to get back to the hood. I waited for ya'll for a little while then I went into the house."

"Did you get some sleep muthafucka?"

"Yeah why?"

"Come here."

She walked over to where Kool Aid was chilling playing with Turtle's raggedy boom box. He glanced up when he seen us approach.

"What's happening Blood?"

"Ay Kool Aid, this nigga talking about he got some good sleep last night."

"Aw my nigga Grumpy, you know we got bumped up by the Sheriffs when we made it back to Compton. They pulled us over on Rosecrans and had us jammed up for at least an hour." Kool Aid explained enthusiastically.

"They searched that muthafuckin car from top to bottom, huh." Reddy added.

"Yeah I was tired than a muthafucka. They had us sitting on that cold ass curb with six or seven pigs surrounding us. Whatever I owe you my nigga we even." Kool Aid smirked.

Reddy and I both laughed. It was something I could put behind me now and move on with my life.

About two months after my drama with Shorty another surprise came knocking at my door. Linda had developed into a relationship that I was cool about. I was still fucking Tamara from time to time so we were still officially together as well. One day I came home from hanging out over Ronnie-Ru's house and both females were sitting on my porch. My mom was in the house but she had told both girls to wait for me outside. If I could have backed out of the driveway I would have done that shit. I stared at both females and they gave me looks that could kill. I took my time getting out of the car. When I opened the car door Tamara was the first to step off the porch. I was hoping these broads would fight and give me a scapegoat out of this shit but they were both smarter than that.

"What's going on Dwayne?" Tamara asked.

My head was lowered like I was doing something but I was trying to avoid eye contact. She glared at me without blinking an eye.

"What do you mean what's going on?"

"Are you dating her or are you dating me?"

"Aw you tripping. It ain't even got to be about all of that. I'm just trying to survive in this rough ass city."

"I'm talking about you two timing both of us and we didn't know anything about each other. Come on now Dwayne look at me."

"Well we've been having problems Tamara. Why are you coming at me with all this static in the middle of a hot ass day?"

I knew Linda was pissed off because she was usually the first person to say something. Now she was sitting on the porch quiet as hell. I didn't know how to ease out of this without everything going to hell.

"So that means that we are dating other people because we've had a few problems. It would have been good to get the memo Dwayne."

"Hold on a minute."

I jumped out the car and ran into the house. Linda hadn't said anything to me while I was passing. She didn't even give me any eye contact. All she did was sit in the porch chair and stare out into the yard. I opened the screen door then quickly ran into my room like I was about to grab something. Once in the room I began pacing the floor. Mumbling to myself while a hole was being burned into the nappy carpet.

"What the fuck you gon' do Grumpy? What are you gon' do?"

I asked myself repeatedly but I didn't see any way out of this. After a few moments of trying to conjure up something my mom walked into the bedroom.

"You need to set it straight with those girls. Which one you want to date Dwayne and don't play any games."

"Mama this is my business so let me handle it."

"No, you are acting just like yo daddy. He would play these same kinds of games so I know what these girls are going through. They both like you a lot because if they didn't they would have left by now. They are waiting on you to choose. So man up and choose which one you want."

I was a little pissed off at my mom but she gave me a look like she didn't care. Slowly I made my way back to the porch. This time Linda stood up when I came outside.

"Hold on Linda."

I jumped off the porch while Linda sat back down. I went out into the yard to meet Tamara grabbing her by the arm to step onto the sidewalk.

"I think we been putting off what's going on with us. I don't see you regularly like I used to and you only come around for a tune up. When you ready to do that thing. We come from two different worlds so we gon' have to go our separate ways."

"Oh so you've been fucking me but now we're from two different worlds? You weren't saying that a few days ago."

"Hold the fuck up Tamara you ain't got to put shit out there like that. We did our thing while it lasted but now it's time to move on. Yo moms and pops looked at me as nothing but a hoodlum anyway. So it's best that we go our separate ways…respect my decision." I firmly whispered.

"You know what, your right. I shouldn't have came to your house without calling anyway. I just wanted to show you my new car my parents got me for college. You take care of yourself Dwayne."

I watched her walk back to the car. I was gon' miss having sex with her. Linda was the bomb too but I didn't know if I was gon' lose her once I walked on the porch. Lifting my head up I walked on the porch and sat next to her. She watched Tamara drive off in a brand new red Honda Accord. Neither one of us said anything for a few moments.

"So you broke it off with her to be with me. I'm flattered."

At this point I thought it was wise for me not to say anything. More than likely she was setting me up for the big break up. I tried to grab her hand but she snatched it away. That made me stand up and start walking into the house. She got up and followed behind me so that was a good sign. When she walked into my room she sat down on the bed and kicked her feet up.

"You know I shouldn't fuck with you anymore." She began.

"Aw don't be like that. That was an old flame that I hadn't broke it off with yet."

"Don't lie to me Dwayne. Or should I call you Grumpy-Ru?"

"I'm telling you it wasn't anything between us. I hadn't seen her in a while. She came by expecting something that wasn't there anymore. You know you my baby Boo."

I leaned into kiss her but she turned away so that my lips landed on her cheek. I started nibbling on her neck and she started getting into it. And as if on cue my mother yelled into my room from the hallway.

"I'm on my way to Ontario Dwayne so I won't see you until tomorrow."

"Okay."

We started kissing the moment we heard the door close. We were butt naked in a matter of seconds rolling on my bed. That was always the cure when you messed up with a female. If you gave her the dick real good she was a little more forgiving. I worked her so tough that day that I put her to sleep. When she woke up I gave her a glass of water and kissed her on the forehead.

"Thank you."

"How are you feeling?" I asked.

"I'm good but honestly I think I'm pregnant."

"Are you serious?"

"I think so. I haven't had a period and I'm always sleepy. That's why I wasn't quick to leave yo ass when you were trying to be a player."

She playfully punched me in the arm. I grabbed her and gave her a big bear hug. She laughed as I smothered her with kisses. After we played around she still was sleepy so she laid her head back on my pillow.

"Go ahead and get some rest and I'm gon' hit the block."

"Nah you should stay here with me and cuddle."

"Come on now Linda. We can chill when I get back. I want to see what's up with my money then holler at some of the homeboys."

"You just got to be in the streets. You better be glad I'm too tired to argue with you."

We kissed then I threw on a Pendleton because of the chill outside. I pulled my gun from behind the dresser and Linda glanced up.

"If you ain't gon' be out too long you don't need to bring yo strap."

"Yeah but…"

"Yeah but nothing Dwayne. The Sheriffs are hot right now. When my homegirl dropped me off we passed two Sheriffs staring into the car of two women. What do you think they are going to do when they see you?"

Against my better judgment I listened to what she had to say. When I first hit Holly street I felt kind of naked. I went on Pannez to check on the little homies who were curb serving for me on the block. Money was rolling in pretty good so I had a nice stash of money coming from one of my little homeboys. We called him Renny-Ru because his name was Lawrence. I had taken him under my wing for the last couple of months. After Reddy hooked me up with another connect I was back making money. Shortly after that she disappeared. Kool Aid and I was working together to keep money flowing in the neighborhood. After chopping it up with the young homie I made my way back to Holly Street where I ran into Kool Aid. He was standing outside of Turtle's house. We had two spots we were serving out of. One was on Pannez and the other was on Compton Blvd. two blocks east of Holly Street in an apartment complex called the Pueblos. He had collected his money and we were talking about trying to set up one more spot.

"Ay Blood let me run in Turtle's house so I can take a leak. I can't take this shit into that nigga's house."

He pulled out a brown paper bag from out of his pocket and sat it on the trunk of his car then ran into the house. I yawned because I was already missing my bed and who was lying in it. I would finish my conversation with him and call it a night. I pulled out the wad of money in my pocket and began counting it when I heard a sound. It startled me for a minute. To my surprise three squad cars pulled up on me. Leading the pack was that asshole Sheriff Cole.

"So what's up Grumpy-Ru? Have you killed anybody lately?"

"What the fuck are you talking about?"

"Someone just lit up the Neighborhood Crips tonight. I thought you might know who it was."

"First and foremost I wouldn't have anything to say to you if I did know. And I just came outside thirty minutes ago."

"So you don't know who did it?" He asked sarcastically.

"Look am I under arrest? I'm about to bounce."

As I began to step off he held up his hand for me to stop. I glanced at him as he walked over to Kool Aid's car.

"What do we have here?"

He unwrapped the brown paper bag to find a thirty-eight six shot inside. I cursed to myself. He looked up at me and smiled then pulled out his handcuffs.

"You better hope there ain't any murders on this gun."

I didn't even feel like replying. He read me my Miranda rights then he handcuffed me. He stuffed me into the back seat of one of the squad cars and before the car drove off Kool Aid stepped out of the back yard. I could tell he felt bad so all I did was shrug. It was nothing he or I could do about it. I would have to swallow the charge. For the first time in a long time I was able to take a deep breath as they drove down the Compton streets. Looking around at my hometown this would be my last hoorah for a long time. There was no telling how much time they were about to hand me. But I was a Hub City Hoodlum, so I had to take it like a man. Besides, it was my turn.

20
GROWN MAN SHIT

It doesn't matter you should drive your own car!
Linda

3 ½ YEARS LATER

Linda came to pick me up from prison in my white Fleetwood Cadillac. On the passenger side was my seven year old daughter. Sitting in the back in a car seat was my two and a half year old son. She had never brought him up to the pen to see me because she didn't want him seeing me that way. I was glad she was smart enough to know not to do that. The sun was especially bright the day I came home. It was warm but it wasn't particularly humid. That was how California weather could be sometimes.

When I walked up to the car my daughter jumped in the back seat with her brother and Linda slid over.

"You know my license is expired by now."

"It doesn't matter you should drive your own car."

Once inside the driver's seat I had to adjust everything to fit my height. I leaned in my car and cruised down the street like I never missed a day on the street. Things were different for me now. I had a family I was happy with so I was ready to slow down. My plans were to go back to school to work as a mechanic and eventually open my own shop. I wanted to know how the homies were doing so I would have to go by the hood and holler at everyone that was still around. Many of us had moved out of the hood to different cities and even different states.

Kool Aid from what I heard was fighting a dope charge that was kind of major. Since I was locked up they had passed a lot of crack laws that targeted people in the hood. You got more time for a lot less crack than what you got for powder cocaine. Kool Aid was caught up in that game and things were different these days. Nowadays a lot of people were out for themselves so the District Attorney could hand certain niggas twenty years and they will fold. Kool Aid and I were a part of the last generations that believed in a code of never cooperating with law enforcement. The streets had been oversaturated with everyone wanting to be thugs but not willing to take what came with being a thug. I never considered myself a thug. I either was a gangster or hoodlum

When I rolled through the neighborhood I got the run down on everyone that had been out when I was locked down. Reddy was into something big because she was always traveling and doing shit like that. She was supposed to be connected to a ring of hustlers. That was all I heard about her. The house she lived in on Pannez was still occupied but when I went by there no one was home. Turtle had moved up to a city called Lancaster which I heard was nothing but a baby Compton. A lot of the homies from the East Side had migrated out there. Ronnie-Ru was around but he was married with a family. He would come around the hood from time to time. Loko had caught a murder charge but he had been a loner for a long time. The homie Timmy-Ru was also locked up on a dope charge. The hood was only a shell of what it once was. What was always crazy about my hood and my city was that Compton for the most part was a working-middle class-community. Most of my homeboys' parents went to work every day and many owned houses. It was a rough middle class community that would make you kill or be killed. That was why a lot of us from Compton were arrogant and proud gangsters.

After checking on all the homies I made my way to Ontario, California. My mother had moved out there and bought a house. Everyone was supposed to meet at her house so that I could see my brother and his three kids. I remember always wanting to challenge him because I wanted to prove I was just as down. One thing I knew about Flintstone was that he loved his younger brother. No matter how much we fought or got into it he had my back. That's what it's about nowadays. I will never forget where I come from but I was now on some grown man shit. What's imprinted in my heart is the experience of a lifestyle and a city that will leave an indelible mark for the rest of my life. Compton helped to shape my swagger, my disposition and my confidence. I had endured a lot and survived a lot more to be able to be on some grown man shit.

Before I left the hood I rolled through the neighborhood just to reminisce on different landmarks. In front of Turtle's house was where I almost got killed by Roccy. Down the street from Ronnie-Ru's house was where Slow was killed and Loko was shot. Looking at that spot made me wonder if things would have been different for Loko. He was never the same after that day. I rolled over on Pannez and thought about Smokey and Pookie. It was a sad moment when those two gangsters ran through my head. A smile finally came back to my face when I passed by Reddy's house again. They don't make too many women like her. I hope to see her again in this lifetime. As I made my left onto Alondra Blvd. off of Holly Street and back to the freeway I took a deep breath. I survived and no one can take that from me. I wasn't just any ole hoodlum I was a Hub City Hoodlum. That meant something to me and I will never forget where I come from.

THE END

COMING SOON

AT

www.ensbooks.com or

eBooks at amazon.com/kindle

COMING SOON
AT
www.ensbooks.com or
eBooks at amazon.com/kindle

GIVE AN INCH – Short story about Reddy-Ru the main character from 'KRACKS IN THE KONCRETE'

The long nosed chrome thirty-eight was pointed at his head. It was nothing standing between him and the barrel of the gun. He stood tall without flinching. If today was the day for him to meet his maker he would take it like a man. She smiled at him with a confidence that racked his nerves. He knew in his heart she knew how to use the weapon she was brandishing.

"How much do you owe nigga?" She barked.

"I owe seventy-five hundred." He quickly replied

"And when did you tell that nigga you were gon' pay him his money?"

"Three days ago…but I had a little problem with getting off what I was supposed to get off."

"All you giving me are excuses. Excuses only benefit the muthafucka that's giving them, nobody else."

The barrel of her gun still was pointing at his forehead right between his eyes. She was a pretty ass redbone with thick luscious lips. If she wasn't who she was he would have tried to run up in her a long time ago. She was beautiful and deadly at the same time though.

"Look Reddy, I can't think with a pistol in my face. I know we can work something out."

"Who said you were supposed to think? Fila been worried about his money and that's some shit he shouldn't have to worry about. We might be passed working something out. How much do you got on you right now?"

"I got forty-five hundred. I'm only three thousand short. Give me a few days and I can come up with the rest." His voice strained.

She thought about his request and considered how she should handle it. She glanced around the room to notice the off white walls covered with WAK paintings. There was a pile of dirty clothes in a trash bag near the hallway to the bedroom. He didn't even have a sofa. A television sat alone in the middle of the floor with a DVD player under it. She could tell he was scraping by to live. He wasn't a sound hustler, she considered. That bothered her about him. If he was lazy about his own money then he wouldn't have a problem being lazy with someone else's money.

"Look here Bobby; I don't know if you are really good on yo word. I mean, you've been hustling for him for three weeks and you still ain't got off that yayo." Reddy shrugged.

"I had to get everything up and running first but once I got into the swing of things it will be easier to move this shit." A glimmer of hope flashed across his face. He quickly attempted to hide it because he knew what she was capable of. He also had to show some strength because she didn't care for weak ass men. Her reputation had preceded her.

"Okay, give me the forty-five hundred and we can go from there."

He walked a couple of feet away from her to reach for a pair of pants. She kept the pistol on him while her eyes remained focused.

"Easy, my nigga, easy." She warned.

He carefully made his way inside of his pocket to pull out a wad of money. Reddy smiled slightly when she seen the cash. She was hoping for his sake that it was the amount he had claimed it to be. Glancing downward at the nappy tan carpet her black high heel boots were planted on. Her pistol slid down slightly enough where he felt a little more comfortable.

"Count the money in front of me." She calmly demanded.

It was mostly large bills from what she could see but she still couldn't calculate the amount. He took his time counting the money until he had gotten to the end.

"That's only thirty-nine hundred, my nigga. You are six hundred dollars short." She shook her head.

"Well this is what I have, can't we work this out."

"See Bobby, you're a bitch ass nigga, as far as I'm concerned. You told me forty-five hundred when you knew you were supposed to have seventy-five. But you couldn't even produce the amount you told me you had. How the fuck am I supposed to trust you?"

"Nah Reddy it ain't like…"

She fired one into his knee cap. He screamed as he fell to the floor. He slid backwards towards his wall wincing in pain.

"Fuck you Reddy." He winced.

"See nigga, you ain't real about this here game. There are consequences when a nigga can't stay true to what he's supposed to be. I was giving you a pass for the forty-five hundred but you couldn't even make that."

She walked up closer to him with her pistol lowered to her side. The white in his eyes were turning yellow as water fell down his face.

"Give a nigga an inch and he tries to take a mile." Reddy lifted her piece, looked him in the eyes then let off four shots. Each bullet pierced his skull. Reddy cleaned off the pistol then sat it down next to him. After pulling out a back-up pistol she pulled the Victoria Secret's Pink Hoodie over her head and walked out the front door.

PaPa Sak is known as the **Kingpin of the Inkpen.** He has self published nine fiction novels under Etched N Stone Books Entertainment, Inc. publishing company. He has been a voice for the poor and disenfranchised for the purpose of enlightening the people of what's going on in urban America. He writes authentic real life stories about real life experiences. The market today is flooded with urban fiction that tends to exaggerate certain experiences in the street. Many of these stories are what PaPa Sak would call tabloid fiction that sensationalizes characters in the streets. PaPa Sak stays true to the streets because he comes from the streets and must stay true to his roots. His genres of literature range in Urban Street, Romance, Fantasy, Sci-Fi and Self Help. He has spoken at various schools, colleges and Correctional institutions. For more information on PaPa Sak and Etched N Stone go visit him at Facebook/Novelist PaPa Sak, www.myspace.com/papasakkingpen, Twitter/papasak71 and the official website at www.ensbooks.com